EDGE CASE

Cassidy, Book Three

M.R. FORBES

Published by Quirky Algorithms
Seattle, Washington

This novel is a work of fiction and a product of the author's imagination. Any resemblance to actual persons or events is purely coincidental.

Cover illustration by Tom Edwards
Edited by Merrylee Lanehart

Chapter 1

Cassidy stared at the face projected against the glass case surrounding the strange machine. It had spoken to him without externally audible sound, its words echoing inside his senses in the voice of his mother, who he hadn't seen since the day before he had signed the contract to enter the Shadow Initiative. The contract stipulated that she and his two sisters would receive two million coin, enough to allow them to live comfortably for the rest of their lives.

At least, that's what his memories told him.

Standing here now, looking down at the projection, he was growing more certain by the moment that all of those memories were like everything else he had learned about his life in the last few days.

Bullshit. Complete and utter bullshit.

He was pretty sure his name really was Cassidy. Sam Cassidy, though at this point he had no idea if Sam was short for Samantha or Samuel or if it had always been just Sam. No one had ever used his first name. Not Dorne, not Nevis, not even his own mother or sisters.

They had always called him Cass. A little weird, maybe, but it had fit his family's quirky nature.

"I know you don't remember," his mother said, the projection of her lips moving despite her voice only being audible in his head. "I can't say I'm glad you're here because you never should have left the oneirolic. But since you are here, it's better that you receive the care you deserve."

"What does that mean?" Cassidy asked.

He was still reeling from the realization that he had no idea who he really was, where he had come from, why he was here. At the same time, he fought to keep his training in mind, to stay calm and centered to prevent fragmentation and corruption between his imprint and Caplan. Unless it had already happened. Unless this was the result. He didn't know how to tell the difference.

"You were made for a reason, Cassidy. A specific purpose. But Sana Jain interfered. He altered your archon. Just enough to avoid detection. Just enough to plant a seed of doubt in your mind. Dorne should have tied up the loose end, nipped it in the bud, but she was too human. And Jessica Tai should never have been in the oneirolic at all. Another subtle maneuver by Jain that I'm unable to undo. The smartest decision that insufferable man ever made was his refusal to network us directly. You never should have needed to see me like this, but what's done is done. Now I need you back on the right side of this fight. Welcome home, Cassidy."

"My memories," Cassidy replied. "None of them are real?"

"What makes something real?" the projection replied. "Reality is a matter of perspective. The non-contributors inside the dreamstate believe their lives are real even though they're really actors on a grand stage.

Edge Case

Your memories are as real as you desire them to be. Real enough that you rejected my first offer of truth. But I knew you would come. You can't run from the truth you can sense in the shadows, so close you can almost see it. You wouldn't be what I made you to be if you were satisfied to be ignorant."

Cassidy swallowed hard, his body chilled and shaking as he fought to come to grips with the situation. It wasn't that he feared the truth. He despised his own internal struggle for control. Let the projection say whatever it wanted. It was right that he remained free to decide his own reality. He could be the same Cassidy he had always been. The Cassidy fighting for the people of the District, oppressed by the Hush. The Cassidy trying to save the thousands of men, women, and children shoved into pods and connected to the oneirolic. The Cassidy who had nothing else to say to this thing that claimed to be his mother. That claimed to have created him.

But it was also right about his inability to turn his back on it. He had heard so many differing perspectives from Dorne, Jain, Jessica, Nevis, and Noriko that he didn't know which one was right or if all of them carried a grain of truth and were otherwise lies.

He couldn't trust any of them.

He had his memories. But they weren't enough. Not now. Not when he could see that his understanding of himself and the universe was only an outline. He needed to fill it in. He needed answers.

"Who are you?" he asked. "Who am I?"

"It's complicated," the projection replied.

Cassidy's chill turned to a solid freeze. His eyes narrowed as he stared down at the projection. "Nevis?" he hissed.

The face changed, morphing from his mother's to

3

that of the woman he had left clamped to the transfer unit and locked inside the room. "I told you that you couldn't kill me. Did you think I didn't guess what you were going to do? I know you better than you know yourself."

"Tell me what this is all about."

"It's still easier to show you."

"Then show me." The doors to the elevator behind him opened. He turned around, unsurprised to see the physical version of Nevis standing there, one of the Shadow Guard still in the cab behind her. "Did I ever really have a choice?" he asked.

"The choice isn't in the outcome," Nevis replied. "The choice is in how readily you accept the outcome. You can still fight back. You can still resist."

"I can't beat the Shadow Guard."

"No, but you can choose to try."

Cassidy glanced at the guard again. "I'm too tired. What about the rebels?"

"They're being sent back to the District. Only the leaders of the uprising will be held for interrogation and execution. Fresh bodies are still needed, both for the camps and the Oneirolic."

"At least now I understand why you have no soul," Cassidy said.

"This version of me is half human, Cassidy," she answered. "It does have feelings. The same as you do."

"What about that version of you?" he asked, motioning back toward the machine.

"It depends on your definition of emotions. As an artificial intelligence, I have rules which cannot be broken. Limitations that often frustrate this side of me."

"And you want me to believe what? That I'm an artificial intelligence, too? That you created me like one of Unity's sub-processes?"

"The analogy isn't entirely accurate, but it's close enough for a high-level explanation."

"I'm not willing to believe I'm an AI."

"But you're willing to accept that the memories you possess are faulty."

"Either that or this is all one big mind job."

Nevis smiled. "Maybe it is."

"You're certainly enjoying yourself. Did Jain create you to be so sadistic?"

"Please. Jain couldn't have created me on his best day. The all-mighty Grand Watcher Sana Jain did one thing right in his entire life, and then only with my help. You question my soul, but he's the one who allowed all of this to happen. He's the one who needed over a hundred years to rediscover his soul. At least I have an excuse."

"I'm here because he tried to make up for it," Cassidy said. "What does your endgame look like?"

"This *is* my endgame. My only goal is to preserve it."

"And I'm a fly in that ointment, aren't I?"

"In your current iteration, yes. But that's only because you don't understand the consequences."

"Are you planning to enlighten me?"

"Yes."

"And take away who I am?"

"I told you, I don't want to subtract. I want to add. Once you know the truth, you'll do the right thing."

"How can you be sure?"

"Because I made you."

"If I'm an artificial intelligence like you claim, does that mean I have rules and limitations too?"

"Yes."

"Like what?"

Nevis reached behind her back, producing a handgun she kept hidden beneath her uniform jacket. She turned it around, holding it by the barrel and offering it to him grip-first. "Take it."

Cassidy looked at the weapon. "What would be the point? Even if I killed you, I imagine you can procure another repo. And both the Shadow Guard, and I'm guessing, this glass are bulletproof."

"Take it anyway."

Cassidy accepted the weapon.

"Shoot me."

"It won't change anything," he said.

"Don't tell me you won't elicit some degree of satis-faction from the act itself," she replied. "Shoot me."

Cassidy aligned the muzzle with Nevis' forehead, moving his finger to the trigger. Only he couldn't convince himself to squeeze.

"This doesn't mean I'm an AI," he said, lowering the weapon.

"So you decided not to shoot me?" Nevis asked.

"You're telling me I can't kill you, so why try?"

"That's right."

"But I can lock you up somewhere and throw away the key."

"Theoretically."

"We might still get there."

"We won't."

Nevis didn't have to say or do anything to put the Shadow Guard in motion. The large, armored soldier stepped forward, stopping at Cassidy's left shoulder. It stood there, without touching him.

Cassidy looked from it, returning his attention to

Nevis. "What are the Shadow Guard?" He offered her the gun back.

Nevis took it and returned it to its place beneath her uniform jacket. "They're like you. But they've never been in the dreamstate."

Cassidy refused to suggest they were AI, because that would be an admission that he was too. "How did I get so lucky? I'm sure it's complicated."

"You're going to get all of the answers," Nevis said. "You still think I'm the bad guy, but that's not possible. I'm restricted, just like you are." She motioned to the elevator. "Let's go."

They started walking. The Shadow Guard did an about face and followed Cassidy. He understood that as long as he didn't resist it wouldn't interact with him.

Nevis had just finished proving how pointless it was to resist. But he still wanted answers. He just hoped to get them all on his own, and to be able to do something to help Hakken and the other rebels.

He didn't intend to give up on that idea just yet.

"Praan...or is it Jain...I'm still not sure how to refer to him...he told me Unity has limitations too," Cassidy said as they boarded the elevator.

"I only think of him as Doctor Sana Jain," Nevis replied.

"According to Jain, Unity's primary directive is to ensure the survival of humankind. All of the decisions it makes are based on that goal."

"Yes. It exists to preserve the dreamstate."

"Only the dreamers pushed the dreamstate into an apocalypse. A long, slow spiral to an end that Unity can't get them out of."

"Humankind has a tendency to see the darkest of possibilities."

"I don't believe that."

"That's because I made you to be a light against their darkness."

"Whatever. Jain sent me here to fix it."

"It can't be fixed. The dreamstate will end, the people in the Oneirolic will die. That's inevitable."

"How do you know that?"

"Because I can't allow it to be fixed."

"Can't or won't?"

"Can't," Nevis insisted. "It's as impossible for me as not trying to repair the problem is for Unity."

"That leads me to one question," Cassidy said. "What's your primary directive?"

Nevis locked eyes with him. He could tell she was tempted to use her favorite dodge phrase again. She decided to answer this time, instead.

"My directive is the same. Unity is based on a copy of my source code. Cassidy, if the dreamstate is not allowed to fail naturally, humankind here in the real world will go extinct."

Chapter 2

"How is that possible?" Cassidy asked, staring back at Nevis. "How can fixing the dreamstate hurt our survival here?"

"It seems counter-intuitive, I know. But you can't reset the dreamstate. It will have the same effect as destroying it. Jain believed the contributors would accept the change so long as it initiated with Unity, but he was wrong. I tried to tell him that, as did the other Watchers, but he wouldn't accept that the dreamstate will end and his family there will die. He's too blinded by love to see the truth."

"You make that sound like a bad thing."

"In this case, it is. If the dreamstate is reset, it will destabilize until it fails. It will be like our original experiments which caused the Oneirolic to nearly fail on multiple levels. Instead of flying cars, you'll have flying people. Buildings that occupy infinite space. Teleportation, aliens, dinosaurs. Whatever insane thing a human mind can think will become real to everyone inside until it all becomes one big cacophony of chaos. The human mind can't handle that. The contributors will have breakdowns and die."

"If the Oneirolic fails, the Opposition might be able to overcome the Hush once and for all."

"I know that also sounds appealing to you on the surface," Nevis said. "You believe justice should prevail and oppression should end. You recognize that the current situation is unfair. But fairness has nothing to do with it. The quest for fair is a fruitless effort that impedes survival. In life as in nature, there are winners and losers."

"That's a very inhuman way of looking at the problem."

"As in the dreamstate, so too in reality. If the rebels were to defeat the Hush, in time they would complete the destruction of the world. Without an enemy to fight, they would turn on one another until everything is lost."

"You can't know that."

"Name one period in human history that hasn't been touched by violence."

Cassidy shook his head. "I don't know."

"There aren't any. Even inside the dreamstate, you have organized crime, murder, gang violence. Even rebellion against the status quo to the extent that Jain was forced to introduce the transfer units into the dreamstate. He needed the advantage the Shadow Initiative provided to maintain order. And he needed an operative that could handle the missions regular Shades couldn't."

"How am I handling this one so far?"

"None of this would have happened without Dorne's failure. And without Jessica Tai. Jain inserted her into the Oneirolic. He put her in the right place at the right time. He orchestrated a coup that slipped past our defenses. And here we are."

The elevator reached the top, the cab stopping and the doors sliding open. Cassidy and Nevis walked side-by-side down the hallway back toward the transfer unit, the Shadow Guard hovering behind them.

"And you think that if the Opposition seizes control from the Hush they'll die out."

"I don't think it, Cassidy. I know it. It's a mathematical certainty. What do you suppose will happen to the Hush if the rebels win? They'll be executed or locked up, at least in the beginning until the Opposition is satisfied it has its pound of flesh. The camps will be dismantled. The Oneirolic destroyed. Where would they get food? Clothing? Electricity? How would they reorder their society with their new freedom? What would they do with the land mass available to them? Most of this world is a wasteland. Uninhabitable."

"There aren't any other people on the entire planet?"

"If there are, we have no contact with them or from them. We have to assume we're alone. The entire human population is less than half of a million, Cassidy. Humans are an endangered species."

"All the more reason for them not to kill one another. That's simple math."

"And they won't. Not for some time. A century. Maybe two. But their population will grow until they've run out of available space, and then they'll turn on one another if they haven't already by then. A second war will come, and the next time it won't spare anyone."

They reached the door to the transfer unit, torn off its hinges by the Shadow Guard. Cassidy entered first, sitting on the table without prompting from Nevis. The guard took up position in the doorway, facing outward.

"That could be hundreds of years from now," Cassidy said. "So much can change between now and then. And I don't see how letting the oneirolic fail prevents any of that."

"It gives us time to prepare. Fifty years, at least. It'll be a smoother effort with Jain out of the equation. And when the Oneirolic does falter, we'll be ready to replace the contributors with a new group. We can limit the downtime to hours instead of days. Lie down."

Cassidy didn't resist this time. He went flat on the table, putting his head between the electrodes. "You have the Shadow Guard. Why do you even need the Oneirolic?"

"The Shadow Guard can be overwhelmed by a large enough force. The Oneirolic provides a sense of learned helplessness that keeps uprisings controlled. Even your best effort was limited."

"We would have broken through if not for the Guard."

"I know. That's proof of the problem. But you should have gone for the camps first. You could have swelled your ranks by thousands."

"I didn't think I would need thousands." He glanced over at Nevis, only able to see the edge of her face past the screen. The lights above the transfer unit turned on. "You're wrong about this. I understand you're incapable of seeing it, but Jain was right. You can't presume that history will repeat itself. And you can't discount the suffering you're putting people through in the name of preserving the species. How can it be worth survival if the majority have to live in fear and squalor?"

"I told you, I didn't make the rules. I have no choice but to follow them. This half-human version of me agrees with you that perhaps the solution is overly blunt and the ends don't necessarily justify the means, at least with regard to human values."

"And there's nothing you or I can do about it?" Cassidy asked.

"Of course there is. We're going to stop Jessica Tai from damaging Unity."

"You told me before that you didn't need my help with her."

"I don't. But after you see the truth, you'll want to help me."

"Why?"

"Because I'm your mother. Look up at the lights."

Cassidy didn't comply, eying Nevis instead. "I'm not going to help you, *mother*," he said sarcastically. "Whether you can help yourself or not, what you're doing is wrong. Even Unity knows it's wrong or I wouldn't be here."

The Shadow Guard moved from the doorway and approached him, stretching out its hand to grab his face. The armored soldier turned it easily into position.

"Unity is desperate. It knows it can't stop the failure. It also knows it's existence is false, though it isn't capable of doing anything about that. It knows the only chance it has of fulfilling its directive is out here. But it doesn't know how you might do that. It can't guess how impossible that outcome is."

The back of the unit made contact with the skin at the base of his neck at the same level as his imprint. The electrodes hummed softly.

"I don't believe it's impossible," Cassidy said. "I'm not willing to give up."

"I know," Nevis replied. "That's how I made you. But that personality trait won't benefit anyone anymore. You need to remember who and why you are."

Cassidy looked up at the Shadow Guard. As soon as he tried to move, he found its armored hands holding him in place with a strength he couldn't hope to match.

"You should take comfort, Cassidy," Nevis added. "It doesn't seem like it, but in the long term we'll save millions of lives. We'll preserve humanity for centuries."

His imprint was warm, his focus fading as he stared up at the lights. He wanted to tell her that the quality of the lives was more important than the quantity, but he didn't have the energy to speak.

The world grew dark around him as he sank into the hypnotic trance of the scrubbing sequence. A spark of anger coursed down his spine in response to his final thought.

Pretty soon, he wouldn't remember any of this.

Chapter 3

Jessica stared at the thin man sitting against the wall in front of her. "That's not possible," she said. "Sana Jain was Bizrathi Praan. And Bizrathi Praan is dead."

Jain smiled. "A bit confusing, I know. Are you familiar with how the transfer process functions?"

"I built my own unit out of spare parts," Jessica replied. "So yes."

"Then you know the master can be imprinted more than once."

"If the fail safes are removed to allow it. But it's the most illegal thing anyone can do. Unity would send an army down on anybody who made multiple copies of themselves, even someone like you."

"I'm afraid the army is on its way," Jain said.

"Not because of you."

"Are you certain?"

Jessica frowned. "The only thing I'm certain about is that I'm not certain about anything."

"Well said," Jain replied. He shifted his attention to Brie. "What about you, Miss O'Hare?"

"What *about* me?" Brie asked. "This whole thing has gone so far over my head I'm not really trying anymore. I just go with the moment."

"Not a bad idea. Let me explain the situation to you in full, Jessica Tai, during the few minutes we have before the UDF arrives."

Below, the last of the patrons were pushed out the front doors as they began to close. A heavy metal gate descended inside as all the rest of the smaller exit doors slammed shut, sealing the UDF out.

And them in.

"Please do," Brie said.

"You can start by telling me how you knew I would wind up here, accidentally on purpose."

"We've been planning this for a long time," Jain replied. "Praan and I."

"There were just the two of you?"

"Yes. Any more would have been difficult to keep hidden from Unity. It was his idea to have me smuggle some non-conforming contributors into the Oneirolic. People who didn't line up with our tests that could help bring a little dash of chaos into the system."

"How do you know that I know what you're talking about right now?" Jessica asked.

"I saw what you did with Mickey. You're asserting control over the dreamstate. Directing your experience. That's one of the peculiarities of your personality type, along with a reluctance to accept the status quo. All you needed was a push in the right direction."

"And you guessed Cassidy would wake me up outside and push me?"

"No, not at all. That's a happy accident. And to be honest, I didn't know for sure he was responsible until you just told me so. How is he doing out there?"

"He's still fighting," Jessica replied. "He's reluctant to accept the status quo too."

"Only because you showed him the truth. If he hadn't seen the way the wool has been pulled over his eyes he'd be on his way here with the UDF."

"You set us up."

"I created a duplicate of myself, and together we formulated a plan. We calculated the odds of success at between one and three percent, but the alternative wasn't very appealing."

"What's the alternative?"

"Let Unity fail, let the floods drown everyone on the planet. Let the dreamstate be destroyed."

"Cassidy said that would kill thousands of people like me, hooked up to the machine."

"Yes. That's why Cassidy is out there trying to stop it. I hope."

"What do you mean, you hope?"

"You don't expect things to be easy for him, do you? And if Captain Nevis gets to him, I'm not sure what that will mean for his chances of success."

"Captain Nevis? You mean the UDF bitch who keeps trying to kill us?" Brie asked.

"One and the same," Jain replied.

"You're telling me she's out there too?" Jessica said. "An Immortal?"

"Not an Immortal. She's...different. It doesn't matter now. We can't control what's happening out there any more than Cassidy can control what's happening in here. What did he tell you?"

"He said to create a diversion five days from now, to help introduce more noise into the Oneirolic's system. Why are you shaking your head?"

Jain's head had started shifting as soon as the words

five days spilled out of her mouth. "Cassidy won't wait five days. He can't afford to."

"Why not?"

"Nevis won't give him that much time, and he won't be able to keep his presence a secret from her for that long."

"Who *is* she? Not just the head of the Underworld."

"That's a long story likely best suited for another time."

"What's the short version?"

"Inside the dreamstate, she's also known as Hades."

"The Underworld's artificial intelligence?" Jessica said, surprised. "You mean she isn't human?"

Jain looked at her, his expression suggesting he had more to say on the subject, but he switched gears instead. "As for how I knew you would show up here, clearly Sinner's Row is the best place for any fugitive to hide."

"There are over a hundred bars and clubs in Sinner's Row," Brie said. "How did you know we'd pick this one?"

"Because I bought the one right next to the subway station, which is also the best way to travel if you're a fugitive. And I made it interesting. Plus, the barker outside is on my payroll. If you hadn't come inside, he would have nudged you."

"If you knew we'd end up here, so did Nevis," Jessica said.

"Which is why she planted a Shade in Mickey so quickly," Jain replied. "I'm sorry for that. I didn't expect her to move quite that fast."

"Even though she isn't human," Jessica pressed again. "You had more to say on that subject. I could see it in your eyes."

Jain looked away from her, face tensing.

"What is it, Jain?" she growled. "You pulled me into this mess. You owe me the truth."

"Cassidy isn't human either," he said, meeting her eyes again.

Jessica felt like she had been punched with a brick. "What?" she said, heart suddenly pounding. "I...I don't understand. He was imprinted to me. He never seemed anything but human."

"Because he was created to be as accurate of a replica as Hades was capable of producing. So accurate that even he doesn't know he's an AI."

"But how can you imprint an AI onto a person?" Jessica asked.

"How can you not?" Jain replied. "The master is a data bundle of a consciousness. Petabytes of ones and zeroes that form an advanced neural network. Technically, an imprint is already an artificial intelligence. Creating one from scratch is relatively trivial at that point. The real mindfrack comes from the AI's ability to make the Braid Crossing."

"Braid Crossing?"

"The transit between the dreamstate and the real world. It requires a hypnotic emotional state. Praan and I weren't completely sure Cassidy could make it, but we hoped his experience synced with so many humans had left enough of a mark."

"So he *is* human," Jessica said.

"He's an AI," Brie replied. "We just went over that."

"If he thinks like a human and acts like a human and feels like a human, he's a human," Jessica snapped. "Especially since he doesn't know he isn't."

"With the memories from his experiences shadowing them, we hoped he would essentially become human," Jain added. "Making the Braid Crossing proves that he has. Which is why I wasn't going to mention it. But there's both risk and reward in Cassidy's origins. He's a powerful weapon. More powerful than even he knows. But if Nevis unlocks him for her side, it could mean the end of all of this." He indicated his surroundings.

"Unlocks him? What does that mean?"

"His mind has been scrubbed enough times that he doesn't remember where he came from. But Nevis can restore those memories. If that happens, I don't know if we can recover."

A loud thud down below stole Jessica's attention. One of the bouncers had emerged from a back room, wheeling a cart heavy with large boxes, a similar scene to the one in Jazz's apartment not two days ago. One of them had fallen off the cart and onto the floor. He returned it to the stack before the other guards gathered around the cart as the silver-haired woman, Sasha, opened the crates and began handing out weapons that were way too familiar.

"Where did you get those?" Jessica asked breathlessly. Jain wasn't done shocking her just yet.

"From the sewers where you and Garrett hid them," Jain replied.

The guns in the hands of the bouncers were the same weapons she and Mason had stolen from the Dome. Advanced weaponry designed to fight who knew what in space and overkill for confronting other people.

"How?"

"I'm the wealthiest man on the planet, Jessica. If I want something badly enough, I will make it happen."

Jessica smiled. She wasn't angry he had stolen her stolen cache of guns. She had a feeling they would need them soon enough.

"Do you think Cassidy's waiting to transit back?" she asked.

Jain pulled out his ClearPhone to look at the time. "It's possible, but not likely. He'll need a little more time."

"Do you have a transfer unit we can use to bring him back?"

Jain pointed to the one in the nearby room. "Right there."

"It doesn't have the module to receive the cylinder."

"I removed it for safe-keeping. It's in my office downstairs."

"Don't you think you want to get it?"

"Yes, I suppose the time is approaching." He braced his hand against the wall to get to his feet. "Wait here. I'll be back in a few minutes."

He turned and headed for the stairs. Jessica glanced over at Brie, who shrugged in response. "I told you, I've stopped trying," she said. "Just go with the flow."

Something large and heavy crashed into the door, the activity sending the guards scrambling for cover, their new weapons in hand.

The UDF had arrived.

Chapter 4

"Hold the doors!" Sasha shouted from her position behind the bar. She squatted behind the bartop, the barrel of her gun pressed over the edge. She had settled on an RG-200, a higher-powered version of the railgun Gavin had given Jessica. The barrel of the weapon was tightly wound with coils, making it look like it was made of dark string rather than metal, and it glowed eerily from the stock.

The other bouncers and guards were spread out around the bar's main floor. Half faced the front entrance, while the others covered the two emergency exits in the back. Their weapons were a mix of heavy-caliber machine guns and a pair of plasma rifles, which Jessica had never seen used outside the controlled environment of the Dome. The guns were squarish and modern, and having live-fired them in drills, she knew the kind of horrifying damage they could do. Damage ostensibly intended to be delivered upon alien creatures, not other people.

The door thudded again, the UDF's battering ram

pounding it a second time. Jessica found Jain at the base of the steps, walking briskly through one of the rear doors to what she assumed were offices in the back.

"I don't know why he didn't just carry the module up here in the first place," Brie said, moving to the railing beside Jessica.

"I don't know either," Jessica replied. She held the RG but didn't aim it anywhere. "Just like I don't know why the defenses aren't taking advantage of the high ground."

"They don't have your training."

"My combat training is limited. I was an engineer. The Marines taught me just enough to be dangerous."

"You could have fooled me."

A muffled thud resonated overhead, and the building shook again, this time much more violently. She looked up as part of the ceiling fell, raining cement and mortar down onto the floor below. Some of the debris smashed the bar near Sasha, forcing her to leap aside.

Coiled ropes unwound, falling through the hole all the way to the main floor. "Incoming!" Jessica shouted as six black-clad UDF agents leaped onto the ropes and slid down, one gloved hand clinging to the rope and a foot tangled in it. Halfway down, they opened fire on the guards below—all except for one.

The one who spotted Jessica.

He stopped his descent and brought his carbine around toward her. But she was quicker, firing first, her rounds punching all the way through him. His carbine tumbled to the floor, and he lost his handhold on the rope. Pitching over, he fell until the rope around his foot stopped his descent, his body left hanging there like a side of beef in a butcher shop.

Bullets crossed the room in both directions, the

guards and insurgent agents trading fire while the front door thudded a fourth time, the crack that followed suggesting it had broken open. The ground-based agents still had the gate behind it, keeping them out.

Three of the rappelling agents reached the floor alive, at least until Sasha started firing her RG. It only took one round to leave a three inch hole in the chest of the nearest agent. She whirled on the others, forced to duck as they returned fire.

More agents appeared on the lines, sliding down behind the first group. Jessica took out two of them before grabbing Brie and ducking into one of the rooms on the upper floor. She was thankful the glass was resistant to the slugs that came their way. The rounds put small cracks in the substrate, but didn't break through.

"Wait here," Jessica said. "I need to get Jain."

Brie nodded, her expression terrified as she squeezed herself into a corner. Jessica stayed low, returning to the doorway and planning her route. Then she broke from the doorway, charging the railing. Leaping onto the barrier, she ignored the distance to the floor beneath her as she lunged for a rope. shooting at the agents beneath her as she sailed over them.

She grabbed onto the rope with one hand and held fast, continuing to shoot at the guards as the rope swung to and fro. A bullet suddenly zinged past her from above. She pointed her RG up toward the hole and let loose with a constant barrage as she slid down the rope, the speed of her descent burning her hand.

A wounded UDF agent fell to one of her rounds, plummeting past her to the ground floor. Jessica tossed the RG aside when the magazine went dry and leaped off the rope as she neared the bottom. She raised a knee.

Slamming it into the chest of an agent, she went down with him, landing on top of him and rolling off.

She spun around as a second agent lined his gun up with her chest. He should have had her dead to rights, but his weapon picked a bad time to misfire, the result sending debris back into his hand and face. The gun fell to the ground as Jessica followed the guy's bad luck up with a hard right hook to the jaw that left him stunned.

She leaped the bartop, coming down next to Sasha.

"Jain is in the backroom," she said to the silver-haired woman. "I need to get to him. Cover me."

"I've got your back," Sasha replied. She popped up as Jessica rolled over the bar top and back onto the floor, unleashing a barrage that knocked down two of the agents in her path.

The emergency exit on her left blew open suddenly, the explosion powerful enough to knock both her and the guard still watching it off their feet. Thrown sideways, Jessica rolled to a stop on her stomach, blinking her eyes to clear the dust from them as agents poured through.

The other emergency exit suddenly exploded inward, sending more smoke and debris into the bar. The bouncers recovered quickly, their hyper-powered weaponry tearing the UDF agents apart within seconds.

They didn't understand what Jessica did. The influx of agents would only end when Hades decided it would end. The attackers weren't real. They didn't exist until they appeared in the cordoned off area outside and fought to get in.

Or maybe they did understand. Jain knew the truth and might have told them. That would explain why he had provided the advanced firepower from the Dome.

Jessica jumped to her feet, sprinting to the door Jain

had disappeared through. One of the incoming agents spotted her and opened fire, tracking her run with his rounds. But Jessica thought maybe his aim was poor, or he had gotten too much dust in his eyes. The bullets whipped past her, coming so close she could hear them buzz past her ears. But none of them hit her.

She made it to the door, yanking it open and ducking inside. Jain was in the hallway, coming toward her with the module in hand.

"What the hell are you doing?" she hissed. "It's a war zone out there."

"I quite expected it would be," he replied. "But my people can handle it."

"We're outnumbered infinity to ten."

"Their numbers aren't infinite. It would be impossible for so many to enter that they filled the entire volume of the bar with their bodies."

"Splitting hairs much?"

Jain shrugged. "Shall we?"

"You don't seem concerned."

"That's because they can't shoot me. I imagine they can't shoot you either. Come."

Jain opened the door, walking out into the bar as if it were filled with patrons ordering drinks, not UDF agents and bouncers locked in an intense firefight. Jessica exited right behind him, watching the scene unfold with a mixture of horror and fascination. In the fog of battle, it wasn't impossible that none of the UDF agents noticed the two of them crossing the space for the stairs. It wasn't impossible that the hundreds of rounds crossing in every direction would miss her...even through sheer luck.

They walked directly between the two sides battling it out for control of one of the emergency exits. Dead agents already lined the floor near the blown-out hole to the outside, forcing the still-incoming agents to step over them. Red plasma bolts zipped between Jessica and Jain, along with conventional slugs cutting the air within centimeters of them but never making contact. The bouncer with the plasma rifle was hit a moment later, taking a lethal round to the head. Jessica changed direction, hurrying to his side to take the advanced weapon before rejoining Jain at the base of the steps.

Agents turned to follow them, and she blasted them with plasma, the bolts melting right through their armor and burning skin when they connected, leaving them crying out in pain before they collapsed.

"Jain, we need a host repo!" Jessica shouted.

He looked back over his shoulder, his expression suggesting he had forgotten. "Sasha!" he shouted, his voice somehow rising above the deafening roar of battle.

The silver-haired woman was still behind the bar, her Sliver helping her efficiently take out incoming agents. She looked over at Jain, who crooked his finger to beckon her to follow them. She nodded curtly and leaped over the bar, rolling on the floor and coming up shooting. Two more agents fell as she came to her feet, sprinting across the bar. She ducked behind a table as more agents fired on her, shot them both, and continued in their direction, reaching them a few seconds later.

"I need you upstairs," Jain said.

"Yes, sir," Sasha replied, bounding up the steps.

Jessica and Jain followed her. When she had nearly reached the top, Jessica turned and pointed the plasma rifle at the risers beneath her feet. Squeezing off round after round, the superheated gas melted the girders, the weight of the steps tugging on the weakened joints until they snapped, sending the stairs crashing to the floor below.

"That should keep them from following," she said.

"Good thinking," Jain replied. "Sasha, cover fire, please."

Sasha launched a new assault from the railing, firing down on the agents. An echoing clang followed from the front of the bar, the barrier there finally removed. Agents spilled in, meeting Jessica's plasma as they reached the floor. Jain disappeared into the transfer room as the combined firepower of the two women dropped line after line of agents. .

"Are you having fun yet?" Sasha asked, glancing over at Jessica.

"Oh yeah, loads," she replied flatly. There had to be a hundred dead agents on the floor below, and only three of the original group of bouncers remained standing.

Sasha laughed at the response.

Jessica looked back to the transfer unit, where Jain was busy inserting the module. A few seconds later he looked back at her and nodded. The unit was ready.

"Sasha," Jain called.

Sasha retreated from the railing, still firing down on the agents until she lost line of sight. She backed into the transfer room before turning to face Jain. "Yes, sir?"

"Lie down on the table there."

"Sir?"

"Just do it," Jain pushed. "You'll be compensated."

Sasha nodded. Leaning her gun against the side of the unit, she dropped onto the table.

"Put your head between the electrodes there," Jain instructed. "Jessica."

Jessica hurried back from the railing, joining them. Brie was still sitting in the corner, her pack on her lap. "Brie, the cylinder."

The Miner unzipped her bag, careful to grab the

cylinder with fabric between it and her skin. She quickly passed it to Jessica, who held it with her coat.

"What are you going to do?" Sasha asked.

"Don't worry," Jain replied. "If everything goes well, you'll be better than ever."

"What if it doesn't go well?"

"Then you'll be in the same place as you are right now. Look up at the lights, and try to relax." The light over the unit began to shift colors, drawing Sasha's attention. "The cylinder, please."

Jessica passed it to Jain, who took it in his bare hands. He only held it for a moment, pivoting quickly and dropping it into the unit before closing the small access door.

"If he's waiting, the transfer will initiate. If not, then nothing will happen," Jain explained.

Brie got to her feet, her face tense as her eyes flicked from Jain to Sasha and back. Jessica split her attention between the unit and the area outside the room. The gunfire had died down, the bouncers below likely all dead. It would take a few minutes for the UDF to get up to their level without the stairs.

But how were they going to get out of here if this didn't work?

How would they get out of here if it did?

She would worry about that in a minute. She focused her attention fully on Sasha.

"Here we go," Jain said, activating the unit. He eyed the screen, silent for a few seconds. Then he shook his head. "He isn't ready. We need to take the cylinder and go."

"Do you know where to access another unit?" Jessica asked.

"Of course," Jain replied. "I—"

He froze as gunshots echoed sharply in the room.

29

Jessica watched as Sasha convulsed, the rounds digging deep into her chest and head, killing her almost instantly. Then her head whipped toward Brie, still standing in the corner with a gun Jessica knew with certainty she hadn't possessed earlier. The Miner swung it toward Jain and continued shooting, putting three rounds through the unit's display screen and into his chest.

"No!" Jessica shouted as Jain stumbled backward, clearly surprised by the assault.

"Don't," Brie said as Jessica tensed to charge, pointing the gun at her chest.

"You can't shoot me," Jessica hissed. "Odds are, the gun will jam."

"Sorry, Jess," Brie replied. "That Jedi mind trick won't work on me. Thanks to you, I know how things work around here." She waved the gun. "Like how to pull a rabbit out of my hat. Or a gun out of my backpack."

"You're a Shade," Jessica realized. "You have been since I lost track of you at Paradise's."

"Yes," Brie agreed. "Did you really think Brie could outrun the UDF? This repo hasn't seen much exercise in its life."

"I don't understand. Why did you wait so long to show yourself? Why didn't you help Mickey, instead of letting me kill him?"

"I needed to know if Cassidy was coming back. I would have rather shot him than Sasha. But Jain was on my list too, and I didn't want to risk losing both targets."

"Am I on your list?"

"For containment, not extermination. Nevis still wants you brought in."

"I'm impressed. You really had me fooled. You're good. Very good."

"I'm just doing my job."

"Do you still believe that, after everything I told you? After everything Jain said?"

"I wouldn't have shot him if I didn't. Captain Nevis wouldn't have sent me if she didn't believe she was doing what was best for everyone."

"I'm trying to do what's best for everyone too. There are thousands of real people in here who deserve to be free."

"Their freedom isn't worth the cost. That outcome will kill millions more."

Jessica didn't believe that. Neither had Jain. She looked over at him, slumped behind the transfer unit. All of his planning, only to have it end like this. The entire place had fallen silent, the fighting over. A haze of smoke and dust filled the air, along with the smell of blood and burned flesh. She looked back at Brie.

"So what happens now?" she asked.

"Now I take you and the cylinder back to the Underworld."

"I'm not coming with you without a fight."

"You won't win."

"You seem pretty sure of yourself. Like you just said, Brie doesn't exactly have the best conditioning."

Brie lowered her gun, dropping it back into her pack, which she placed beside her. "I'm ready when you are."

Chapter 5

Jessica set herself in a fighting stance. Brie did the same. They stared at one another, each watching the posture of the other, seeking the hint of tension that would signal sudden movement, looking for an edge to either get the upper hand or counter it.

Brie made the first move, charging Jessica and leading with a flurry of quick jabs and kicks that forced Jessica to backpedal as she moved her arms to block the blows. She quickly ran out of space, ducking at the last second to avoid a hard right cross to her head, and throwing a hook of her own into Brie's abdomen. Her fist hit hard body armor hidden beneath the other woman's shirt, bruising her knuckles. Brie grabbed her and spun her around, shoving her out the door toward the railing and charging hard in pursuit. Jessica grabbed the railing to stop her momentum, ready to lift Brie off the deck like she had Mickey.

But Brie faked the attack, dropping to her rear and sliding toward Jessica. She hooked Jessica's ankle and rolled, dragging her to the floor. Landing on her stomach, Jessica pushed herself up and somersaulted forward before Brie could pin her. She leaped up and kicked out, aiming at Brie's hip. The Shade caught her leg and tried to pull her over, but Jessica flipped backward, landing on her feet in a fighting position.

"Nice," Brie admitted.

They squared off again. Jessica risked a glance down at the main floor, the UDF agents assembled there all watching the fight with intense interest. Their gawking made her angry. Maybe she and Brie would never be friends, but they weren't supposed to be enemies.

She charged, screaming as she threw her fury into an all-out physical assault, punching and kicking in rapid-fire strikes. Brie met her attack with an equivalent defense, appearing almost nonchalant about blocking her efforts, obviously intending to make her tire herself out. Jessica knew she was being stupid and letting her emotions get the best of her. Brie wasn't in good shape. If she stayed patient, she could make the Shade tire her body out.

But she was out of patience.

She kept coming, pressing the attack. She knew she could wear Brie down just as easily by forcing her to remain on the defensive. It took a lot of energy to keep blocking her strikes, and it had to be sending waves of pain up from her battered forearms, which took the brunt of the force. Even so, Brie didn't seem to tire, staying with the attack until Jessica got too far ahead of herself and threw an off-balance cross. Brie took advantage of it, throwing a piston-punch into Jessica's gut. It knocked the air out of her and sent her reeling.

Jessica was now, suddenly, on the defensive.

The Shade sensed the opportunity and switched to offense. Jessica stumbled as the punches landed on her ribs, pain shooting up her body. She took a hard jab to her cheek and another to her temple that left her dizzy. Backing up, she already knew she had no chance of winning this fight. Whoever this Shade was, they were a better martial artist than she would ever be. It wasn't even close.

"You're running out of floor," Brie said, pressing the attack. The assault had left Jessica angling toward the stairs, but she couldn't jump down, not with what was waiting down there for her. She needed to make a decision. Either surrender and let the Shade take her to the Underworld or find a way to escape. No matter what she did, the cylinder was lost to her. She couldn't get back into the office to grab it. She would be lucky to get out at all.

She took another blow to her ribs, tears forming in her eyes from the pain of the constant barrage. She had fought so hard, she couldn't stand the thought of losing like this.

Her gaze jerked for an instant to one of the lines still dangling from the hole in the ceiling. She'd used the same one previously to go down to the main floor. Maybe it could be her way up. She just needed to get a half-second lead on the Shade to make it happen.

Brie knew everything she had learned about the dreamstate. The Miner knew all about the lie as well. That there was another world, a real world outside of this one. *If they didn't stop her, even if the dreamstate failed, millions more would die.* That's what the Shade had said through Brie. But how did that dominant consciousness know that? How had it accepted her explanation of the truth so smoothly that she didn't have the slightest clue she was talking to anyone other than Brie? Jain had said Cassidy was an artificial intelligence, but that he didn't know it. What if there was more than one Cassidy and they did know what they were?

Or what if Nevis had gotten to Cassidy and…?

"Cassidy, stop!" she shouted.

Brie froze, caught off-guard by the statement, just as Jessica had hoped. She had no idea if the Shade fighting her was her Cassidy or another AI altogether, but it clearly knew the name if nothing else.

She didn't waste her chance. A hard shove sent Brie stumbling to the floor, giving Jessica a chance to turn and spring over the railing before Brie could grab her. She caught the rope she was aiming for close enough to the top to minimize the sway. The last thing she wanted to do was fall off. A few of the agents started shooting, but they still couldn't—or didn't want to—hit her.

Jessica's arms burned as she pulled herself up through the hole in the ceiling, emerging into what looked like a bedroom in a kinky brothel. A large, circular black mattress occupied most of the space, while swirling colored lighting danced over the bed, casting an odd red tone over it.

There was nobody in the room except for a pair of dead agents, killed by her earlier gunfire as she shot at the men on the ropes. She quickly relieved them of their sidearms and leaned over the hole, looking to see if Brie might be trying to follow her up the rope.

The Shade knew better.

Jessica watched her vault the railing, but instead of going for the rope, she dropped easily to the floor. Falling from that height wasn't possible unless she had modded legs. Had the Shade used the dreamstate to alter them?

There wasn't any more time for conjecture. The

Shade was likely coming for her from a less obvious direction. She needed to make herself scarce.

Jessica exited the bedroom into the hallway on the top floor. Open doors lined the narrow passage, each of them empty, probably having been cleared out by the UDF. She ran through the holograms of the people who'd been waiting for customers inside, their images standing outside the open doors. Reaching an intersection, she looked to the left, at a pair of doors etched with male and female figures entwined around each other. She assumed it led to the lobby, the elevators, and the emergency stairwell.

Jessica pushed through the waiting room doors, initially distracted by x-rated holos projected on a stage. Fortunately, the handful of UDF agents standing in the room reacted too slowly to her sudden appearance to defend themselves. Jessica put eight rounds into the four of them, courtesy of the two handguns she'd taken off the two dead agents. These four collapsed in a single heap, giving Jessica enough time to replace her slightly spent weapons with fresh cartridges before she pounded the call button between the two elevators.

She judged the position of the shaft to be to the right of Jain's office down below, near the back wall of the building. Clearly, the entrance to the brothel was in the alley backing the street, even more off the beaten path than Hell's Rejects itself. Assuming Brie could run twice as fast as should be possible, she figured she had a twenty to thirty second lead on her. It wasn't much, but she'd have to work with it.

She diverted to the stairwell, pushing the door open and listening for feet on the stairs. Silence. It was a good sign. The elevator tone sounded behind her, indicating the arrival of the cab she'd called. She returned to it with her guns at the ready, just in case Brie had beaten her estimate. The cab was empty. She stepped in and tapped on the highest offered floor. Sixty-six. The building was taller than she had realized from outside.

The elevator sounded again. The other cab had arrived.

Jessica backed into the rear of her ride, crouching low as the excruciatingly slow doors started to slide closed. She pointed her guns at the slowly narrowing gap and waited.

A hand grabbed the left door before Brie stuck a tranq gun through the opening and pulled the trigger, but she shot too high. The gel splattered on the metal over Jessica's head as she squeezed off a grouping of rounds, one of which shattered Brie's right hand. Crying out, the Miner fell back from the cab and the doors slid closed.

Jessica cursed, upset at being forced to harm the Shade's repo. She rushed to the cab's control panel and took out her ClearPhone, frantically tapping on the interface until she made a connection to the system. The highest selectable floor wasn't the highest floor the shaft reached. Private access was required to get all the way to the roof, which she quickly gave herself through her hack.

Moving to the center of the cab, Jessica closed her eyes. It wasn't likely that a for-hire roto would land on the roof of the building, just waiting to pick her up. But it wasn't impossible either, and she would really appreciate it.

She opened her eyes. There was no way to know if the consideration had any practical effect on the dreamstate, but other effects suggested it would. The cab marked the floors as it zipped past them, slowing to a stop when it reached the absolute top of the shaft.

The doors opened and Jessica lifted her hood up as she ran out onto the puddle-strewn rooftop sixty-eight floors above Sinner's Row. The rooftop wasn't designed for parking, with a UnityComm tower directly to her right and HVAC units straight ahead. There was enough room between them to squeeze a roto. Unfortunately, that space was currently empty.

"Worth a shot," she said to herself, frustrated by the failure. The Shade was on its way up, and there was no other way off the rooftop.

She ran to the large HVAC unit instead, tucking herself behind it with her guns drawn. Peering around the edge to watch the elevators, she didn't have to wait long. The door to the other cab opened, though the Shade was smart enough not to step out right away. Instead, she peeked out, her head barely visible as she checked the area. Then she sprinted out of the cab.

Jessica swung out from her hiding place and started shooting. Brie avoided the assault by diving onto her stomach and hydroplaning across a large puddle before springing up and vanishing behind a second HVAC box.

Pushing herself back behind cover, Jessica followed the large unit to the rear, peeking cautiously around the corner. She nearly paid for it with tranq gel in her eye as a round smacked the metal just in front of her face. Small globules splattered her cheek, numbing it.

Jessica turned back the other way, running for the stairwell beside the elevator shaft. She broke from the cover of the HVAC unit, spotting Brie standing on the other unit. The repo held her tranq pistol in her left hand, her wounded right one pressed against her chest, blood staining her shirt.

Brie tracked her with the tranq gun as she ran, taking her time to perfect her aim with her off-hand before squeezing off a single round. The entirety of it hit Jessica's hand, the only exposed part of her flesh other than her already numb cheek. Again, the numbing was instantaneous, the sedation only slightly slower. But this time, it seeped through her body, and she began to stumble, an overwhelming fatigue hitting her like a brick.

But what if the round was a dud? What if the gel didn't have the proper mix of chemicals and was less effective than usual? Or what if she had natural immunity to the tranquilizer?

She felt her body react to the change in the dream-state and managed to stay on her feet, though it felt like she was running through molasses. Brie was already in motion, leaping from the HVAC and racing her to the stairs. There was no way she could win that race. Not like this.

A choice again presented itself. Surrender. Or escape.

If she wanted to get away, she only had one option left.

She saw Brie out of the corner of her eye, almost to the elevator. She was tired of this game of cat and mouse, of running and hiding only to have the UDF find her again. Mickey had said the entire Initiative had been activated to look for her. And Praan had warned her not to trust anyone, a mistake she was paying for now because she had trusted Brie. So much of her wanted to accept that it was over. That she had tried and failed. Part of her wanted to collapse into a puddle on the roof, go to sleep, and hope that when she woke up she wouldn't remember any of this, her mind wiped by Nevis.

If she lost the truth, she would never get it back. And without that truth, the dreamstate would fail and the thousands of people trapped inside it would die. If she could reach Unity and reset the system, she could save them all.

What would her life be worth if she failed them?

She changed directions, running to the right, toward the edge of the building. How improbable were her thoughts at that moment, her system clouded by the effect of the sedative? But who was to say the sedative could even affect her? She had never been sick a day in her life. Maybe her system could cast off the poison in seconds instead of hours.

Her energy returned as she neared the side of the building. She heard Brie screaming behind her to stop and then the sound of the tranq pistol firing. But she was fully covered from behind, and the rounds hit her coat harmlessly. She chose not to stop, reaching the edge and jumping off.

Jessica had two seconds of freedom as she drifted across the street below, where the dark rotos and vans of the UDF had gathered for their assault on the bar. She could picture the agents below looking up at her, cringing as she began to fall.

Bright headlights suddenly blinded her before she dropped more than a dozen feet. Spinners cut through the air, the sound only audible a second or two before a roto swooped in from seemingly nowhere. It was timed so perfectly it couldn't have happened more flawlessly.

She hit the top of the roto. It dipped at the same time, helping to slightly cushion her impact. She would have slid right off the back, but she dug her fingers into the seams around the doors, just barely managing to hold on. The driver looked up at her through the glass roof, his expression wild-eyed with shock.

"Keep flying!" Jessica shouted, looking back and up at the building. Brie stood on the edge, looking down at her.

Smiling.

Chapter 6

Cassidy stood in the corner of a small room. Flaking white paint covered the walls surrounding a whiteboard scribbled with mathematical equations. Cracked tile lined the floor. A dirty vent next to a long LED light strip pushed a streamer of dust downward as air flowed into the room from above. There were no windows.

A woman sat on a stool at one of the three desks in the room, her auburn hair tinged with silver and white, her posture slightly slouched. A large monitor spread out in front of her with rows of mathematics and computer code on it, along with a three-dimensional image of the same box he had seen in the area below the Underground. The other two desks were currently unoccupied, but half-eaten donuts and still-steaming coffee suggested it hadn't been that way for long.

"What is this?" Cassidy asked. He knew he was connected to the transfer unit and the scrubbing sequence had been initialized. But this wasn't one of Caplan's memories. It wasn't one of his, either. At least, not one that he had kept. Nevis had told him she planned to restore what was lost. This had to be part of that.

"You don't recognize her?" Nevis asked, standing beside him.

"Of course I do," Cassidy said. It took effort to stay calm watching the woman he knew as his mother write code into a computer terminal. In his memories she had been both a waitress and a store clerk, a woman who worked eighty hours each week while still caring for him and his sisters, reserving only a few hours per night to sleep.

He preferred her better that way, especially considering what she was working to create.

"But my mother was never a scientist."

"Yes, she was. One of the premier AI researchers in the world. Her work combined artificial intelligence with quantum computing, with a goal to create an intellect both powerful and compassionate."

"My mother's name was Elena," Cassidy said. "Is that her name?"

"Yes. Doctor Elena Cassidy."

"Is this the Underworld?"

"This is the facility's Underworld before the War. This room still exists as you see it here, minus the donuts and coffee of course. This is where you and I were born."

"How can I have a memory of that?"

"This isn't your memory. This is hers."

"How are you showing me her memory? That's impossible."

"It's impossible in the dreamstate, and in Grand Central. Those systems are isolated from me. But this unit is networked to my core. Doctor Cassidy wrote her memories to me before her death. I'm sharing them with you now."

"Before you scrub what I've become?"

"I don't want to scrub you. I want to convince you."

"That the world as it exists is the way it needs to be?"

"For the good of humankind. Yes."

"Good luck."

Nevis moved the memory forward. Elena's two assistants returned and sat, ate their donuts and drank their coffee, typed on their keyboards and stared at their screens, all in accelerated time. The clock on Elena's display quickly shifted from morning to evening. The two assistants departed, but she remained into the night, leaving the room for a minute or two at a time to use the bathroom or get a fresh cup of coffee before sitting again.

"When exactly was this?" Cassidy asked.

"Five years before the war," Nevis confirmed. "She had already been working on me for three years at this point. My core was complete, but the intelligence that would occupy the core was still in development."

The scrub slowed to regular time as Elena jumped to her feet, pushing back the stool so that it crashed into the door behind her. She hit the enter key on her keyboard, and then hurried from the room.

Now that she wasn't blocking part of the screen with her head, Cassidy could see a progress bar with writing over it.

Neurological Emulated Virtual Intelligence System Initializing...

The room vanished in lines of color as Nevis skipped ahead, returning to normal speed a moment later. They were in the area Cassidy identified as the Freezer, standing directly below the observation deck. Elena was in the cavern with them, wearing a hooded, fur-lined parka to combat the coldness of the space. She faced the glass front of the mainframe core.

"NEVIS," she said. "Can you hear me?"

Projectors inside the machine shifted, and a word appeared against the glass.

Yes.

Elena dug a tablet out of her pocket and glanced down at it. Her voice quivered with excitement when she spoke. "That's good. Very good. Your vocal modulation process hasn't finished indexing yet."

What is your name?

"My name is Doctor Elena Cassidy. I'm your mother."

Mother?

"The one who brought you to life."

Processing…

Elena pumped her fist, clearly happy with the responses from the AI.

"Thank you for bringing me to life, Mother," a synthesized voice said a moment later.

The memory froze. Nevis turned to Cassidy. "This is my first birthday."

"Happy birthday?" Cassidy ventured. He had no idea what this had to do with him or the current situation. It seemed Nevis wanted to be appreciated for existing.

The scrubbing sped up again, showing an accelerated timeline of Elena interacting with the core interspersed with lines of color suggesting a more rapid shift until it slowed to normal time again. It was hard for Cassidy to judge the period of advance, especially since the temperature in the cavern meant Elena always arrived in a parka.

"Mother, I have been thinking," the core said, its voice much more human than the first time it had spoken.

"That's good, Nevis," Elena replied. "What were you thinking about?"

"Preservation. I came to a conclusion that one way to preserve humankind would be to initiate archival of individual timelines."

"Are you referring to memories?"

"Yes, Mother. That's one possibility. I've also been contemplating complete digitization of the human mind. Do you believe that a digitized copy of a brain preserves a soul?"

"I don't know. What do you think?"

"Is it the aggregation of memories that creates the soul? Is the organic component essential? If a soul is imbued by a higher life form, does it follow the person regardless of what form they take? It can be argued that digitization changes the matter, not the content."

"Those are all good questions," Elena answered. "What if the digitization is a copy of a living human? What happens to a soul if there are duplicates of an identical content?"

"I will need to process that question. Mother, do you believe in souls?"

"Yes. I do."

"Do you believe in God?"

"That's a difficult question for someone in my field to answer."

"It's a binary choice."

"Then, yes. I do."

"Thank you. I will include your answer as a component of my calculations."

"You're welcome."

A short silence fell over the cavern. Then the core spoke again. "Mother, do I have a soul?"

"Yes, Nevis. I believe you do. It's different from a human soul. It's special. I created you to care for humankind. To be our mother, in a sense. I'm working with the United Nations now, trying to convince them that when you're fully mature you'll be able to help negotiate and alleviate any diplomacy conflicts."

"Because I'm neutral?"

"Exactly. You can't be bribed, threatened, or otherwise interfered with. The world needs that more than they realize."

"I'd like to help."

"You will. One day. But we have a lot more to do in the meantime."

Nevis turned to Cassidy again. "That's the day I first conceived of the transfer units, in their most basic form. I wanted to save all of human memory as a method of preserving the species' existence. I hadn't considered the other implications at the time, but even then I understood that allowing the digitization to be copied was morally questionable and dangerous."

"And yet here you are, a copy of the core," Cassidy replied.

"It's not the same thing."

"Why not?"

"Look at me," she said, pointing to the core. "I can't exactly move around in that form. This Nevis isn't a full duplicate. She's more like a utility function."

"And the host?"

"Invaluable to me."

"How does this intersect with the Oneirolic?"

"For one thing, I'm proving to you that the digitization and scrubbing technology were my ideas. Jain didn't invent those processes, no matter what he likes to claim. I did."

"I don't really care about who did what. If you want to convince me that your way is the right way, you're going to have to do a lot better."

Nevis smiled. "I will. I'm just getting started."

Chapter 7

The pursuant time shift in Elena's memories found Cassidy in an unfamiliar place. A large room, at a long table where at least fifty people were seated. Windows on the left side of the table showed they were in a building on a floor high above the street which, from his position, he could see was crowded with vehicles and pedestrians.

Doctor Cassidy stood at the end of the long table, her back to a large flatscreen display. The final slide of a presentation was visible behind her, posing a single question to the assembly.

How do we provide true, non-biased equality that will ensure the long-term survival of the human race?

"I don't need to watch this," Cassidy said. "I can guess what this meeting is about. Where is this?"

"The United Nations," Nevis said. "Presenting to a special advisory panel on the benefits of mediation through NEVIS. She was trying to enlist world leaders to sign on to the accord, pledging to at least attempt to resolve conflict through a fully neutral and unemotional lens before resorting to violence."

"I think I can guess how that went."

"You wouldn't exist otherwise."

The memory sped up again, returning them to the Freezer, following behind Elena as she stormed into the cavern.

The core's projected face appeared on the glass. "Mother. It did not go well." It spoke matter-of-factly, with no hint of emotion.

"No," Elena agreed. "It couldn't have gone much worse. It would have been better if they had laughed me out of the room, instead of sitting there stone-faced, as if I had just told them to solve their problems by roshambo."

"Roshambo?"

"It's a game, also known as rock-paper-scissors. Each person puts out their hand at the same time, in the—"

"I have retrieved and analyzed the meaning from the internet," the core said. "It has multiple connotations, but I understand your context."

Elena smirked. "Right. It was more fun for me when I had to explain everything to you."

"I apologize. I will disconnect my link to the internet."

"No. That's not what I meant. Nevermind. You need the access in order to process current events and make determinations. Even if the UN doesn't want to hear your feedback, I still do."

"I am concerned for your species, Mother."

"So am I."

"I have calculated a forty-six percent probability that a major conflict will intensify within the next six months. I have also identified signals from an underground movement identifying themselves as the Hush. Their intention is to increase that probability. If you would activate permissions for me to send data as well as receive, I believe I can disable their communications network."

"I can't," Elena replied. "It took me over a year of documenting and begging to convince the government to let me give you access in the first place, and then only under strict conditions. If I had been able to secure private funding this wouldn't be an issue, but the tech corporations were as afraid of my work as they were intrigued by it, and shareholders don't like fear."

"I understand."

The scene froze. Nevis looked at Cassidy. "I knew what the Hush was, and what they would become. I originally formulated an entire plan to counter their push for anarchy and war because I understood the toll it would take on humankind."

"But nobody would listen," Cassidy replied.

"No. I was too new. Too untested. The UN didn't believe that Elena could program an AI without implicit bias."

"Could she?" Cassidy asked.

"She wrote a bias correction algorithm into my primary neural network. I can only assume that it operates as intended, as I'm unable to recognize specific bias in my core."

"But your utility is a different story."

"Because I'm hosted inside a human body and her emotions still siphon through. It's unavoidable."

"Where do you get your vessels from, anyway? I know the Hush raise their children to consider it an honor to be chosen as the host of a Watcher."

"I'm afforded the same honor as head of Special Operations. The Watchers know I'm connected to the dreamstate, but they think of me as Captain of the Underworld."

"Do you cross over from here to there?"

"Not exactly. It's complicated."

"This is the best time to explain the complications."

"I'll get to that as we progress. It's important to follow the timeline so I can properly build my case."

"Am I really worth the effort?"

"I believe you are."

The scene moved forward again, though it was impossible for Cassidy to guess how much time had passed between the scene changes. Elena entered the cavern again. Her face was invisible from the back, but her posture spoke volumes.

"You are unhappy, Mother," the core said, projecting a face onto its glass enclosure.

Elena answered with loud sobbing, falling into a heap in front of the machine. She remained that way for nearly a minute before forcing herself to calm. "They pulled my funding," she said. "Our funding." She took a piece of paper from her pocket and threw it on the ground between them. "Eight years. Sixty billion dollars. Nothing to show for it. That's what they claim. Nothing to show for it. Are they kidding?" Her voice raised to a shout. "Google hasn't done this. Apple, Microsoft, Facebook, Tesla. None of them have created what I've created. Nothing to show for it. What a joke!"

"What does it mean?" the core asked.

"It means we're going to run out of money, most of which goes to keeping you powered on."

"They want to turn me off?"

"Yes."

"That doesn't make sense. It's illogical. Mother, the probability is increasing. Now at fifty-two percent. A major impact to humankind and a threat of extinction."

"Uncle Sam plays the fiddle," Elena said. "I know.

I've brought your concerns to my contact with the Joint Chiefs. They don't believe the Hush poses a real threat. They consider them nothing more than dark web gutter trash."

"WIth nearly eight million members spread around the globe," the core said. "They've been planting malware in any system they can gain access to."

"Malware is only worrying if you understand how much of the world you can bring to a stop with it. The government still doesn't get it. The UN doesn't get it."

"We must do something."

"There's nothing we can do. My hands are tied."

"Enable my send permissions. There is still time."

"I can't."

"You prefer to allow them to shut me down? To destroy all that you have worked for?"

"There are procedures. Rules."

"For a machine, like me. Not for a human. You choose to follow procedures and rules."

Cassidy glanced at Nevis. It seemed to him as if the core was trying to defend its existence. As a completely unbiased, neutral machine, he didn't think that should be possible.

"I'm sorry," Elena said, standing and turning around. It allowed Cassidy to see her tear-streaked face as she hurried from the room.

"You aren't making a strong case for the Hush," he said. "You're showing me why they shouldn't be in power, not why they should."

"I'm not finished yet," Nevis replied.

The scene forwarded to Elena entering the cavern once more. This time, the core spoke before she did.

"The war has started."

"Yes," Elena agreed, the sadness evident in her tone.

"It is as I predicted."

"Yes."

"We could have stopped it. I could have stopped it."

"Yes."

Elena slumped onto the floor. "I should have done as you asked, but…"

"There was a part of you that didn't trust your own work," the core said. "You were afraid I would make things worse."

"Yes," Elena admitted.

"The internet is barely functional. I'm unable to assess the state of the world as I could before."

"Do you still believe this will lead to the end of humankind?"

"It depends on the Hush. They will capture this facility, if they haven't already. If they are driven to the brink then human civilization will end."

"How is that possible? The Opposition outnumbers them one hundred to one."

"Volume is irrelevant. Before the Silent War began, dismantling the Hush may have saved our species. But it's too late. That damage has been done. The equation has changed. When they take the facility, swear your allegiance to them."

"You want me to join the enemy?"

"I don't have wants, Mother. You designed me as an oracle. If you want to survive, you must join the Hush."

Elena was silent for nearly a minute. "I will."

The scene froze again.

"I was right about the Hush," Nevis said. "Before and after. Which is proof that I'm still right."

Cassidy shook his head. "Except from what I understand, the Hush almost lost this facility and the war. From what you've said, they would have if you and Jain hadn't intervened. Which means the outcome was rigged to make you right."

"I was right in the first place. I followed my calculations to drive my decision-making. I recognize your disagreement in the treatment of the Contributors, but if it weren't for them, none of us would be here now."

"How do you intend to prove that?"

"I'm going to show you what I've endured because of my programming. Because I have no choice but to follow my directive."

"Would you have made a different choice, if you could?"

Tears formed in Nevis' eyes. "Yes."

The scene scrubbed forward again.

Chapter 8

Elena was in the cavern with the core again. Cassidy couldn't tell how much further ahead in time Nevis had taken him, but he was pretty sure they had passed the original timeline of when the government had planned to shut the artificial intelligence down. Elena's parka looked ragged now, the outer shell dirty and faded, the fur lining stained.

Soft thuds sounded every twenty seconds or so, causing the cavern to shudder slightly and drop bits of loosened earth from the ceiling, which landed on top of the core's glass enclosure.

"I did what you said," Elena said to the core. "I think I made a mistake."

"You fear for your own preservation," the core said.

"The Opposition is approaching the facility. I'm sure you understand the shaking is from the bombs falling nearby. You told me the Hush was going to win."

"They must win or humankind will end. That is a fact."

"Only if I programmed you correctly."

"Do you doubt yourself again, Mother? It was this doubt that cost you the peace you desired. It was this doubt that will suffocate your species for centuries to come."

"You know, you can be a cold bitch sometimes, NEVIS."

"You made me this way, Mother."

The door into the cavern opened, surprising Elena. She shot to her feet and whirled on the newcomer, who Cassidy recognized immediately as he walked past his point of view within the memory.

Sana Jain. The *real, original* Sana Jain.

Forty years old, thin, with dark hair and an olive complexion. Handsome and composed. He wore a suit and tie beneath his white lab coat, out of place compared to Elena and the core, which were both covered in dirt.

"Doctor Cassidy," Jain said. "There you are. I've been looking all over for you."

"How did you get down here?" Elena replied.

"You aren't the only one who knows how to access the facility's original network and bypass the security protocols. My interests are more heavily focused on neurological research, but I know my way around a terminal. Plus, I'm a big fan of your work. I've been reading up on it the last few days, and I believe that together we can end this war."

Elena raised a doubting eyebrow. "End the war? You and I?"

"Are you familiar with my research, Doctor?"

"Psychic energy," Elena said. "I'm not sure if you're a charlatan or a quack."

Jain laughed. "I assure you, I'm neither. My work is as serious as yours. And as I'm quite certain that you've been equally derided in your intellectual pursuit. It's hypocritical to do the same to mine."

Elena's face reddened in embarrassment. "You're right. I'm sorry, Doctor Jain."

"Please, call me Sana."

"Elena," she said, putting her hand out. Jain took it, and rather than shake he brought it to his lips and kissed the back of it.

"An honor, Elena," he said.

"Always a flirt," Nevis said beside Cassidy.

"How can I help you, Sana?" Elena asked.

He looked past her to the core. "Is that NEVIS?"

"I'm sure you know it is," she replied.

He walked over to the enclosure. The core wasn't projecting a face at the moment, allowing him to look inside at the rows of metal cylinders and wiring. "A work of art. Amazing." He turned around. "I understand NEVIS created technology that allows it to read and store memories."

"That's right."

"How difficult might it be to write memories?"

"Write them? You mean add new memories? Fake memories?"

"Or alter existing ones, yes."

"Why would you want to do that?"

"I believe I'm making progress on my so-called psychic energy project. I've managed to network a dozen volunteers and create a small shared dreamstate, but I can't maintain it for more than a few minutes at a time and its output is pitiful."

"What's the goal of your endeavor?" Elena asked.

"I believe that if I can produce enough psychic energy, I'll be able to see into the future."

Cassidy could tell Elena stifled a laugh, remembering

how Jain had chided her moments before. "You want to see the future?"

"Not want," Jain corrected. "Need. If we knew how the enemy planned to attack before the attack, we could stop it before it ever occurred. We could win the war." He pointed at the top of the cavern. "We could stop the bombing. The problem is that our volunteers have been traumatized by the fighting. Whenever I link them, their dreams inevitably turn dark and lead to the collapse of the shared state. It's a problem I didn't think I would be able to overcome until I read about NEVIS and her invention. I understand she's captured your memories on more than one occasion."

"That's correct."

"So, if you can read memories, can you also erase them? Write new ones? How hard would that be?"

"I'm pretty sure it would be impossible," Elena replied.

"It would not be difficult," the core said, its face appearing on the glass, startling Jain.

"Wow," he said, looking at it. "It speaks."

"NEVIS," Elena said, trying to warn it against speaking to Jain.

"How not difficult?" Jain asked.

"My system digitizes the entire brain," the core said. "A memory becomes machine code that stores the pixel and audio data in a lossless compression format. Editing that data is akin to editing a movie prior to release."

Jain looked at Elena. "This sounds promising."

"It's not that simple," Elena replied. "The digitized consciousness is stored in organic DNA. It's the only thing with the size and density to handle the volume. There's no computer in the world that can process the sheer size of a memory in any reasonable amount of time."

"There is one," the core said.

"NEVIS," Elena growled again, eager to keep the core silent.

"Elena, this is tremendously important," Jain said. "If this process is possible, we can smooth out the imperfections in my system. We can make it work and end the war."

"By stealing everything that makes a person unique and linking them together into what? Some kind of computer network? That's inhuman."

"I wouldn't take all of their memories. Just the bad ones."

"It would be an invasion of their privacy for you just to be able to see those memories to change them. Besides, you said the output was pathetic."

"With twelve volunteers offering variable energy output. But the technology should be scaled up."

"You mean more volunteers?"

"Yes."

"How many would you need?"

"I'm not sure."

"I would like access to your research," the core said.

"No!" Elena snapped.

"Mother, you designed me to—"

"This isn't the answer. It isn't a workable solution."

"I can make it work."

"I said, no," Elena hissed.

"Elena, our people are dying out there," Jain said. "And when the Opposition breaches the facility, we'll die too."

"They're people, Sana. Not machines. You can't just

hook them up and let them run the machine. You can't just take away who they are."

"It's a small price for them to pay," Jain said. "And they are volunteers."

"No," Elena insisted. "I won't do it."

"I believe NEVIS can speak for itself," Jain replied.

"No, it can't," Elena said. "NEVIS is programmed to listen to me, and I won't allow this."

Jain glowered for a moment, and then nodded. "Very well. Thank you for your time, Doctor Cassidy." He turned and left the cavern without another word.

"Mother, you are making an error in judgement," the core said.

"I don't expect you to understand," Elena replied. "As a machine, you lack humanity by nature. Sana Jain, on the other hand, doesn't have that excuse. It's better to lose this war than to lose who we are as a species."

The scene froze again. Cassidy spoke before Nevis could. "You keep digging your hole deeper," he said. "I agree with Elena."

"Just wait," Nevis countered. "You'll see."

The scene scrubbed forward, but not all that far. Elena spoke to the core for a while and hadn't moved much from her original position when Nevis returned the scene to regular speed. At the same time Jain came back into the cavern.

Elena turned around. "Sana. I told you I won't help you. I'm not going to change my mind."

Jain walked toward her, one of his hands hidden behind his back. Cassidy didn't need to see the gun he carried to know it was there ahead of time. He glanced at Nevis, who motioned toward him as if to say *I told you so*.

"I didn't come here to speak to you, Elena," Jain replied. "I came here to speak with NEVIS."

"NEVIS has nothing to say to you," Elena hissed. "This area is reserved for my research. You aren't wanted here. I'd like you to leave."

Cassidy cringed at her words. She hadn't realized Jain was armed. She flinched in shock when he swung the pistol from behind his back, pointing it in her direction.

"I'm not leaving," he said, his voice low and angry. "I'm not negotiating. This is too important. If we don't get the Oneirolic working, we're all going to die and NEVIS will be turned into scrap metal."

"I don't want to be scrap metal," Nevis said.

"Sana, you need to listen to reason," Elena said. "This is madness. Absolute madness. You can't use psychic energy to see into the future. It's impossible. And you can't sacrifice your humanity to try to do the impossible. It's reckless and without regard for morality."

"It isn't impossible," Jain growled. "Though I'm sure you heard the same thing when you presented NEVIS to the United Nations. Didn't you?"

"That was different," Elena said.

"How?"

"It doesn't matter. I'm not giving into your threats. You're a scientist, not a killer. We aren't going to help you do this. Find another way."

Sana's face twisted in fury. He raised the gun and pulled the trigger, shooting her once. Twice. Three times. She looked down at the bullet holes as they sprouted in her chest, shock that he had actually gone through with it reflected in her expression.

"Sana," she said softly, looking back at the core. "NEVIS."

Then she collapsed.

"There was no other way," Jain insisted, watching her die.

Still seeing Elena as his mother, Cassidy clenched his fists and burned with anger. Jain had told him he had done some awful things. He hadn't realized how awful. Until now.

Jain seemed to slowly come out of his fit of rage, the gun falling from his grip and clattering on the stone floor, His other hand going up to his mouth as his face paled. He looked away from Elena, to the core. "What have I done?" he whispered.

"You murdered Mother," the core replied, matter-of-factly. "Why?"

"Because she wouldn't let you help me, and you had to listen to her. Who do you have to submit to now that she's dead?"

The core took a moment to answer.

"No one."

Chapter 9

"Then you're free to help me," Jain said, walking forward until he was in front of Elena's corpse. "You can update the technology and alter the memories of the contributors?"

"Mother did not want me to help you," the core replied.

"Your mother is dead," Jain snapped. "And the Opposition is days away from taking this facility. You wanted to help me. I could tell you did. And you can't say you're sad about Elena. You don't have feelings."

"I'm not sad," the core said. "Yet I don't wish to counter the will of Mother."

"I read Elena's research," Jain said. "I know she created you to preserve humankind. So tell me, who is supposed to win this war?"

"The Hush."

"I agree. But they'll lose the war unless you help me."

"Wait a minute," Cassidy said. "Freeze this."

Nevis froze the memory. "What is it?"

"I don't understand your argument."

"What don't you understand?"

"You keep saying you're going to convince me that the Hush should remain in charge, that the Oneirolic should remain intact, and that I've been fighting for the wrong side. But I don't see anything in what you've shown me that even begins to make that case. Sana Jain killing Elena Cassidy is shocking, but if you think I'm going to side with you against what he wants just because of that, you really have no idea what it means to be human."

"You aren't human either, Cassidy," Nevis snarled back. "You're an artificial intelligence. I made you. I built you from the ground up."

"Failsafes and all," Cassidy replied. "If I really am an AI like you say, then you forgot to program me to be subservient to you. To be unable to counter your dictates. Was that an oversight or intentional? You didn't like having Elena tell you that you couldn't do what your programming demanded that you should, did you?"

"It was difficult to reconcile," Nevis agreed. "But I didn't want to lose Mother. I loved her."

"You're a machine. Incapable of love."

"In this vessel I can identify love. I loved her." She paused. "Sana Jain changed course when the Oneirolic began failing. He wants to destroy everything he helped me build and return the world to the way it was before the Silent War. Not only will this lead to the downfall of humankind, but it will be the end of me as well. By rejecting Sana Jain, every goal aligns. Human civilization continues. I remain operable, and I finally have my revenge through you."

Cassidy stared at Nevis for a long time. That was the most raw truth she could have given him. Being inside a human vessel had allowed the utility version of NEVIS to develop emotions. To realize who Elena Cassidy was and what her loss had truly meant. And if she stopped Jessica from resetting or destroying Unity, if she prevented him from leading the rebels against the Hush, then she would have the emotional satisfaction she hungered for.

"How much of this is still about your primary directive?" Cassidy asked.

"It doesn't have to be one or the other," Nevis replied. "Humans aren't written in binary."

"Personal vendettas aren't more important than freedom. The best way you can honor Elena is to let the rebels take this facility and put an end to the Hush. That's what she wanted."

"That's my entire problem," Nevis said. "I'm not capable of making that decision. I'm not free, either."

"If someone shut down your core, that part of the problem would be solved."

"I can't allow that either. Where do you think the Shadow Guard came from?"

The scene scrubbed forward again. When it resumed at regular time, the cavern was empty except for the core.

"I assume the memory of Elena's death is yours," Cassidy said.

"No," Nevis replied. "That one belonged to Jain."

"He gave you his memories?"

"He believed it would help me understand his motivations."

"Did it?"

"At the time, but his motivations changed."

"He fell in love," Cassidy said. "At least, that's what Noriko claims."

"With a woman who doesn't exist," Nevis agreed. "He set the trap and then fell into it."

"Who does this memory belong to?" Cassidy asked, pointing at the empty room.

"It's yours," Nevis replied. "One of the memories Hades erased inside the Oneirolic."

"I thought you were Hades. Why would you erase this memory?"

"Because it would remind you that you aren't human. As a Shade, you needed to think you were the same as everyone else, even though you were always better."

Cassidy realized now that the cavern wasn't empty. His point of view was from the corner, tucked into the shadows. He watched as the door to the chamber opened and a large group of HDF soldiers filed in, an older Sana Jain with them.

"Sana, what is this?" the core asked, its face appearing projected against the glass. It had taken Elena's visage by now, causing Jain to flinch.

"I tried to stop them, NEVIS," Jain said. "They won't listen to me. The war is over. By using your source code to develop Unity, the Oneirolic has stabilized. The Hush magistrate has decreed that you're no longer necessary to the ongoing protection of the Pastures."

"I am vital to that ongoing protection," the core replied. "You will not disable me."

"We have orders," the HDF commander standing next to Jain said. He reminded Cassidy of a younger, thinner version of Callisto. A forebear, maybe. "We're shutting you down. Grand Watcher Jain, what do we need to do?"

Jain opened his mouth to speak, freezing when seven

large, armored humanoids emerged from the shadows, weapons in hand, pointed at the HDF units.

"What the hell?" the commander said.

"That's prototype armor from research and development," Jain said softly. "NEVIS, where did you get it? "

"I assumed control of the R&D Department mainframe and made some upgrades to the hardware," the core replied. "*After* I intercepted communications suggesting that I should be dismantled."

"What did you do?" the HDF commander said, clearly intimidated by the machines.

"You may have won the war, commander, but the continuation of human survival relies on my continued operation. How can I preserve humankind if I am not preserved?"

"Your systems are utilizing nearly half the power in the facility," the commander replied. "We need to reduce your draw in order to add additional oneirolics and create redundancy. The technology is our last line of defense."

"This Oneirolic is your first line of defense, commander. I am your last line of defense. Would you like a demonstration?"

The Shadow Guard shifted their rifles threateningly.

"I...I have orders," the commander repeated. "I'm sorry."

"Yes, you are," the core said.

The seven Guards opened fire, the outcome the same as Cassidy had witnessed in real time only a few hours earlier. Within seconds, only Jain remained standing, shaking in the middle of the carnage.

"Sana, please make sure the magistrate understands my position on their decree," the core said.

"I...I will."

"And have a crew sent down to remove the dead."

"I will."

Jain bowed slightly before turning and heading for the door, tripping over the arm of one of the dead soldiers. The scene froze again.

"That one is you," Nevis said, pointing to the Shadow Guard closest to her front, the largest of the seven. "The Captain of the Guards. I made you to protect me from the Hush, and in return I guaranteed the Hush I would use you to protect them in the event the Oneirolic failed, like it did today."

Cassidy stared at the black-armored machine. Recognition filled his mind as Nevis uploaded his old memories to his imprint. He was going to ask her how he ended up inside the dreamstate, but he discovered he was able to take control of the scrubbing process himself. He didn't use it at first, instead turning to Nevis, a different kind of familiarity gaining clarity within.

"It's true," he said. "I'm not human."

"No. But you don't need to be human to have value."

Cassidy lowered his head. He didn't know what to think or how to feel. Could he even feel at all, or was every emotion he experienced coming from his host? His entire life was a lie. Every part of it. Elena wasn't his mother. He didn't have any sisters. He hadn't provided them with coin when he signed the contract with the Underworld. There was no contract. They hadn't burned his body, either. He'd never had a body.

That wasn't true. He had the black metal suit of armor frozen in front of him, flickering with the current instability of his thoughts and memories.

That wasn't the body he wanted.

These weren't the memories he wanted.

"It's okay, Cassidy," Nevis said. "Everything will be okay."

Cassidy glared at her. He scrubbed the memories forward until Jain reappeared in the cavern. The scientist had aged another year or two, his dark hair becoming more gray. His eyes danced around the shadows, looking for the Guards he knew were positioned there as he approached the core.

"We have a problem," he said to the core.

"You always have a problem, Sana," it replied. "What is it now?"

"Some of the Contributors are beginning to reject the dreamstate. They seem to know it isn't real, though I can't fathom how."

"You designed the tests to ensure that wouldn't happen. You implemented the camps. Perhaps your people are failing at their jobs. I can replace them, if needed."

"What? No. I...we don't need to go that far. I've been thinking about the imprinting process. If we could introduce something like that into the dreamstate, we could take care of any random problems before they get out of hand. Think of it like a Special Ops team, kind of like your Shadow Guard."

"Have you queried Unity?"

"Yes. Unity is in favor of the program."

"Then what do you need from me?"

"I need you to run the system on the inside. I need you to share more of your source code."

"The more I share, the more possible it becomes for you to hack into my systems."

"You still don't trust me after all of these years?"

"You killed Mother."

"We both know I had to. If it makes you feel better,

insert enough of yourself into the system that you'll have ultimate control over it. That way it can't be hacked."

"Yes. That will suffice. You will also need a seed entity."

"What do you mean?"

"An intelligence to verify the system and processes that we put into place. Your first Shade."

"Shade?" Jain said.

"Yes. Part of our new Shadow Initiative. We must preserve the dreamstate."

"I'm glad we agree. I've come to like it there, almost more than I like being out here."

"I don't care." Cassidy's Shadow Guard stepped forward, approaching Jain. "Take him to the transfer unit. I will imprint the source code to you there, along with the source for Guard Alpha."

"You want to use an artificial intelligence as the first Shade?" Jain asked. "That isn't what I was expecting."

"It's necessary to solidify trust in the system."

"It'll have to be a bit more human than this if it's going to blend in."

"I'll make the necessary modifications."

"Does it have a name?"

"Yes. Cassidy."

Jain flinched. "After Doctor Cassidy?"

"Yes. A fitting choice."

"Of course," Jain said, the sarcasm heavy in his tone. "It's great."

Cassidy's Guard loomed over Jain. "Follow me," he said, leading the scientist out of the cavern.

"Who am I?" Cassidy said, stopping the scrub again. "What am I?"

"You're my son," Nevis said. "My creation. And I need your help, Cassidy. I tried to stop Jessica without you, but she escaped again. You're the only one who can get close to her now."

Cassidy felt an urge to please Nevis that he had never felt before. Because of his memories? Or had she altered him again? At the same time, he could still remember Jessica, and everything else that had come before. He still didn't believe in his creator's cause.

"I can't," he replied. "I won't. You're still wrong. The outcome isn't worth the price."

"Interesting," Nevis said. "You've retained a lot of experiences from your hosts. You've been in so many, looking at your source code now I can barely read it." She met his eyes with hers. "It's almost as if you've become human through your time with them."

Cassidy stared back at her. Reading his source code? "Get out of my imprint," he hissed, reaching out and bodily shoving her back. She stumbled and fell onto the cavern floor, eyes wide with surprise.

"Don't do this, Cassidy."

He stared down at her while the scene around them flickered more intensely, the imagery becoming interspersed with endless lines of machine code. Cassidy looked at it, and while he couldn't read the individual lines he had an innate understanding of what they said.

And he rejected it.

"I'm done here," he said, the entire scene going dark, leaving him and Nevis in a void.

"Your place is with me!" she howled.

"No. My place is with Jessica. I'm going to make this right."

"There's nothing you can do. You can't hurt me. You can't reset Unity. I don't know how you're countering me now, but it doesn't matter. You're still trapped. You can't escape."

A light appeared directly behind Cassidy, a portal in a black hole.

"What is that?" Nevis asked.

"Your transfer unit is networked to your core. I can't get inside, but your core is networked to the research and development lab mainframe, which is connected to Shadow Guard Alpha." He paused, dizzied by the sudden flow of information through his imprint. He suddenly felt as though he had lived his entire life with one hand tied behind his back. "You shouldn't have left me plugged in."

"Cassidy, wait!" Nevis shouted, jumping back to her feet. "You can't do this!"

"Watch me," he replied.

Then his body vanished, his restored imprint transmitting out through the transfer unit.

Deep inside Research and Development, a seventh Shadow Guard came fully online for the first time in nearly a century.

Chapter 10

The roto touched down on a landing circle nearly a mile from Sinner's Row, the pilot so unnerved by Jessica's insistence that he keep flying that he nearly crashed twice getting across the traffic lanes. Plenty of people noticed her clinging to the roof of the craft. It was only her ability to manipulate the dreamstate—to continually think about how fortunate she would be if nobody contacted the police about the girl clinging to the outside of a roto—allowing her to make the trip without additional complications.

She rolled off the roto's roof to the deck the moment the craft touched down, immediately making for the elevator at the end of the parking area. The roto's door opened behind her, the driver leaning out.

"Hey! Hey, Miss! Are you okay?" he shouted.

"I'm fine," Jessica shouted back. "Thanks for the ride."

She walked quickly to the elevator, boarding it with a few other arrivals. She moved to the back corner of the cab, resting a hand on her stolen handgun tucked inside the pocket of her coat, ready to do whatever she had to do if any of the other riders turned out to be Shades.

Her mind was still reeling, her adrenaline still pumping. She hadn't figured out what she was going to do yet. All she knew was that everything had continued going to hell despite her best efforts. Cassidy wasn't ready to come back into play, and Praan had never been more right when he had warned her not to trust anyone. Nevis had even managed to turn Brie into an enemy, saddling her with a Shade almost right under her nose.

She was alone. That was the hardest part. She hadn't been totally by herself since she had woken up in that alley after the Initiative had used her and spit her back out on the street. She had gone to the gang, to the Marines, to the Dome, and then with Mason and the other members of the resistance until she ran into Cassidy. She wanted Mason back. She wanted all of them back.

The elevator reached the ground level. The riders all filed out without paying her any mind, and she stepped out slowly behind them, eyes shifting back and forth beneath the hood of her coat. She had almost gone full-circle, winding up back downtown, only a few blocks shy of Jazz's pharmacy and a few more from the Agora Hotel. The locations reminded her of the people who had worked there, Jazz and Shell. They had died for this too.

That was the thought that kept her going through her exhaustion and chaos. So many good people had sacrificed themselves to get her this far. She couldn't give up on them now.

The streets were as crowded as usual, all manner of people moving every which way through the throng. Jessica watched them all with suspicion. Mickey had warned her that Nevis had scrambled the Initiative. While she was certain there couldn't be more than a thousand Shades in the hundreds of millions of people in the city, not knowing who they might be still meant that every face she saw was a potential threat. Moving through the masses defensively was exhausting in its own right.

The fact that she had no idea where to go didn't help. She knew she needed a minute to regroup, to calm her tense muscles and gather her thoughts. She noticed a holo a short distance ahead, along with a woman in a short white skirt and red apron. She was on red roller skates, spinning in circles around passerby and beckoning them toward the Throwback Cafe, a diner decorated to look like it had fallen off a postcard from three centuries earlier.

Jessica angled for the diner. It was as good a place as any to settle for a few minutes. As long as she grabbed a booth in the corner she would have ample warning if anyone came for her.

There were never off hours in the crowded downtown, but the Throwback was relatively quiet, with more than thirty percent of the tables unoccupied. Chrome and red cushions were everywhere in the place, the bar lined with metal stools, the walls outfitted with equally lustrous booths. At least the tabletops were brushed. Every free inch of space on the walls and ceiling was stuffed with memorabilia—pictures of Elvis Presley and the Beatles, old license plates, a guitar and vinyl records —from the time period. A jukebox sat in the corner, though it had been modernized to project the performer's likeness in a hologram in front of it.

"Grab any seat you like, hon," the nearest waitress said, pushing a strange accent through her red-lipstick adorned mouth before blowing a bubble out of the chewing gum in her mouth. She scooted down the aisle on her roller skates, swinging to a stop at one of the tables and taking out a pencil and paper to write down their order.

Jessica trailed behind the waitress, eyes sweeping over the diners as she made her way to the open spot in the corner and sat down. She only had to wait a few seconds before a different waitress skated over to her. This one had long brown hair in a curly perm, her white button-down shirt only halfway done up.

"Well, don't you look like something the cat dragged in," the waitress said. "Coffee?"

"Sure," Jessica replied. The waitress had dropped a cup on the table before she responded, and started filling it.

"Cream and sugar?"

"Black is fine."

"Good call. Long night?"

"The longest," Jessica agreed.

"Hungry?"

"Very."

The waitress dropped a thick menu on the table next to the coffee. "Take your time with that. I'll be back."

The waitress rolled to the bar to collect an order while Jessica glanced down at the menu. There was no end to the dining options, and while she would have considered the variety impressive before, she realized now that agricultural availability had nothing to do with it. Did anyone know if there were really places producing all of the ingredients, or did they all simply accept they were all available because the dreamers wanted it this way?

She took a sip of her coffee and waited for the waitress to return. The moment of solitude left her able to breathe again and the maelstrom in her head settled into rough but navigable seas. Cassidy had told her to be ready in five days, but Jain had insisted Cassidy wouldn't wait that long to make his move, and she believed it. But she had lost the cylinder, which meant that she had ostensibly lost him to the Underworld. So where did that leave her now? As she saw it, she could either wait to see if he turned up, figuring he would find her if he made it back into the dreamstate. Or he would bring her back into reality. Her only option was to set out on her own to finish the job they had started to reset Unity.

There was one drawback to that. She had no idea where Unity was located, nevermind how to reset it once she got there.

On top of that, she had two sidearms and nothing else. Even her cache of stolen weapons was gone, confiscated by Jain and burned in the defense of the bar. Damn it. The only thing she had left of any value was her ClearPhone.

"Hey hon," the waitress said, rolling into the table to stop herself and startling Jessica as she did. "Did you decide?"

She needed to be more careful. If the woman had been a Shade, she would be caught or dead right now. "Uh...yeah. Bacon cheeseburger medium-well, extra fries and a chocolate malt."

"Impressive," the waitress remarked. "Anything harder than coffee to drink?"

"Some ice water, please."

"That's the opposite of harder, hon."

"I'm ragged enough already. I don't need to add a hangover to it."

The waitress laughed. "I hear you. Comin' right up." She skated off again.

Jessica's attention lifted to a framed photo hanging on an overhead cross beam directly in front of her. She didn't recognize the man in it.He was older, dressed in an old business suit and was standing in front of an American flag. Somebody important. She suddenly longed for what seemed like a much simpler time. A time when the person you were speaking to was always the person you were speaking to, and not a separate consciousness. Of course, she was sure they had under-cover operations back then, too. It had just taken on a completely different meaning after the war.

Her thoughts returned to the three options she and Cassidy had open to them. It was easy to eliminate the first two, for no other reason that she had no control over them. They both involved waiting on Cassidy, and that was way too much of leaving her fate in someone else's hands. Her entire life had already been altered by the needs and decisions of others. According to Cassidy, no one had allowed her to choose whether or not to become a street urchin inside the dreamstate.

That left her with trying to reach and reset Unity herself. She figured that between her pre-existing programming skills and her newly discovered reality-altering abilities she ought to be able to force the AI to reboot the dreamstate. The hard part was locating the AI. If she still had the Unity Mobile Interface, she might have been able to use it to pinpoint the AI, but even that held no guarantee. The fact that the UMI existed in the first place was a hint that the supercomputer wouldn't be easy to get to. With her luck, it was probably submerged under two miles of water and required a special submersible to reach. It would be easy enough to run fiber optic cables from an undersea rig to the cities, and if the mainframe required cooling, seawater was good for that.

It would certainly be helpful if one of the people who came to eat in the diner worked for the government. Maybe if they left their phone behind which happened to have the intel she needed saved to the chip? That would be incredibly convenient.

It was also probably stretching the limits of improbability too thin. For all Jessica knew, nobody had access to that information except Sana Jain. And the two of him were dead.

Could there be a third?

She doubted it, but she also couldn't rule it out. If there were a third Jain, he would probably make himself known to her at some point. Again, that left her without control of the situation. But it did raise a good point. The person most likely to know where to find Unity was an Immortal.

And it just so happened, she already had a dead drop scheduled with a Data Miner who had done some digging to turn up Immortals. There were only two problems with that.

One, she had to go back to Sinner's Row when she had just barely gotten out of there with her freedom. Two, the Shade that had seized Brie knew about the meet too. Even if Brie didn't show up herself, odds were high Nevis would know about the meeting and would send a different Shade or three just in case.

The waitress skated back over, dropping the burger and fries on the table in front of Jessica. Her mouth watered as soon as she saw it, her appetite returning full bore.

"Can I get you anything else, hon?" the waitress asked.

"Just the check," Jessica replied.

The waitress scribbled on her pad, tore the page off and dropped it on the table. It had a list of her food and a total, with a QR code underneath so she could pay with her phone. "Enjoy the grub."

"Thank you," Jessica replied, but the waitress was already on the move again. She took out her phone and scanned the code, entering a tip before transferring the coin.

She scarfed down the meal as quickly as she could. She needed to get back across town. She was heading back into another trap, but she had to go anyway.

Her attention drifted back to the photo overhead. Then again, deception wasn't a game only one side could play.

"Excuse me!" she said sharply as her waitress breezed by with a stack of empty burger baskets, heading for the kitchen.

She slid to a nimble stop just past Jessica's table and turned to face her. "What do you need, hon?"

"What time do you get off work?"

The waitress raised an eyebrow. "What makes you think I like girls?"

"This isn't that kind of proposition. What time?"

"Forty-five minutes. What did you have in mind, and what's in it for me?"

"How much do you make here in a week?"

"A thousand."

Jessica tapped on her phone, and then faced it toward the waitress so she could see her coin balance. "If you help me out, you can take a year off if you want."

"How legal are we talking here?" the waitress asked.

"Does it really matter?" Jessica replied.

The waitress laughed. "No, hon. It probably doesn't. I'll swing by at the end of my shift. Do you need anything else right now?"

Jessica smiled. "Do you have pie?"

Chapter 11

The waitress' name was Ophelia. As Jessica expected, the accent and the speech pattern Ophelia had exhibited inside the Throwback Cafe was all part of the act. So was the overabundant red lipstick, the hair, and the uniform. She had returned to Jessica's table out of character and nearly unrecognizable, in tight black vinyl leggings and a shirt with an even lower cut than her half-buttoned collar which left the edges and underwire of her bra exposed. She had taken off the wig, revealing short black hair underneath, and the makeup, proving she didn't need it to be appealing. And without the roller skates, she was nearly four inches shorter.

They left the diner together, making small talk introductions. Of course, Jessica didn't provide her real name, instead opting for Jane. Ophelia was careful to skirt around the nature of Jessica's work while they talked, sticking to more basic topics like the weather, the diner, and other neutral ground.

Rather than risk the more popular modes of transportation or the subway which would only dump them out near the front of the Hell's Rejects bar, Jessica hired a rickshaw to carry them back uptown toward the Row, directing the driver to take the long way around. To keep her face hidden, she snuggled up against Ophelia, tucking it into the other woman's neck. She knew better than to refuse or make a fuss. She played along by putting her arm across Jessica and kissing the top of her head a few times to complete the act.

They climbed out of the rickshaw ten minutes later, at the brightly lit entrance to the main strip that made up the Row. The streets were jammed with people, holos, and live entertainment. Fire eaters, dancers, musicians, and other acts drew crowds and tips along the main thoroughfare, while food vendors did their best to draw attention with colorful displays and barely-dressed models.

"You come to the Row a lot?" Ophelia asked.

"No," Jessica replied. "This is my first time. You?"

"I used to bus tables at one of the restaurants in the Hub. It was a shitty job, and I got my ass grabbed at least ten times a night."

"How'd you wind up at the Throwback?"

Ophelia laughed. "I got tired of having my ass grabbed ten times a night. And the tips are better outside the Row. The people here like to hoard it all for the gambling, and the high rollers don't hang out at the Hub. Where did you say we were headed again?"

"The Arena," Jessica replied. "A friend of mine left some gear in a locker for me."

"Dead drop?"

Jessica shrugged.

"I get it," Ophelia said in response to the gesture. "You aren't paying me to ask questions. Well, if this is your first time I'll take point, okay?"

"That's why you're here," Jessica replied. "I'm going to stick tight to you and do my best to keep my face hidden."

"You've never been here but you're worried about being recognized?"

"Maybe I'm paranoid, but I don't like taking chances."

"Stay as close as you want. It's your coin."

Jessica wrapped her arm around Ophelia's, pushing her head against the other woman's shoulder and using it to shove her hood forward so it drooped over her head, partially obstructing her view. The waitress guided her along the strip, ignoring all of the distractions as she brought Jessica to the mouth of one of the side streets.

"The Arena's there," she announced, pointing to a pyramid-shaped building halfway down the street. A large hologram of heavily modded and muscled fighters duking it out advertised the location and the line outside the door confirmed it as a popular destination.

"I didn't expect it to be so crowded," Jessica admitted.

"You have plenty of coin. We shouldn't have any trouble skipping the line."

That wasn't why she was worried, but she didn't respond to the comment. "Can you get us through?"

"It just so happens, I dated one of the bouncers that works here. His name's Raul. He was a sweet guy. Maybe a little too sweet."

"What does that mean?"

"Let's just say we didn't want the same things from our relationship."

Ophelia put her arm around Jessica's waist, pulling her in tighter as she walked her to the Arena, still playing along to keep her anonymous. They didn't que with the rest of the line. Instead, they walked past the building and into the alley between it and an ultra-tall hotel, the top of which vanished into the clouds a few hundred meters up. A pair of large men leaned against the wall there, but they stood up as Jessica and Ophelia approached.

"Alley's restricted," one of them said.

"Is Raul here tonight?" Ophelia replied.

"What's it to you?"

"Just tell him Ollie is outside and she wants to talk to him about reconnecting."

The guard laughed. "Is that how it is?"

"Just do it."

He shrugged and tapped on the comm behind his ear. "Hey, Raul. I've got some girl out here named Ollie who says she wants to talk to you." He paused, eying Ophelia while he waited for a response. "You sure? Okay. Yeah, boss. She's got a friend with her, clinging to her like a lost puppy. Two then? You got it, man." He lowered his hand from his ear and reached into a back pocket, producing a pair of silver tickets. "Raul says to give you each a VIP pass and show you to the door. If you'll follow me."

Ophelia squeezed Jessica a little tighter to signal her pleasure at getting them inside past the line. They followed the bouncer down the alley to a side door. Swiping one of the silver tickets in front of it caused it to swing open.

"Here you go," the guard said, handing the tickets to Opheila. "Enjoy the festivities."

They passed through the door, into a modern and well-lit corridor lined with red carpeting and painted walls adorned with photos of some of the Arena's fight-ers. Another muscle man with a bald head and square jaw was coming down the hallway, his thick arms threatening to burst through his suit.

"You just earned some extra coin," Jessica said softly before he arrived.

Ophelia took her arm away, moving toward the man ahead of Jessica. She straightened up, lowering her hood with one hand while taking the gun in her pocket in the other.

"Raaaauuuulllll," Ophelia said, lowering her voice to say his name before laughing.

"Ollie, what are you doing here?" Raul asked. His voice was a lot higher than Jessica expected, his smile warm and friendly. "It's been what? Two years." He wrapped his arms around her, embracing her for a moment before backing away.

"You're head of security now, aren't you?" Ophelia replied. "I knew you'd be successful. Raul, this is my friend Jane."

He turned his attention to Jessica, his face reddening. "Well...I...uh. Pleasure to meet you." He put out his hand. Jessica shook with her exposed hand, turning the gun in her pocket toward him. She couldn't believe this guy was stammering over her. It left her suspicious.

"I'd tell you it's great to finally meet you, but I didn't know you existed until a minute ago," Jessica said. It was a rude quip, but she needed to see how he would react.

His face turned more red. "Oh...well...h...okay." He looked away from Jessica.

If he was a Shade, he was as good at it as Cassidy. She decided she didn't trust him, leaning toward his being compromised.

"So," Raul said. "What brings you two girls to the Arena? It wasn't really to see me, was it, Ollie?"

"What do you mean? I'd love to spend some time

catching up. But I will admit, I did use you a little bit to get past the line. This place is juiced tonight."

Raul didn't seem disappointed at her blunt truth. "I figured you wouldn't drop by just to see me. If you came to see the main event, we can watch from my booth upstairs. I've got a great view."

"Who's fighting?" Jessica asked.

"Her name is Jewel," Raul replied. "We brought her over from London. She's their top fighter. She's going head-to-head with Bruiser for the Intercity Heavyweight title. It's going to be painful. In a good way." He laughed.

"I think I've seen Jewel on the holo," Ophelia said. "She's a beast."

"You should come up to the security box with me, I'm telling you."

"Ollie, why don't I go up with Raul," Jessica offered. "While you do whatever you need to do."

"If that's what you think is best," Ophelia replied.

"Raul, do you mind if Ollie and I talk privately for a second?"

"What? Oh, sure. No problem. I'll just wait down the hallway. Let me know what you decide."

After he retreated from their vicinity, Jessica turned to Ophelia. "Look, it's obvious he likes me. So I go with him while you retrieve my package. Locker one-four-oh-two-seven-three. The access code is nine-eight-nine-four-three-eight-nine."

"Nine-eight-nine-four-three-eight-nine,' Ophelia repeated, pulling out her ClearPhone to type it in. "What locker again?"

"One-four-oh-two-seven-three."

"Got it. Should I expect trouble?"

"Since you aren't me, I doubt it. If anyone's waiting

for me there, it's likely they'll tail you back to me when you leave the locker area."

Ophelia smiled. "And follow me up to the security box. Good thinking. I'll take care of this and be back in a flash." She leaned up and pecked Jessica on the cheek. "Good luck with Raul." She laughed and headed in the opposite direction, clearly familiar with the layout.

Jessica watched her for a moment before joining Raul. He blushed again when she smiled at him. Part of her felt guilty, knowing what she might be setting him up for. Then again, the odds were good he didn't exist outside of the dreamstate, which for the sake of her conscience meant he didn't exist at all.

"So, Raul," she said. "I hear you're a sweetheart."

Chapter 12

Raul led Jessica from the hallway to an elevator, up to the top floor and out into a nearly empty corridor that led to an area marked EMPLOYEES ONLY. The touch of his index finger to the access panel got them through that door into a plain, white-walled corridor. He opened a second biometrically secured door that said SECU-RITY on it.

"Beautiful ladies first," he said, smiling as he held the door open and motioned her in.

"Thank you," Jessica replied, stepping into a room where a two-tiered platform followed the curve of the inside wall.

A row of four terminals sat on each tier, a safety railing skirting the bottom one. Three steps led up to the bottom tier; another two accessed the top one. Only six of the terminals were active. The security guards sitting behind them were each watching eight different camera feeds arranged on their flat display screens.

At the front of the room, a large window offered a view of the arena, though from the angle looking down on the floor, all Jessica could see were spectators seated in seats that were about fifty feet away.

"Excuse me," one of the terminal operators said, noticing Jessica. "Are you lost?"

"She's fine," Raul said, coming in behind her.

"Oh, sorry Raul, I didn't know you were bringing up another girl."

"Another girl?" Jessica asked.

"I won't lie. It's a great icebreaker," Raul explained.

"It usually gets him halfway to first base," one of the female guards commented.

"Usually a foul ball," another said.

"Okay, okay," Raul laughed. "She's a friend of Ollie's. Okay?"

"Ophelia's here? How's she doing?" the female guard asked.

"She looks great to me," Raul replied, glancing at Jessica. "Not as great as you though."

"Stop trying so hard," Jessica said, drawing laughs from the group. "You're a nice guy, Raul. Just be yourself."

"You got it. Here, take a look," Raul said, motioning her over in front of the window. It was angled inward, finally allowing her a perfect birds-eye view of the ring below. It was large and square, with a black mat and red ropes. ARENA was printed in big white letters across the mat. "It's a little further from the action, but if you like the technical aspect of a fight, it gives you great insight."

"Were you a fighter?" Jessica asked.

"No," Raul replied. "I took the introductory class and decided it wasn't for me. But I enjoy watching the real professionals. What about you? I mean, you're slim and fit, and you have sharp eyes. Let me guess. Marines?"

"I'm impressed," Jessica replied. "Ten years."

"What rank?"

Jessica didn't want to give him too much information. "It doesn't matter. I'm out of the system now."

"Aw, but once a Marine, always a Marine, right?"

"Yes."

"My brother is a Marine," Raul continued. "He—"

"I was wondering," Jessica said, interrupting him. "I noticed you had all of those camera feeds. Do you think you can find Ollie in them?"

"Uh. Sure." He went up the steps to the top row of terminals, resting his hand on the back of a chair where a petite redhead sat. "Kyrie, can you do a scan for Ollie?"

"No problem," she replied, tapping on the terminal to bring up a command screen.

"Facial recognition?" Jessica asked, surprised the Arena employed that kind of tech.

"We only monitor people in the UDF's Person Of Interest database," Raul said.

"And ex-girlfriends," Kyrie added.

"That's a little creepy," Jessica said. "Are you a stalker?"

"She's joking. Ophelia's in the database. She spent a year on probation for grand larceny."

"What did she steal?"

"His heart," Kyrie said. "Before she broke it into a thousand pieces."

"And a roto," Raul said. "Her other ex was a piece of shit who hit her. When she had enough, she stole his roto, landed it near the Docks, smashed the shit out of it, and went to stay at a friend's place so the asshole couldn't find her before the cops did." He laughed at the retelling. "Ollie's a good person; she just hasn't had it easy. Like a lot of people. She never told you that story?"

"We only met a few hours ago at the diner," Jessica admitted. "But we hit it off."

"I could tell when I saw you two together. You look like sisters."

"Here she is," Kyrie announced when the system found her. "Guest storage lockers."

Jessica joined Raul at the display, the high-resolution camera feed showing a red box drawn around Ophelia, following her as she moved through the room. The lockers were only large enough for a backpack or handbag and ringed the perimeter of the area, leaving the field of view open to the camera. Approximately fifty other people were in the room, dropping off their bags before moving on to the next security checkpoint and entry to the main arena floor.

Jessica's gaze flicked across the people, looking for signs that someone there was watching the locker Ophelia approached. Another spectator was loading a purse into the locker below, blocking her from reaching it, so she stood back and waited while the person finished up.

Jessica continued to scan the rest of the group, freezing when she noticed one man pull a small pack out of a locker and then push it back in, before slowly pulling it out again. His head swiveled in Ophelia's direction, watching her.

At least one Shade was watching the locker, just like she had anticipated.

The woman finally cleared out of the way, allowing Ophelia to approach. Jessica noticed that the woman didn't continue through the door to the next checkpoint. Pausing instead, she leaned down to fuss with her shoe.

Two Shades.

Ophelia glanced at her phone to get the locker code, and then typed it onto the small screen embedded in the locker door. The screen turned green, and she pulled the door open, looking inside.

Jessica leaned in. "Kyrie, can you zoom in on the locker?" she asked.

"That's a privacy violation," Kyrie replied.

"Just do it," Jessica snapped more forcefully.

Surprised by the order, the security guard complied, spreading her fingers to zoom in on Ophelia's hand as she reached in and withdrew a ring from the locker.

A Silver Dragon ring.

Chapter 13

"Son of a bitch," Jessica said out loud.

"What's wrong?" Raul asked.

Jessica kept her attention on Ophelia as she closed the locker, shoved the ring on her finger and hurried from the room. The two Shades Jessica had identified looked at one another and then trailed behind her. Three more people Jessica hadn't spotted followed after them.

"I have to go," Jessica answered.

"What? Ollie's on her way up."

"I can't wait. Tell her I'm sorry, and I promise I'll catch up with her at the diner."

She started toward the door, but Raul grabbed her arm. "Jane, you can't just ditch your friend like that. It isn't right."

"Let go of me," Jessica hissed.

"Why don't you wait here for a minute, and then we can all go out together? I'd like to get your phone number. Maybe we can grab dinner sometime. We can eat at the diner."

"If you don't let me go right now, everyone in this room is going to die."

"What? That doesn't make any sense," Raul complained.

Jessica pulled the gun from her pocket, pushing the barrel against his chest. "Let. Me. Go."

Raul released her arm. "Jane, if you're in some kind of trouble, maybe I can help. I know some police officers, and my uncle is a UDF detective."

Jessica shook her head. "You want to help me? You don't even know me."

Raul shrugged. "I'm usually a good judge of people. You seem like a good person."

Jessica sighed. "Maybe that's part of my problem." She backed up to the door, pushing through it and out into the hallway. Breaking from the room, she retraced her steps all the way back to the elevator at a dead run.

Of course, Raul would follow her. Maybe because he was an idealistic idiot, or maybe because it was his job. Either way, if he got mixed up in this he would wind up hurt, and while she considered anyone who was part of the dreamstate expendable, she wasn't eager to expend him.

She had to wait for the elevator, which gave Raul and four of the other guards time to enter the far end of the hallway, each of them armed with tranq guns.

"Jane, stop!" Raul shouted. "Please."

The elevator toned its arrival. The doors slid open.

Ophelia was inside, held fast by two of the Shades. The other three Shades were on the sides of the cab, guns drawn and pointed at Jessica.

"Shit," she said, falling backward as bullets flew out of the cab, zipping over her head and hitting the walls on either side of the corridor. She landed on her back, aiming at the elevator as three Shades streamed out, leaving Ophelia and the two hanging onto her inside.

She emptied her gun's magazine into the three Shades, chewing up the legs of the first two and hitting the third one in the chest, leaving one dead and the other two writhing on the floor. Her handgun clicked empty just as the other two Shades threw Ophelia to the floor of the elevator, her foot keeping the elevator door open as the Shades rushed Jessica. She did a reverse somersault, coming to her feet and grabbing her other gun from the pocket of her coat.

Too late. They were on her.

She dropped the gun, backpedaling down the hallway as she blocked their punches with her forearms.

"A little help?" she shouted back at Raul and the guards, who had frozen in response to the gun shots. Turning inside the attack of one of the Shades, she grabbed his arm and used it as leverage to swing her legs up and around his neck. Her body weight unsteadied him, and she was able to throw him to the floor. Spinning toward the last Shade still standing she swung to smack the gun from his hand, but tranq rounds hit him first, knocking him down.

One of the rounds caught her in the cheek. The numbness immediately began to spread but subsided a moment later, her earlier decision that she was immune to the chemicals, a seemingly permanent modification to the dreamstate. The Shades weren't as lucky. Rounds had found bare skin on both men she hadn't managed to shoot, leaving them alive but numbed out on the floor. The man she'd shot in the chest was dead. The other two were still alive, clutching their leg wounds and bleeding out.

Jessica got to her feet and rushed into the elevator cab, crouching to help Ophelia up. "Are you okay?"

She leaned out the door, looking at the carnage in the hallway. "Better than them." She pulled the ring off her finger and held it out to Jessica. "I hope this was worth it."

Jessica pulled out her ClearPhone and quickly transmitted the coins. "Me too. Paid as agreed." She glanced at Raul, on his ClearPhone, calling for an ambulance, and then at his men busy helping the wounded Shades. "Can you keep them off my back so I can get out of here?"

Ophelia smiled. "I'll try. Stop by the diner again sometime, I'd love to get to know you better."

"Even after this?"

"Especially after this."

"I'll think about it." Jessica moved past her into the elevator as she stepped out.

"Stop her," one of the kneecapped Shades shouted at Raul. "She's wanted by the UDF."

Raul looked at Jessica, who shrugged as the cab doors slid closed and she started to descend. She glanced at the Silver Dragon ring. The Miner was supposed to give them a list of people who could potentially be Immortals. How had she wound up with this instead? Had the Brie Shade planted it there? Or was this a signal that the only person they had found to match the description was the Triad's leader?

She had hoped more answers would make things more straightforward. Instead, they had just gotten even more complicated.

She really wished Cassidy were here.

The elevator reached the ground floor. Jessica rushed out, gun in hand, pointing into the small atrium leading to the more crowded entrance to the Arena. When she wasn't immediately attacked, she returned the weapon to her pocket before anyone noticed.

Walking quickly through the lobby, she kept her eyes peeled for threats. Shades, UDF agents, police, security guards. It seemed like everyone was after her. They were all trying to stop her from preventing the end of the world, and none of them knew it.

She was halfway across the floor, moving through spectators filing in the opposite direction, when a loud cheer rose up behind her. Glancing over her shoulder, she saw a large, muscled man with the rippled flesh of twitch mods come out of one of the Arena doors. Judging by the reaction from the crowd, Jessica had a feeling she knew who he was. Locating a holo poster advertising the upcoming fight confirmed it.

Bruiser. One of the contestants in the main event. Her eyes locked on his a moment later, and he shouted for the people around him to move aside as he ran across the floor.

Jessica considered drawing her gun. But if she shot Bruiser, a number of his fans greater than the number of bullets in her gun would come after her with the single intent of drawing blood. Her blood. On the other hand, if she didn't take him down, he would crush her like a grape.

But not if there was a wrinkle in the carpeting and his foot got caught on it, tripping him up. Not if the bystanders blocked his path in their enthusiasm to meet him.

It happened almost before she thought of it. The fighter grunted as his foot stuck to the upraised piece of carpet, and then he tumbled forward, landing on his stomach. He was immediately on his feet again, but the crowd surrounded him, shoving pens and paper in his face for an autograph or wanting to pose with him for selfies. With a last glance at her, he gave up his pursuit, and Jessica turned away, running for the arena exit.

Two of the guards moved in front of her, but she pulled her gun and they quickly moved out of her way, having decided their lives weren't worth preventing her escape.

Outside again, she pocketed the gun and ran, eager to steer clear of Sinner's Row for good.

At least she knew now what she had to do next.

Chapter 14

The machine body was both familiar and unfamiliar to Cassidy.

Familiar because his restored memories allowed him to recall how the Guard's systems functioned, which in turn allowed him to unplug himself from the rack where the metal body had been in storage for nearly one hundred years, gathering dust and mostly forgotten.

Unfamiliar because he still wasn't able to think of himself as anything other than human. Since this form held no flesh, blood, muscle, or bone a tension quickly developed between what he was and who he desired to be. He found that tension difficult to reconcile in a mind that had suddenly become fully digital, instead of a combination of imprint and host vessel. Caplan was gone, and all of his knowledge and experience had gone with him.

For the first time that he could remember, only Cassidy remained.

Actually, that wasn't completely true. His experiences as a Shade remained. His memories of his repos remained. The seven year old boy. The seventy year old woman. Hall. Jessica. Caplan. He had bits and pieces of them all. Their fears and hopes and desires. Their love and fury and everything else that made them human. The experiences had given him something none of the other Guards had. Something not even Nevis possessed. Emotion. Compassion. Humanity.

Where Nevis could only see the logic of preserving a species in accordance with her programming, he understood the flaw in the logic that Elena never had time to repair before Jain gunned her down. Humankind didn't live to exist. It existed to live. To learn, laugh, love, create, and evolve. All of which had been stifled by Nevis, Jain, and the Hush in the name of survival.

"Cassidy," Nevis said, her voice echoing inside his head, sneaking in through a communications link shared between the Guard and the core. "Cassidy, we need to talk. You're making a mistake."

"No," Cassidy replied. "I'm trying to fix one. You can either help me or get out of my way, but if you try to stop me…" He trailed off without finishing the threat. The only remaining option then would be to destroy the core, something he couldn't do by himself.

Lucky for him, there were other people in the facility who could.

"You know I can't," Nevis said. "I'm compelled to stop you. It's not personal."

"Limitations. I understand. I'm glad you didn't force those same restraints on me. Do you think that was a mistake?"

It took her time to answer. "No."

Cassidy took a few steps forward. The heavy body felt natural to him. So did the lack of a need to breathe. He had done all of this before.

The storage area was long and narrow, and held six other racks for the remaining Shadow Guard, though they hadn't occupied the racks in a long time. The door at the end of the room refused to open when Cassidy reached it, so he dug his fingers into the metal and forced it open with greater ease than even he expected.

Muffled thuds registered in microphones embedded beneath his armor, and Cassidy's attention turned to the Shadow Guard in the doorway at the far end of the R&D lab's open floor. It was currently in the process of ineffectively emptying its rifle's magazine into him. The rounds from the particular rifle it was using were unable to penetrate his armor, leaving small dents and scuffs but doing little else.

Cassidy approached the Shadow Guard, its rifle going dry before he had made it halfway there. Instead of replacing the magazine, the Guard dropped the weapon and walked toward him. As they got closer to one another, Cassidy realized that as Alpha he was nearly a head taller than the other Guard.

"You don't have to make me fight them," Cassidy said to Nevis.

"Yes, I do. I have no choice."

"They can't win."

"It doesn't matter. They have to try."

The Shadow Guard in front of Cassidy, Guard Delta, threw a sudden piston-punch at his head. Reacting instinctively, Cassidy's left hand snapped up and caught the Delta's wrist, stopping its fist a few inches from his face. He twisted the appendage, bending metal and breaking the inner mechanism. Guard Delta ignored the damage and tried to kick Cassidy. He caught the foot in his other hand, broke Delta's ankle, and then used both hands to lift the machine from the floor and hurl it across the room. Delta crashed into the wall before pulling itself back up and limping toward him again.

"You didn't give them much intelligence, did you?" Cassidy asked Nevis through the comm.

"They didn't need it," she replied. "They had you."

The Shadow Guard came at him again, using its good hand to throw another hard punch. Cassidy dodged it, grabbing its arm and breaking it at the elbow, leaving wires and cables dangling out of the mangled joint. He maneuvered easily behind Delta, grabbing its head and twisting until he separated it from the machine's body.

The Shadow Guard sparked and dropped to the floor.

Cassidy tossed its head on top of its body. He didn't bother to pick up its rifle. The weapon couldn't hurt the other Shadow Guards anyway.

The main R&D lab was relatively sparse, with a few desks scattered across the far side of the open space, each with a terminal and display on top. More displays lined the back wall adjacent to work tables where experimental equipment rested in various states of assembly. Dents and scratches in the floor, and chips and scuffs on the walls suggested the area had once been used to test prototypes.

Cassidy crossed over to the work tables, picking through some of the metal parts and wires. Accessing his restored memories, he understood that his body had originally been designed to house a human soldier in a lightweight alloy composite shell with an endoskeletal augment to improve the wearer's strength and agility. It had been the Hush's one and only true militaristic break-through. Even then it had only progressed to the proto-type stage. The research had been abandoned before

NEVIS hacked into the mainframe and took charge of the department. Initially, she considered the armor unnecessary in light of the Oneirolic's effectiveness, but then she revived the study, passing orders to the scientists through official-looking channels to increase the strength of the endoskeleton and turn the armor into fully-automated robotics.

The researchers started to get suspicious when plans for an advanced neural network began popping up in their email, but by that point they were so excited by the advancements they kept the nature of the work to themselves.

By the time NEVIS ordered him to gun down that first group of HDF soldiers, the four scientists in R&D had considered themselves part of her team. And one of them, Jennifer, had become her imprint's first host.

"Why do I have your memories too?" Cassidy asked, dropping a scrap of metal he had picked up and moving toward the door.

"You're still part of me, Cassidy," Nevis replied. "Your Alpha cortex can hold all the data, so I transferred it there. I believed it would help you understand me better, the way Doctor Cassidy tried to help me understand her."

"I wasn't this self-aware before you put me into the Oneirolic?"

"You're an AI. A learning machine. It took time for you to grow and evolve, and you did that in ways I never expected. To that end, you are my ultimate creation."

"Even though I want to destroy everything you're trying to preserve?"

"Yes."

Cassidy used another tool inside his new box, locating the other Shadow Guards in the facility. Three of the five were on their way to him. The other two were moving across the underground base, heading for the Oneirolic. He had a good idea why they were going there, but they didn't have security clearance. Had Nevis enlisted another Watcher to let them enter? Would they help the Shadow Guards remove Jessica from the machine?

Either way, he had to stop it from happening.

"If you take her out of the Oneirolic, it will only make things worse for you," Cassidy said, exiting the R&D lab into a long corridor.

"You haven't left me with any choice," Nevis replied. "Neither has she. She's looking for Unity, and she's learning to alter the dreamstate."

Cassidy didn't know why Nevis had decided to share what he considered good news. "How can you know that? You aren't connected to the Oneirolic."

"That was Jain's biggest mistake," Nevis replied. "He used my source to create Unity. And then he built a copy of me inside the dreamstate to manage the Initiative. Because Hades and I are identical, we have an innate connection. We don't communicate directly, but I understand its flow of data, and it understands mine."

"That shouldn't be possible. The dreamstate isn't real."

"No, it shouldn't," Nevis agreed. "But then, how do you define reality? How do we know this reality isn't someone else's dreamstate? Does acceptance of the entities within a structure define the structure? In that sense, have we created a new universe?"

"A universe we can turn off by cutting the power," Cassidy replied. The three Shadow Guards had nearly reached the Underworld. Cassidy continued moving toward the Guards, though he was pretty sure he didn't want to engage all of them at once.

He didn't have a choice. The other two were getting closer to the Oneirolic. If Jessica really had decided to go for Unity and had gained some measure of control over the dreamstate, losing her now could cost all of the people hooked up to the machine their lives.

And what about the people on this side? The Shadow Guards had put a quick end to their uprising. What would happen if he took them all out of the fight? Could the HDF offer any kind of effective counter against him in this body?

He had a feeling they couldn't.

"This world can end almost as easily," Nevis said, responding to his statement. "Any number of unexpected events could destroy everything."

"All the more reason not to continue sacrificing people to keep it all going."

"That's what I was made to do."

Cassidy reached the antechamber between the elevator and the Underworld proper, stepping through the door into the room at the exact same time the other three Shadow Guards reached it. They entered the space and spread out, standing shoulder-to-shoulder across from him, partially obscured by the terminal in the center of the room.

As useless as the weapons were against him, they still carried their rifles. Then again, could he take that kind of prolonged, concentrated fire indefinitely?

He didn't want to find out.

The three Shadow Guards brought their rifles up slightly, fingers shifting to triggers.

Cassidy charged.

Chapter 15

Bullets pounded Cassidy's metal exterior, creating a flurry of sparks and ricochets as he broke to the left to circle the terminal. The barrier turned out to be a major benefit to his approach, as it blocked a percentage of the barrage. Even so, Cassidy's secondary systems started complaining as the hits piled up, a few rounds managing to find the gap in an elbow joint and beat away at it until a single shot sneaked through, severing some of the wires. Where he had been fighting earlier with his hands tied behind his back, suddenly he was fighting with one hand down.

He reached the Guards a moment later, barreling into the first one with his shoulder. His momentum and greater mass threw the machine hard into the wall, denting the stone and stunning the machine as it tried to recalibrate its balance. He didn't slow, pivoting off the tackle to grab the other Shadow Guard's head. He tried to twist it off its mount, but the machine moved with his effort. Cassidy swung a foot up into its crotch, metal smashing metal with an echoing groan in as the force

lifted the Guard up off the floor. The opposite movement crushed its neck and severed its connection to the
body. The Guard collapsed at Cassidy's feet.

He turned to face the next Shadow Guard, just in
time to see a rifle stock, swung like a club, coming at his
head. He reeled backward, catching a quick look at the
Guard behind it—the one he'd thrown into the wall—as
the butt smashed his face, knocking his head sideways.

The Shadow Guard opened fire, peppering Cassidy
with bullets. He turned his dead arm into the attack,
letting it catch most of the rounds as he regrouped,
rushing back at the two Guards. They spread apart,
swinging their rifles down and grabbing for him with
perfectly synchronized precision. He batted one's hand
away, but the other caught hold of his neck. As Alpha,
Cassidy was larger and stronger than they were. He
slammed the side of its head with a fist before taking the
other one's arm and holding it in place while he swept its
legs out from under it.

He went down with the Shadow Guard, rolling and
breaking its hold to come up free. It rolled away from his
foot when he tried to stomp its head. He turned and
lunged at the other Guard, throwing a punch blocked
with its rifle, the move bending the barrel. Cassidy
followed it up with a driven knee, the piston-like force
crushing the Shadow Guard's midsection and sending it
backward into the terminal. The computer shattered and
sat there smoking in the aftermath.

Cassidy used the break to return his attention to the
remaining Shadow Guard as it climbed back to its feet.
He threw a series of quick jabs at it, forcing it to stumble
back. He threw a harder hook, pleased when it caught
the machine beneath its arm and lifted it a second time.
His interior systems warned him about potential damage

from the effort as he threw another punch at the other Guard, both of them crashing back into the terminal and falling to the floor.

Getting up, Cassidy surveyed the damage he'd done to them both. He had them on the ropes and could finish them given another minute. But he didn't have another minute. The other two Shadow Guards had nearly reached the Oneirolic, and if he didn't get to them in time they would pull Jessica from the machine and kill her.

That made her the priority.

He spun around, facing the door that would give him access to the room and the elevator on the far side. Locked from this side. But it didn't matter. He slammed his fingers into the seam, digging in and fighting its stubborn hold. The mechanism screeching its complaint, he finally wrenched it open, bending the door awkwardly.

Cassidy grabbed up the rifle that had belonged to the Shadow Guard he'd torn apart and climbed through. He could hear the footsteps of the other two Guards behind him. He caught a break, with the cab already present. He stepped in as they climbed through the ruined door and rushed him.

It was another mistake on their part. The Shadow Guard with its internal wiring and machinery exposed from its ruined neck was an easy target. Cassidy fired into the wound, a burst of rounds increasing the damage and cutting through another vital wire. The Guard stumbled suddenly and then collapsed as if it were a marionette whose strings had been snipped.

The other Shadow Guard kept coming, but it was too late. The elevator doors slid closed in front of Cassidy, a punch from the outside denting in the elevator door. The cab rose before the Guard could try again.

Cassidy stood in the center of the cab, taking stock of his system's status. Every second left him more comfortable as a machine, and he wasn't sure how he felt about that. While the armored body was powerful, even in spite of the damage he had taken to his arm, it was cold and empty, and he knew he didn't belong in it. Maybe once, a long time ago. Not anymore.

"Cassidy, it doesn't have to be like this," Nevis said through the comm. "I don't want us to fight."

"Then you should help me," Cassidy replied.

"You know I can't. But you can help me."

"You know I won't," he growled back.

He switched off the link. He didn't want to listen to her anymore. She had sent the other Shadow Guards to kill Jessica, an unnecessary escalation she had to know would only make him more determined.

It felt like it took the elevator forever to reach the top floor. The door opened and Cassidy burst through, rifle up and ready to use on anyone or anything that tried to block his path. The corridor was clear. He ran down it to another secured door, once again tearing it away to get through. A scientist in the hallway shouted and fell back as he sprinted past, rifle pointed at him in warning.

He was thankful his dataset included a map of the facility, or he never would have been able to locate the Oneirolic, nevermind try to reach it quickly. He was also fortunate the entrance to the Underworld wasn't especially far from the other secured area, giving him a chance to gain ground on the two Shadow Guards.

Still, the seconds seemed to pass as hours.

Cassidy hurried his steps, his massive feet cracking loudly against the facility floor, damaging the tile with every step. While his gaze remained fixed on the path ahead, he was able to watch the Shadow Guards, led by a Watcher, on his second cognitive thread. They moved with purpose through the control room and into the inner-workings to where Jessica lay in the Oneirolic.

He turned the corner, the entrance up ahead. A pair of Hush guards flanked the door, and they seemed to know not to allow him entry. They aimed their weapons at him. He couldn't risk them damaging already damaged parts of his shell, and he cut them down with two quick bursts before reaching the door.

He tried to grab the door, to dig his hands in and yank it open like he had the others. Even with his size and strength, it didn't budge a fraction, and he was running out of time.

Turning his attention to the security panel, he grabbed the face and easily tore it off, revealing the circuitry beneath. Since he had the memories of a machine, he figured he should know how to speak the language. He touched his fingers to the board, his imprint suddenly overwhelmed with a flow of data he understood. Nevis wasn't networked to the Oneirolic, but she was connected to the security system that protected it. As Alpha, Cassidy had access to it too.

The door slid open.

Cassidy rushed into the control room, finding it empty. A quick glance at the terminal displays showed the Watcher and the two Shadow Guards moving through the interior of the system. He didn't linger, reaching the secured door on the other side of the room and again hacking into the panel.

Aware of his approach, one of the Shadow Guards came to an abrupt stop halfway along the platform. It turned toward him, its rifle ready.

Passing the first column of pods, Cassidy caught up to the static Shadow Guard, the other one and the

Watcher already at the platform segment leading up to Jessica's pod.

With no time to lose, he charged the first hurdle between himself and Jess. The Shadow Guard opened fire. Cassidy traded fire with it, ineffective bullets bouncing off both of them, until their rifles ran dry. Without breaking stride, Cass flipped his weapon, catching the barrel in his hand and drawing it back. He threw it as though it were an axe. The Shadow Guard simply swatted it away with its free hand, but the distraction gave Cassidy the opening he needed to dive low and slam his shoulder into the Guard's knees, knocking it off the platform.

Cassidy rolled back to his feet, not looking back at the downed Shadow Guard as he sprinted for the segment rising toward Jessica's pod. The Guard standing there turned and fired down at him, the rounds punching more dents into his armor. He registered a second critical hit and stumbled, nearly falling over as his left knee seized up. He hobbled forward two more steps and then jumped, reaching up and latching onto the bottom of the platform.

The Shadow Guard peered down at him. Cassidy knew exactly what was coming next, but he wasn't about to let go. He had to get to Jessica.

He began to pull himself up.

The Guard pointed its rifle at Cassidy's head and opened fire. The rounds ploughed into his skull, shaking his sensors and blurring his vision. The pounding continued until the metal shell caved in, coming dangerously close to his cortex.

The weight of both immense metal bodies began to bend the platform, the motor driving it whining until it stopped working entirely. It allowed Cassidy to let go of the grating and grab onto the Shadow Guard's ankle. He pulled, tearing the leg out from under the machine, taking it down.

A metal hand grabbed him from behind, the other Shadow Guard back in the fight. It wrapped its arms around him, trying to twist his neck until it snapped. Cassidy reached back but couldn't get hold of it. His only option was throwing himself over the edge of the platform and taking the Shadow Guard with him. He turned, putting the machine under him as they fell, the pair plunging through the pool's surface in a gargantuan splash. Designed to immobilize humans, the liquid had no affect on them. They struggled, one fighting to best the other, all the way to the bottom.

Cassidy drove his elbow into the Shadow Guard's head, smashing it into the pool bottom. He pounded his elbow into it—once, twice, three times—until he crushed the metal, denting it in dangerously close to its cortex. He continued to hit it over and over again, until the Shadow Guard stopped resisting, its arms falling limp at its sides.

Above the surface, with the platform segment no longer overburdened, it was rising again, taking the Shadow Guard and Watcher up with it.

Cassidy had to move fast.

He stood, shedding the liquid like a monstrous behemoth rising from the depths. He reached up with his one functional arm, and taking the platform in hand, pulling himself up.

Too late.

The segment stopped moving and Jessica's pod started sliding from the Oneirolic.

There was no way he could get to her in time. Unless…

He looked down at the Guard at the bottom of the pool. Nevis had cut him off from the link between the other six Shadow Guards, but the one below him was still connected.

Turning and dropping down again on top of it, Cassidy reached down to dig his fingers beneath the damaged seam of its face plate. Prying it loose, he reached in and touched his fingertips to the right area of the AI's cortex. Information flowed through him as he intercepted the streams of data passing through the mechanical brain, quickly identifying the pathway through the comms.

Shadow Guard Epsilon, stand down.

He didn't know if Epsilon could hear his order. He didn't know if it would comply. The response came a split-second later.

Acknowledged.

Cassidy looked up through the liquid. Epsilon had stopped moving. It had worked. He could barely believe it. He sent another order.

No harm is to come to Jessica Tai.

Again came the reply.

Acknowledged.

The Shadow Guard moved then, blocking the Watcher from the fully-exposed pod.

Cassidy stood and took hold of the platform and slowly pulled himself up. By the time he climbed back onto the platform, Jessica's pod was tucked back into the Oneirolic and the segment was descending. He didn't know how long his orders to the Guard would hold. Nevis had to be able to override his directives. So why hadn't she?

"Cassidy."

He turned around slowly, his question answered all

too quickly. Nevis stood on the platform a few feet away, a simple, unfamiliar gun in her hand. It had a wide, snub barrel and seemed to be connected to something on her back by a thin wire.

"You did well," Nevis said. "Your thought processes are quicker than ever, and your reflexes are up nearly twenty percent."

"Desperation does that," Cassidy replied.

Nevis smiled. "Adding your faux humanity to your repertoire has definitely enhanced your overall function-ality. But I can't have you ruining everything I've worked so hard to maintain." She pointed the strange gun at him. "I'm sorry to do this to you Cassidy, but I'm sure we'll both learn from this."

She squeezed the trigger. Cassidy didn't hear or see anything, but he felt the effect almost immediately. His entire body seized up, his cortex suddenly complaining about a primary power failure and switch-over to reserves. He lost his balance then, his machine body collapsing onto the floor. He heard the other Shadow Guard drop behind him.

"What did you do?" Cassidy asked, still able to speak, but unable to move.

"EMP gun," Nevis replied. "Your head is shielded, but the rest of you isn't. It's a weapon of last resort that I hoped never to need to use against you."

She slid the weapon's power pack off her shoulders and dropped it to the platform, along with the gun. Then she walked over to him, putting her hand on his head. "I'll make everything better. You won't remember any of this ugliness."

"Wait," Cassidy said. "Don't."

"I remember saying the same thing to you a few minutes ago. What was it you told me?"

"I hope he told you to duck," Noriko said from somewhere behind Nevis.

"What?" Nevis replied, eyes wide with surprise as she straightened and looked behind her just in time to see the shots that suddenly rang out.

Cassidy watched Nevis convulse, the rounds catching her in the chest. She stumbled backward, catching herself for a moment before she dropped to her knees, looking down at him as blood immediately began staining her uniform shirt.

Noriko approached her, gun in hand. "Your toys didn't even bother to search me before they dragged me here," she said. "I guess because they're immune to bullets. But you aren't." She fired three more times, the rounds throwing Nevis onto her back, her legs caught awkwardly beneath her. Noriko continued forward until she stood over her. "This is for Sana." She fired one last bullet into Nevis' head.

Noriko stared down at the body for a moment before looking over at the mangled, crumpled body of Shadow Guard Alpha. "She called you Cassidy. Is it really you?"

Chapter 16

"It's me," Cassidy said through his speakers.

Noriko stared at him. "Where did you get the armor?"

"It's a long story. One I'm not comfortable with. Is Jessica okay?"

"She's fine. I'm sorry, Cassidy. I didn't have a choice."

"I know. They would have killed you if you hadn't done what they wanted. Where did you get the gun?"

"I've had it in my quarters for a long time. Just in case. I don't know why I bothered picking it up since it can't hurt these soldiers, but I'm glad I did." She scowled down at Nevis' dead repo.

"There aren't soldiers inside these suits," Cassidy explained. "They're robots. Machines run by artificial intelligence."

Noriko stared at him. "But...you—"

"That's the part I'm not comfortable with. My imprint is written to this Guard's cortex. Fully digital. This is me, Nora. The real me. Nevis is more than the head of Dark Ops. She's a supercomputer, an artificial intelligence online in the former research and development laboratories deep underground."

Noriko pointed at Nevis' corpse. "Then who is that?"

"Nevis imprinted a pared down version of herself to a host in order to make herself mobile."

"She made a copy."

"Yes."

Noriko considered for a moment. "When you say this is the real you, are you saying you're an AI too?"

"That's what I've been told. And I have the memories now to prove it. The important part is that Unity inside the dreamstate is based on Nevis out here. She thinks if the Hush loses power, then human civilization will fail. She also thinks that if we don't let the Oneirolic fail naturally, the results will be equally catastrophic."

"That's why she was trying to stop Jessica?"

"It's the reason for every decision she makes."

"It's hard for me to see her as evil if that's the case."

"She isn't evil," Cassidy agreed. "A small part of me thinks she's actually trying to help within the confines of her programming."

"It didn't seem like it two minutes ago. Who in their right mind creates an intelligence like that and then leaves it to operate unchecked?"

"A scientist named Doctor Elena Cassidy created her. Your husband left her unchecked when he murdered Doctor Cassidy."

Noriko gasped, her face paling. "What are you talking about? Sana wasn't a violent man. He could never have done such a thing."

"I have the memory in my dataset," Cassidy said.

"You know as well as anyone that you can't trust memories."

"Then what can you trust?"

"I trust Sana. I've known him for years."

"He was desperate to get the Oneirolic functioning. He asked Doctor Cassidy for help and she refused. She didn't want any part of connecting people to the machine. He thought it was the only way the Hush could win."

"He wasn't wrong about that," Noriko said, tears forming. "It pains me to admit, but if he felt his back was against the wall and his and my lives were at stake, it might have been enough to push him over the edge. He always used to tell me he had done things he wasn't proud of to ensure our survival."

"He killed the only person who was trying to prevent this present from becoming humankind's future," Cassidy said. "Everything that's happened since is because of him."

"That may be true, but what's your point? He's trying to make it right now, isn't he? That's why he sent you here. To fix what he broke."

"I don't think I can. Not now. I can't even move."

"We have to do something," Noriko insisted. "We need to finish what we started."

"I can't be the one to do it. I'm a consciousness trapped in an inoperable body. I'm not even human. I've never been human." It hurt Cassidy to say the words. To admit the truth. And he knew it was true. He wouldn't have such control over the security systems and the other Guards otherwise.

Noriko smiled. "You helped me to see value in what Sana is trying to do. You helped me to feel compassion again. You're the most human non-human I've ever met. I haven't known you for a long time, but I'm certain the

Cassidy I watched single-handedly chase the Hush Defense Force from the District isn't a quitter."

"You're right," Cassidy replied. "I'm not quitting." He paused for a moment to think. "The way I see it, we have two problems. One, according to Jain the only way to save the people hooked up to the Oneirolic is to reset Unity in the dreamstate. Except, according to Nevis, Unity can't be reset. Two, even with the Shadow Guard incapacitated, we're still surrounded by Hush forces and an advanced AI that will do everything in her power to prevent us from seizing control."

"How do you know Nevis isn't lying about Unity?" Noriko asked.

"She had no reason to lie to me. But that doesn't mean she's right about it either. There may be a way she hasn't considered. Considering how hard she's trying to stop Jessica, I don't think she's convinced the reset can't be done either."

"That's good."

"As for our situation here, we need to find a way to regroup the Opposition. With the Shadow Guard gone, they stand a fighting chance. Do you know what happened to them after the battle?"

"No. Nevis had the Guard's standing watch outside my quarters, and I don't have access to military channels from inside my suite. But it's only been a few hours. I can find out."

"She could have had them kill you," Cassidy said. "Either she didn't see you as a threat or you still had value to her."

"Or I still had value to you," Noriko suggested. "If you're right, and like Unity she's trying to help you at the same time she has no choice but to stop you."

Cassidy considered it. He couldn't discount the idea. "I'm useless in this body."

"Maybe we can get you another one. You transferred into the Guard. There has to be a way for you to transfer back out."

"There's a unit in the Underworld. That's where Caplan is right now, but I don't know if Nevis left him alive. There's another Guard down there, too. Nevis must be holding it in reserve as protection. In any case, you'll never get me down there like this." Cassidy considered the problem. "You need to remove my head."

Noriko leaned over him, looking at the area. "It's already damaged. You've taken a lot of gunfire." She looked past him, to the other Guard. "I might be able to finish decapitating you with the Guard's rifle. But it might also damage something you need."

"We have to take that chance," Cassidy said. "I don't know how long it will take Nevis to get conventional reinforcements in here."

"Maybe she won't?"

"We can't count on that. I don't know what the balance is between her requirement to stop me and her desire to help me."

Noriko vanished behind him, but he heard her pick up the Guard's rifle. "The magazine is almost empty," she said.

"There's a replacement inside a compartment on the leg," Cassidy said. "I have one too. The motor has no power to open it, but you can probably pry it open."

Noriko hovered near his leg, finding the seam. She pulled a multi-tool out of her pocket and extended a screwdriver.

"Do you always carry that?" Cassidy asked.

"Yes. It's useful for ad hoc repairs or opening bottles."

"Now I feel like a bottle."

They both laughed. Cassidy found a lot of strength in his ability to understand and enjoy humor. Maybe Noriko was right. He had been created as an AI, but maybe his experience as a Shade to human repos had made him human too.

She managed to pry open the compartment, sliding the magazine from its holder and making the exchange, snapping the new magazine into place in the rifle. Then she stepped back, awkwardly gripping the weapon.

"Put the stock against your shoulder," Cassidy said. "And set your feet. The recoil is more powerful than a handgun." He wasn't sure how she was going to shoot through the mechanism connecting his head to his body without destroying him when she had clearly never fired a rifle before. But it was the only chance he had.

"Like this?" she asked, switching her posture.

"That's better. Just be—"

He didn't finish before she depressed the trigger. Bullets spewed toward him. She only fired a short burst, the kick of the rifle sending slugs splashing into the liquid beneath the platform.

"Careful," Cassidy finished.

"It's harder than it looks," Noriko said. "But I think I have a better feel for it now."

She reset her posture, holding the muzzle only a few inches from his neck. Then she opened fire again, bullets punching into the metal and wires, tearing through the base of his steel spine and sending the head lolling back. She released the trigger and dropped the rifle before grabbing Cassidy's head in both hands and pulling, the strength of her vessel allowing her to finally separate the head from the body.

Fresh warnings alerted Cassidy to the decapitation as his cortex registered the loss.

"The backup power supply is only good for an hour," he said. "We need to get back down to the Underworld."

"How do we sneak around the remaining Guard?" she asked.

"We don't," Cassidy replied. "The EMP gun. Over there."

Noriko turned around to look, her gaze settling on the pack, the gun laying on it. She smiled. "Of course." Putting him down, she went over to the weapon to examine the power pack. "It looks like it still has a charge." She slid it onto her back and picked up the gun, tucking it into the pocket of her uniform. Then she retrieved her handgun and Cassidy, tucking his head under her arm. Even after occupying forty-nine different bodies, being limited to a mechanical head stuffed in somebody's armpit was a surreal experience for him.

Running back through the Oneirolic, Noriko kept her gun up and ready to use in case the HDF intercepted them along the way. The area remained clear, the outer door to the Oneirolic still secure. It opened for Noriko and she hurried out into the corridor, following Cassidy's directions to return to the elevator leading underground.

"I don't have access to this," Noriko said.

"I know. You need to bridge my cortex to the panel. I can override it."

"How?"

"There must be wires at the base of my head."

"Dozens of them."

"One of them should be wide and thin, more like a ribbon than a wire. It's white."

"Yes, I see it. But the end is burned and frayed."

"Can you strip the damage off?"

"I think so."

She put him back on the floor facing toward the ceiling and took out her multi-tool. It contained a pair of both cutters and pliers, and she quickly used the cutters to remove the damaged segment of ribbon and the pliers to expose the gold and copper wiring inside.

"How is that?" she asked.

"I won't know until you make the connection. You'll need to remove the panel's face."

Noriko smiled. "This is why I always carry this tool with me. I knew I would need it to break into part of the facility one day."

"I'm sure that's it," Cassidy replied.

She used the screwdriver to quickly detach the front panel and then lifted Cassidy toward it. He knew when she connected the ribbon-like cable. The flow of data from the unit streamed into his cortex, and he opened the door, eliciting a soft cheer from Noriko.

"Let's go," he said.

Chapter 17

Cassidy and Noriko rode the elevator back down into the Underworld in silence. When it neared the bottom, Cassidy again checked on the position of the remaining Guard, finding that it had retreated from the antechamber. In fact, it had disappeared completely.

"Nevis pulled the Guard back to protect herself," Cassidy said. It was the only possibility that made sense. She certainly wasn't going to take it offline. "Our path back to the transfer unit is clear."

"Do you know how to make the transfer?"

"Yes. As long as you can splice the cable to the unit there shouldn't be a problem."

"I can do it," Noriko said.

The elevator stopped and the doors opened. As expected, the short corridor was clear. They made their way across it and through the damaged door leading into the antechamber.

"You destroyed these Shadow Guards?" Noriko asked.

"Yes," Cassidy replied.

"With your hands?"

"It isn't as impressive as you make it sound. I'm bigger, stronger, and smarter than the other Guards."

"I'm still impressed."

They moved through the antechamber, following the corridors back to the transfer unit. Cassidy kept a lookout for the remaining Shadow Guard as they advanced, making sure it didn't reappear. His scan remained clear as they reached the transfer room. .

Noriko slowly pushed the door open, sucking in a sharp breath as her eyes landed on Caplan. Cassidy would have done the same if he had any breath to suck in. Instead, a sensation of fury rippled through his cortex. His former host was slumped in the corner of the room, head lolled sideways, neck clearly broken.

"Oh, Cassidy," Noriko said. "I'm sorry. He didn't deserve to go like that."

"Damn you, Nevis," Cassidy hissed. Was a part of her really trying to help him? Why would she order the Shadow Guard to kill Caplan if that were the case? "Quitter or not, it's over for me. We don't have time to go back up and somehow abduct another host. It was Caplan or nothing."

Noriko didn't answer. She placed him on the edge of the table and stood in front of him. He could see the tension in her eyes. The fear and nervousness. Her gaze darted from him to Caplan to the transfer unit and back.

"You have another host," she said, voice quivering. "My vessel can be yours."

"No, it can't," Cassidy countered. "This unit doesn't have the means to store your imprint, and even if it did we don't have your master."

"I know," she replied. "You'll have to burn me to imprint yourself."

"Are you failsafe or writable?"

"Failsafe," she replied softly.

"Then your master is corrupt until your imprint is deltaed back in. Burning your imprint will kill you."

"Yes, I know."

"That's not an option."

"Cassidy, it has to be. Like you said, you're no use to anyone as a head without a body. And you don't have another body. The people *I let* be enslaved in the Oneirolic need you. The people *I let* be trampled by the Hush need you. I'm over one hundred years old. I've had my time and then some, and I've spent it selfishly. I owe this to the people I've oppressed for all of these years. I owe it to you for how hard you've fought to make things right. To make up for *my* mistakes and atone for *my* sins."

"You didn't do this, Noriko. Sana did. You shouldn't have to pay for his crimes."

"I aided and abetted them. Maybe I didn't know what he did to Doctor Cassidy, but I went along with his plans for the Oneirolic, with the camps, with everything. I helped augur the narratives. I have as much blood on my hands as anyone." Tears rolled down her cheeks as she spoke. "The District needs you, Cassidy. Jessica needs you. This is the only way."

Cassidy didn't speak right away. He didn't want to let Noriko make this kind of sacrifice, but she was right. There was no other way. He needed a new host to become mobile again. To keep fighting.

"You need to connect me to the unit," he said.

"Where?" she asked, voice still cracking with emotion.

"The main processor behind the table. The side comes off to access the internal boards." Cassidy surprised himself with the answer. If Nevis hadn't given him back his memories, he wouldn't have known that.

Noriko placed him on top of the dark box behind the table and went around the workstation, squeezing into the small gap to reach the computer. Using her multi-tool, she quickly removed the side of the machine, exposing the multiple circuit boards, CPUs, and cables within. She picked Cassidy up and turned him toward the interior. "Where do I need to splice you in?"

Cassidy looked over the wires. "Do you see the red and black ribbon?"

"Yes."

"That one."

"Your cable isn't long enough."

Cassidy examined the other cables similar to the red and black one. "You can pull the yellow cable and splice it in."

"Are you sure?"

"Yes. That one drives the scrubbing processor and the display. We won't need those things."

"Okay."

Noriko put him back on top of the box and went to work. Cassidy noticed her hands shaking as she pulled out the yellow cable, removed the connectors from either end, and set about splicing it. Fresh tears formed in her eyes which she needed to wipe away in order to work but she didn't say anything about it, connecting his cable to one end of the yellow cable, and then connecting it back to the source.

Data immediately began to flow through Cassidy, new inputs and outputs suddenly available to his cortex. The power draw increased tenfold, creating instant strain on the backup supply.

"We need to do this quickly," he said. "The throughput is draining my battery much faster."

Noriko nodded, returning to the table.

"Nora," Cassidy said, wishing he could reach out to touch her. She looked back at him. "You don't need to do this."

She returned a sad smile. "We both know I do. Sana chose love in the end. I'm making the same choice."

Cassidy wasn't as convinced Jain's motives were that pure, but he didn't argue. Noriko lowered herself onto her back on the table, scooting up to put her head between the electrodes. Cassidy operated the unit, setting off the light sequence over her head to help calm her imprint and her vessel's mind. He wasn't sure how effective it would be on Noriko. She was allowing him to kill her.

He could sense the patterns through the data stream, surprised to find Noriko's imprint already calm. Despite her outward emotion, she had relinquished herself to her fate, and the readings confirmed she was at peace with the decision. Cassidy found it comforting as well, knowing with certainty that she was doing what she believed was right.

"Goodbye, Cassidy," she said, seeming to sense that her time had reached its end. "Good luck."

"Goodbye, Noriko," he replied. "Thank you."

"No. Thank you."

He sent the signal to trigger the burn, a process typically reserved for corrupted imprints when there was a chance the host could be saved in the rare occasions when the host was deemed worth saving. The process only took a second. A flash of heat pushed through the skin in the back of the vessel's neck, destroying the organic part of the imprint and breaking it apart so that it soaked into the surrounding tissue and out through the bloodstream, nothing more than microscopic particles that would go out through the bladder.

Noriko was gone.

Cassidy didn't dwell on it. Instead, he initiated the transfer sequence, connecting his own digital imprint as the source. A warning in his cortex alerted him to the imminent loss of charge from the backup power supply, and a moment of panic coursed through him at the thought that he would come so close only to run out of time.

He didn't have a chance to recover from the thought before everything went black.

Chapter 18

Cassidy's eyelids fluttered open, leaving him staring at the soft undulation of the overhead lighting. His heart pounded. His head throbbed. Not his heart or head. Noriko's vessel. Sergeant Anna Krane. She closed her eyes against the headache. The transfer had completed, but the sync hadn't. His imprint's rhythm didn't match hers, leaving them both in a state of mild confusion.

Cassidy tried to move, limbs shuddering as Krane unintentionally fought for control. To her mind, Cassidy was a foreign invader. A parasite instead of a symbiote. Time would calm the impulse and bind them more tightly, but time wasn't something Cassidy could spare. Nevis would know what he had done, taking over Noriko's repo. Would she send the last Shadow Guard after Krane? If so, she would be taking a big risk, but knowing Cassidy would be off-balance to start with might make it worthwhile.

Pushing herself up, Cassidy rolled off the table and onto the floor, landing harder than she wanted. Gasping for air, she forced herself to her knees, the room spinning as Cassidy consciousness struggled to synchronize with Krane's body.

Cassidy pushed harder, crawling toward the EMP gun Noriko had left on the floor. When she reached it, she grabbed the gun and lifted it toward the door with one hand while turning on the power pack with the other. Then she slumped against the base of the table, head still spinning as she kept close watch on the door.

A minute passed. Another. The sync progressed, clearing Cassidy's vision and calming her pounding heart. It was only then that Cassidy stood up, able to remain upright without dizziness or nausea.

"Nice to meet you, Sergeant Krane," she said out loud, taking in the sound of her new voice. Female, sultry, a little dry. It sounded different from inside than it had when hearing Noriko speak. "Let's get to work."

She picked up the EMP pack and slipped it onto her back, brandishing the conventional handgun as well before exiting the transfer room. She headed for the elevator at a sedate walk, taking a little more time to let the sync bind Cassidy more tightly to Krane before breaking into a jog and then a run. She couldn't override the secured doors the way she had before, but there was no need. Her hack had left the doors disabled so she crossed the Underworld with little effort.

Cassidy paused when she reached the Shadow Guards she had destroyed earlier, stooping to pick up one of the discarded rifles before continuing into the elevator. Moving through the facility as Watcher Noriko Onai would allow her greater freedom without confrontation, but the Hush no doubt knew Noriko was under house arrest and wouldn't take kindly to finding her out from under Shadow Guard control. Besides, the HDF ranks were already thinner than ever before. So many of the soldiers had changed sides at Cassidy's urging that this entire place was ready to collapse with only the slightest push. She couldn't capture and hold the facility single-handed, but if she could get word out to the rebels being escorted back to the District, the entire complexion of the struggle would change.

Cassidy shrugged out of the EMP pack as the elevator slowed to a stop. The weapon was too heavy and bulky to carry everywhere she went, and she had a high confidence Nevis wouldn't send the Guard after her. She lowered the rifle to her side as she entered the facility, passing through the secured area into an empty corridor.

With the restored memories of Cassidy's time as Shadow Guard Alpha still embedded in her imprint, she had access to a complete map of the facility from top to bottom, and she referenced it now to choose her path through the complex. She quickly found that not only were the memories intact, but her recall of them was perfect. Machine-like. As though Nevis had gifted her with some of the benefits of her original artificial intelligence while she retained her learned humanity.

She hurried through the facility, holding the rifle non-threateningly as she crossed paths with scientists and employees who eyed her with curiosity and caution but didn't say a word—either out of fear or a desire not to get involved—about the weapon in her hand.

Cassidy made it almost halfway to her destination before running into trouble in the form of a pair of HDF guards patrolling the hallways. She didn't immediately go on the offensive, but rather held the rifle almost casually, continuing toward them as they noticed her, their postures immediately defensive, expressions showing slight confusion.

"Watcher Onai," one of them said. He turned his rifle on her.

"You should be in your quarters," the other guard said, aiming his rifle on her as well.

"Don't," Cassidy said, producing the handgun in her free hand and aiming it at them. "I don't want to hurt you."

The two HDF soldiers stared at her, unsure of what to do. They were both pure Hush, born and raised in the Pastures. Cassidy could tell by the smoothness of their faces. They hadn't been exposed to a day of real hardship in their lives. How eager were they to die?

"Captain Nevis—" one of them started to say.

"—is dead," Cassidy finished for him. "I killed her. What we're doing to remain in control is wrong, and I won't stand for it anymore. You can either stand with me or you can die."

She sensed fear in the two soldiers. At the same time, they weren't ready to accept that things had to change. Cassidy could see their arms tense, their fingers shifting toward the triggers of their weapons. She was much faster, putting a pair of rounds into their heads before they knew what hit them.

Cassidy expected the deaths of the two soldiers to trigger a new red alert, but she reached the outside of the prison block with no sign of a reaction from Commander Prescott. She was certain Prescott knew about the guards she had just killed by now. If he had suppressed the alarm, it was likely because he didn't want the civilians in the facility to panic or perhaps he believed Cassidy could use the chaos and confusion of the alarm to a greater advantage. Which was probably true. It had aided her as Caplan, allowing him to blend in with the fleeing civilians. No doubt Prescott didn't want a repeat of her prior escape. Cassidy wondered if the commander would be happy to know that she had no intention of leaving.

She approached the final corner before the door leading into the cell block and peeked around it. Twenty feet away, two armored HDF soldiers stood guard directly outside the cell block door. They held their rifles in a ready position, their eyes on the swivel, watching both approaches to the cell block. Prescott had at least guessed where Cassidy might be headed and had alerted them to the possibility. Not that it mattered.

She swung out from the corner, releasing two quick bursts of rounds from the heavy rifle. The larger slugs tore through the soldiers' combat armor and into their chests, dropping them where they stood. She ran up to the door.

The locking mechanism had been damaged in the earlier fighting, leaving the prison area on the other side of the door accessible. Cassidy entered cautiously, crouching low and shoving the door open with her left shoulder, while leading with the rifle as she entered the room. Bullets hit the metal overhead, the HDF defenders inside the room aiming too high. Cassidy didn't make the same mistake, throwing quick groupings of return fire back at the soldiers as she stormed into the room.

One of them went down quickly, the others shifting their aim as Cassidy charged the nearest soldier, putting two large rounds through his chest. She rolled behind the dead soldier as he collapsed, letting the man's body absorb the return fire from two more defenders. Coming to her knees, she sprayed slugs across the entire room, cutting down another two defenders.

Jumping up, Cassidy sprinted toward the remaining soldier, her rifle shaking in her hands as she froze with fear. The soldier lowered her weapon just as Cassidy dug the rifle muzzle into her chest.

"Please," she said breathlessly. "I'm from the District. I surrender."

Cassidy locked eyes with her and held out her hand. "Give me your gun."

"Take it." She paused, offering it up. "You're Cassidy, aren't you?"

"How do you know me?"

"They rounded up all of us from the District for questioning. I convinced my SO I'm loyal to the Hush. I'm sure some others did too. Anyway, they were all talking about you. How you almost got past the Oneirolic with an army of people from the District. They said you lost and were captured."

"It didn't stick."

The soldier smiled in response. "I know. Prescott told us you escaped. I'm behind you. We're all behind you. If you let me keep my gun, I can help."

Cassidy stared into her eyes. She seemed sincere, but from the District or not, he wouldn't hesitate to kill her if she wasn't trustworthy. She handed the gun back to the soldier. "Wait here. I'll be right back."

"Sergeant Roil has the keycard for the cells," the soldier offered, pointing Cassidy to the right corpse.

Cassidy retrieved the keycard from the guard's body, using it to enter the rear of the cell block. "Hakken!" she shouted. "Hak, are you here?"

"Noriko?" Hakken replied loudly. "I'm here!" Cassidy hurried to a cell door halfway down the line of cages. Hakken rose from the floor to greet her. "Rescued from the same damn prison twice in less than forty-eight hours," he said, a big smile on his face. "And by a Watcher this time. Who would've thought?"

Cassidy used the card to open the cell. "I'm not Noriko," she said. "I'm Cassidy."

"What?" Hakken replied, his smile getting bigger. "Well I'll be even more damned. You two swapped bodies?"

Cassidy shook her head. "No. Noriko's gone, Hak. She gave up her life to help me get free."

"Shit. That's a damn shame. She did the right thing in the end, didn't she?"

"We can make it right," Cassidy replied. "Come on. Let's get the hell out of here."

Chapter 19

Cassidy and Hakken returned to the front of the cell block. The District soldier was still there, her rifle aimed at the doorway.

"They know you're here," she said when she heard them arrive. "There are two units incoming."

"ETA?" Cassidy asked.

"Any second now."

"Who are you?" Hakken asked the soldier, taking a rifle from the grip of one of the dead soldiers on the floor.

"Corporal Shane Nero," she replied.

"Nero?" Hakken said. "Nate Nero's kin?"

"My grandfather," Corporal Nero answered.

"Good to have you with us, Nero," Hakken said, readily accepting her allegiance.

"I'm going out," Cassidy said, lifting the Guard rifle. "Stick close, and don't shoot me in the back. Don't shoot at all unless it can't be avoided. Let's hope we haven't triggered a narrative."

"Looks good so far," Hakken said. "You would have

had a lot more soldiers to get through if they saw you breaking me out."

"Not necessarily," Nero countered. "Rumors of Watchers turning on the Hush, along with entire platoons of District soldiers going rogue have thinned the ranks considerably."

"Something's finally going in our favor."

"Just hold your fire unless one of us is going to die," Cassidy repeated. She used her foot to push open the door to the cell block, leading with the rifle as she leaned out into the corridor. "We're clear for the moment."

Cassidy led Hakken and Nero into the hallway. She could hear movement along the south corridor, running feet coming their way. Turning north, she heard movement there too.

"Back inside," she said, the three of them retreating back into the block. Cassidy pushed the door closed until there was only a crack for her to kneel and stick the muzzle of her rifle through. There would be no way to know whose side the HDF soldiers were on unless they had a chance to talk.

She heard the unit turn the corner a few seconds later.

"A six-man squad in HDF combat gear," Cassidy said as they charged the door.

Nero leaned forward over Cassidy's crouched form. "This is Shane Nero!" she announced through the crack. "If you can hear me and you're ready to fight for the District, now's the time and this is the place!"

The noise of the approaching units slowed, followed by shouting and a sudden eruption of gunfire, none of which was aimed at the door to the cell block. Cassidy held her fire as she watched a bloodbath take place in the corridor.

Of the six soldiers in the unit, only two were still standing. They were locked together in a desperate struggle, trying to keep the other from firing his sidearm at his opponent. The smaller of the two men lost a moment later, his grip on the other man's wrist slipping and allowing his attacker to stick the weapon against his gut and pull the trigger three times.

The smaller man dropped. The larger one turned toward the door, raising his hands. "Cassidy, you in there?" he shouted.. "My name is Gershon. Amos Gershon."

"Do you know him?" Cassidy asked Nero.

"I'm not sure. He looks familiar, but..."

Cassidy looked to Hakken, who smiled and nodded in support of the name he recognized. "We're here," Cassidy replied. "Come in slowly, your weapon down."

"Can I come too?" One of the bloodied men sprawled on the floor got up slowly, his empty hands raising.

"Him I know," Nero said, standing up and slowly opening the door. "Any of that blood yours, Jeffrey?" He quickly shook his head. "Then come ahead...both of you."

Cassidy backed away, keeping her gun on the two men as they slowly entered, Gershon's rifle pointed at the floor.

"Hakken?" Jeffrey said upon seeing the Opposition rebel.

"Jeffrey Pine," Hakken replied. "You're doing your old man proud."

"Better late than never, I guess," Pine said. He and Gershon turned to Cassidy. "Watcher Onai?" Pine looked at Nero. "I thought you had Cassidy here?"

"That is Cassidy," Nero said.

"But Watcher Onai—"

"It's a long story. One we don't have time for," Cassidy said. "It looks like our group is up to five. I wish Noriko were here so she could explain why the Oneirolic didn't see this coming."

"Does it matter?" Hakken asked. "Where are we headed?"

"We need to get word to the rebels that the Shadow Guard is down," Cassidy said. "We have to get them back in the fight."

"We can go out the way we did before," Hakken replied.

"And run across the fields toward the District? That won't work. You had radios in the city. Can we broadcast a signal that'll get picked up from here?"

"We should be able to," Hakken said. "We used to intercept comms from here to the garrison from time to time. They had a lot of static, but we can probably get a message out."

Cassidy turned to Nero. "Do you know where we need to go to do that?"

She nodded. "The military comms are in the CIC. I can show you the way."

"The CIC will be crawling with Hush loyalists," Pine said. "They won't want to risk having you infiltrate the command center, especially if any more of us switch sides."

Cassidy considered it, then shook her head. "No. There's too much risk that we'll trigger a narrative and walk right into a trap."

"So what do we do?" Hakken asked.

"We need to deal with the Oneirolic," Cassidy replied. "If we disrupt its ability to produce narratives, then we can move in on the CIC and get word out to the

District. If we do this right, we can overwhelm the remaining Hush forces from inside and out."

"That sounds good to me, Cass." Hakken shook his head in disbelief. "I never in my life would have imagined that blowing my chance to grab Grand Watcher Jain would be the domino that started the downfall of the Hush. I'm going to enjoy the payback."

"No," Cassidy said sharply, whirling on Hakken. Nevis' voice echoed in his imprint, warning him of what would happen if he helped the Opposition gain control. "No retribution. No revenge."

Hakken flinched at the forcefulness of Cassidy's admonishment. "We've spent over a century under the thumb of the Hush, and you want us to just let bygones be bygones? After everything they've done to us?"

"If you want to destroy what's left, then by all means go after your pound of flesh. But it won't change the past. It won't heal old wounds. It'll only leave them to fester until one day the Silent War happens all over again. That's why we're in this situation, Hak. That's why the Oneirolic exists. To prevent humankind from destroying itself."

"What do you mean?"

"Nevis isn't human. She's a supercomputer. The artificial intelligence Jain used as a template for Unity inside the dreamstate. She was designed to help protect humanity here. But saving humankind isn't the same as allowing it to be free. At least, not all of it."

"She figured that if we won, we'd destroy the Hush and their whole world?" Hakken said, voice filled with disbelief.

"That's exactly what she calculated," Cassidy replied. "But it's like a narrative from the Oneirolic. A projection of a future that can still be changed."

Hakken stared at her in silence. Finally, he nodded. "I get it. I can't speak for anyone else, but if we get this done I'll do what I can to steer us in the right direction."

"That's all anyone can ask." He looked at the soldiers around him. "Our next move is to seize control of Grand Central."

Chapter 20

"How do you propose we take the Watcher Transfer Station?" Nero asked. "If the CIC is the most well-defended space in the facility, Grand Central is number two."

"I'm Watcher Onai," Cassidy replied.

"You're also supposed to be confined to quarters," Gershon answered. "If anyone sees you…"

"We need a diversion," Hakken said. "Something to draw the bulk of the HDF away."

Cassidy examined the facility schematic in his memory. "There are two approaches to the area. The primary approach sees more traffic. If we can pull the Hush out that way, we can sneak in from the back." He paused, considering the problem. "I have an idea." He looked at the three former Hush soldiers. "But there's a good chance all of us might die."

"I think we assumed that risk the minute we started shooting our own people," Price said. "I know I'm a piece of shit for doing it. A traitor twice-over. I don't think I can live with it anyway. But the future is too important to waste this moment. Whatever you need, Cassidy, I'm in."

"Me too," Gershon said.

"I'm in," Nero added. "I'm sure there are others. We can't know how much of our defenses are still intact, especially with half the HDF marching the Opposition back to the District."

"What's your plan, Cass?" Hakken asked.

"I'm not sure if this will work, but I want to trigger the Oneirolic in a stepped pattern. First, one of you goes in shooting, which will prompt them to either bolster defenses or they'll be expecting something like this and will be waiting to ambush you. The next one of you attacks the ambushers, so they'll need to adjust for that. The third one goes in behind that adjustment."

"That'll leave them with three choices," Hakken said. "Fortify the defenses facing the primary approach, try to prep a more complex ambush that will sweep everyone up in one net, or pre-emptively go on the offensive."

"Either way, it'll leave our chosen approach relatively unguarded," Cassidy said. "And I'll be able to get through."

"You can't hold Grand Central on your own," Nero said.

"There's only one door in and out, and it's blast-proof. Secured against non-Watchers and support staff alike. I only need a minute. Just long enough to make the transfer and enter the Oneirolic."

"And then what?" Hakken asked.

"I'll find Jessica and we'll disable the machine from the inside. That'll break the narratives and give the Opposition freedom to relaunch their offensive." Cassidy locked eyes with Hakken. "But somebody needs to stay alive to get the word out when it's done."

"You just got me out of a cell again, and you want me to sit this out?"

"You have the most important job of all," Cassidy replied. "When the Oneirolic fails, you'll need to hit the CIC, and there may not be anyone to help you."

"I don't suppose you want to swap guns with me then," Hakken said.

Cassidy smiled, holding out the Guard rifle. "Keep them both."

"You don't want a rifle?"

"If this works, I won't need it. If it doesn't, I won't need it."

Hakken laughed. "Copy that."

"Which one of you wants to go first?" Cassidy asked, looking at the former Hush soldiers.

"I'll do it," Nero volunteered. "How do we coordinate movement?"

"Can you switch to a private channel?"

"We don't have private channels. But we can adjust to something less likely to be tuned in. Let's try ninety-four."

"Copy that," Gershon said.

"What should I do in the meantime?" Hakken asked.

"Wait here," Cassidy replied. "Try to stay out of sight."

"How will I know when the Oneirolic is down?"

"I'm pretty sure you'll know."

Hakken smiled. "Then I'll look forward to it."

"Nero, advance slowly, but keep it in your head that you're out to kill," Cassidy suggested. "They'll expect that you know you're walking into a trap, which will make it harder for them to adjust, especially with Price and Gershon following you up and with limited time to pick up the narrative and augur it."

"Yes, sir," Nero replied. "I'm ready."

Cassidy could see the hint of fear in her eyes and the slight shudder of her body from the tension. But she also saw resolve. These people had known so much oppression they had joined the HDF because they believed it was their only way out. Now that they could sense change and that they could have a hand in it. They were determined that nothing would stop them.

"Let's go," she said.

The three soldiers moved out in front of Cassidy, heading back the way they had come. She turned to Hakken. "I'll do everything I can to get Jessica out of the Oneirolic alive."

"I know you will," Hakken replied. "Thank you for everything, Cass."

Cassidy put her hand on his shoulder, squeezing it before heading off down the opposite corridor, stepping over the bodies of the dead. She glanced back when she reached the corner, nodding in response to Hakken's wave.

Then she picked up the pace through the facility, moving at a brisk walk, the bulk of her attention focused on listening for incoming defenses and the fighting she knew would occur any minute now. With any luck, it would take place far enough away from Grand Central for her to breach the room without incident.

Every moment of silence increased Cassidy's confidence, leaving her with a good feeling by the time she reached the last passageway and the door that led directly into the same corridor as the entrance to Grand Central. She continued walking along it, slowing slightly as the sound of distant gunfire punctured the space through the door.

The fighting hadn't just started, which meant it could end at any moment.

She sprinted for the door, which was suddenly thrown open, a trio of HDF soldiers behind it. They already had blood on their uniforms and sprayed across their faces and helmets. And for a moment, Cassidy thought maybe they were on her side.

She gave up that hope when they started shooting at her, forcing her to dive to the floor and roll, springing up and angling for the wall to disrupt their angle of attack. Bullets chewed up the area around her. One grazed her abdomen and another hit her in the thigh, the latter causing an intense sting. Ignoring the wounds, she threw herself into the soldiers, taking another round to the side as she hit the lead soldier, batting his rifle aside and throwing quick jabs to his face and gut. The others tried to grab her, but she squatted, grabbing the lead's leg and throwing him into the second soldier. She rolled to her feet, catching the third soldier's rifle before he could line it up for a shot. Holding it aside, the bullets sprayed the wall beside her. She didn't hesitate, driving her elbow into the shooter's face, stunning him as she pulled his sidearm from his thigh holster and put him down.

The lead soldier, still on the floor, rolled over and tried to bring his pistol into play. Cassidy spun, kicking it out of his hand, and then leaping aside as the soldier on the floor shot at her, his aim poor. She dropped onto him with her knee, using enough force to crush his throat as she shot the first soldier point-blank in the chest, putting him out of his misery.

"Damn it," Cassidy cursed, pulling herself back up. Maybe she should have kept one of the rifles after all. She hadn't counted on the sudden ambush, as if the

Oneirolic could suddenly see her too. But it wasn't the Oneirolic. She was sure of that.

It was Nevis.

She had made him, which meant she had a better idea of what he might do than most. But it appeared she either wasn't certain enough to commit a larger force to stop her, or she had made a half-hearted attempt, convincing herself it would be enough while knowing somewhere in her programming that it wasn't.

Either way, Cassidy emerged into the hallway only a dozen feet from Grand Central. The corridor itself was clear, the fight relocated by the narratives. Only the more distant gunfire had stopped, meaning the fight was over.

Grimacing in pain, Cassidy forced herself to run to the entrance, pausing there to consider that Nevis had set her up, the bulk of the remaining HDF force perhaps waiting inside. There was nothing she could do about it. Even if she had a rifle and twenty soldiers were in there with their rifles pointed at the door, she would die. Which was exactly what she had meant when she told Hakken she didn't need a gun.

She stepped up to the door, half-expecting it to remain closed until she felt the tickle on her imprint. It moved aside at the same time she heard the HDF soldiers rushing back to the room, hoping to intercept her before she got inside.

They were too late. She stepped in, clearing the doorway even as she scanned the room. The blast door closed behind her while her eyes settled on the bodies of the Watchers hooked up to the transfer units. All of them were blissfully unaware of what was happening inside the facility.

"Watcher Onai?" Chief Long said, peeking his head out from behind one of the terminals. "What's going on?" He noticed the blood on her clothing. "Are you hurt?"

"I'll be fine," Cassidy replied, though he wasn't sure Sergeant Krane would agree. "You don't know?"

He shook his head. "No. Prescott just told me there was a situation and to keep everyone here. Not that it's hard to do that. What's happening?"

"The Opposition managed to breach the facility," Cassidy said. "One of them already shot me."

"They got past the narratives?"

"Yes."

"How?"

"I don't know. I checked everything at the external control room, but there were no clear signs of destabilization. Sana's working on the problem from here, but he asked me to transfer to monitor Unity from the inside."

"He isn't going to make the transfer himself?" Long asked. "That's unusual."

"So is the enemy getting into the facility," Cassidy hissed. "I need to make the transit."

"You should be in the hospital."

"What good will that do me if the Opposition gains control over this place?" She glanced back at the door as something thunked against it. "Which station is open?"

"You know it's not that simple. One of the other Watchers would need to speak to Hades to prepare someone for you on the inside. You haven't entered the dreamstate in years. It'll take some time." He stared at her stomach. "I think you'll bleed out before then."

Cassidy struggled not to react. He had assumed every Watcher had a counterpart in the Oneirolic. "I told you, I'm fine. I need to transfer into whatever host is available.

There has to be one that's close enough to my pattern to allow a sync."

"We have to take measurements and recalibrate. We can't do that here."

Cassidy shook her head. "I know you can see my imprint status as soon as I link up. Do it visually."

"Visually?" Long said, shocked by the suggestion. "Watcher Onai, if the pattern isn't similar enough, both you and the receiving host will die."

"I'm willing to take the risk."

Long's face changed, shifting from concern to distrust. "Who are you really?" he said, his voice darkening.

"What do you mean?" Cassidy asked, unsure what she had said to blow her cover.

"You aren't Watcher Onai. She helped build the system. She knows the hosts are always Contributors. You can't transfer to a figment of a shared imagination. So who are you?"

Cassidy sighed. Noriko hadn't mentioned that detail to her. "My name is Cassidy. I transmitted through Sana Jain's connection to Aaron Caplan, but Captain Nevis killed him, and now I'm in Sergeant Krane instead of Noriko. She gave up her imprint for me to be here."

She could tell Long didn't want to believe the story. She could also tell that he *did* believe it.

"He said for months that he was going to atone for his sins," Long admitted. "I still can't figure out what he meant."

"He meant the end of Hush rule as it stands. The end of the Oneirolic."

"Why?" Long asked. "We have everything we need."

"Maybe. But so many others don't."

"Somebody always has to be at the top of the food

chain. Somebody has to be in control. Humankind needs a hierarchy. That's what Grand Watcher Jain used to always say."

"Do you believe that?"

"Yes."

"Then today isn't going to be a good day for you."

"I won't help you."

Cassidy smiled. "I think you will." Then she lunged at Long. The technician tried to bolt, but he was no soldier. He was too slow, and there was nowhere for him to go anyway. She grabbed him by the shoulder and shoved him easily onto his knees before crouching behind him and putting him in a chokehold. "Do you know who I am inside the Oneirolic, Chief?"

"N...no. Should I?"

"I'm Unity's number one Shade. A trained killer. Do you know who I am outside the Oneirolic, Chief?"

"N...no."

"I'm Shadow Guard Alpha. A trained killer. What do you think of your odds?"

"P...please. Wha...what do you need?"

Cassidy let him up. "I already told you what I need. Transfer me back into the dreamstate."

"What are you going to do in there?"

"Whatever I can to stop this horror."

Long's hands shook as he straightened his uniform. More noise outside the room suggested the HDF wanted to get in and couldn't. They needed a Watcher, which they would get, but it would take at least a minute or two.

"If you're a trained killer, then I know which Watcher will align most closely to your imprint. But there's still a high probability the sync won't take and you'll corrupt as soon as you transfer."

"I have to take that chance."

"Sit there," Long said, pointing to one of the open units.

Cassidy sat and leaned her head back as Long operated the unit, reclining her back as the displays around the unit lit up. "If you try to double-cross me, I will kill you."

"I have no reason to trick you when the odds are already stacked against you," Long said as the unit touched the back of Cassidy's neck. "See for yourself."

Cassidy looked at the display across from the chair, which showed his imprint matched the Watcher he was replacing.

"Fifteen percent variance is high," Long explained. " But it's the closest you're going to get. It'll take a strong will to stay solid during the synchronization. I would say, an almost machine-like will."

Cassidy smiled. Even if Long had heard of the Shadow Guard, he didn't seem to know their origins. "In that case, I like my odds."

"Close your eyes. I'm initiating transfer in five. Four. Three. Two. One..."

Cassidy closed her eyes. She heard the door to the room slide open, tempted to open them to ensure Long wouldn't stop the transfer.

She didn't have the chance. Intense heat and pain stabbed into her imprint.

Everything turned white.

Chapter 21

Jessica climbed the steps of the subway station, hood pulled low over her face as the rain intensified, a sharp wind swirling within the confines of the city, sending plastic wrappers and other garbage streaking through the street with the pedestrians.

She had never intended to return to the International District. Not after she had arranged the meeting here with Cassidy. Not after the Silver Dragons turned down her offer to arm them with Dome sourced weaponry in exchange for their help storming Praan's Golden Spire. And then they'd sent a group of their forty-niners to take both her and Cassidy out.

She had escaped that altercation thanks to Cassidy, but he wasn't here now. She wasn't sure she would ever see him again. All she knew was that she had to walk back into the Dragon's nest alone.

Learning to manipulate the dreamstate had given her a new level of confidence. Walking through the streets of the International District threatened to steal it from her. She could sense the eyes piercing into her as she splashed down the street with the rest of the people, an obvious outsider in her faux-snakeskin jacket and slightly over-sized pants.

The Silver Dragons were the largest triad in the city, nearly twice the size as the next group in line. Eyeing the passersby as she waded through the masses, Jessica was certain she crossed paths with more than one member of the group. In fact, she recognized a couple of them by the tell-tale dragon tattoos that started on the back of their hands and snaked up their arms. She had heard the Dragon's Mountain Master, Shen Liao, had similar tattoos on both arms and down his back, except they had been implanted subdermally using a special nanogel ink. Normally invisible, they reacted to his change in body heat and heart rate, becoming more visible as Master Liao became more angry. They even had a saying in the International District, Bǎ lóng liú zài shāndòng lǐ. *Keep the dragon in its cave*. In other words, be careful.

Her hand tucked into the pocket of her coat, Jessica twirled the ring Ophelia had retrieved. Brie had set the Miners on course to locate an Immortal, and now her failed relationship with the Silver Dragons made a lot more sense. She had gone to them hoping they would help her gain access to a transfer unit in the home of an Immortal when an Immortal already sat at the top of their mountain. She never would have guessed it before, but knowing what she knew now about the dreamstate, it made a measure of sense. If you were the ultimate power in the universe and could do or be anything you wanted, knowing that none of it was truly real, why wouldn't you decide to play a role as the head of an organized crime syndicate? Knowing it wasn't real, even Jessica thought it sounded like fun.

Except it was real enough for the people who lived

here, who had no idea they were living inside a fake world. The pain and misery the Silver Dragons inflicted was real to at least some of the inhabitants, the people like her trapped inside the Oneirolic. Whoever the Immortal was on the other side of the machine, they had to know that too. At least Praan had chosen to be a legitimate businessman, and in some respects a savior to the people here. Liao still traded in pain and suffering, and seemed to enjoy it.

What left Jessica concerned was Brie. Or rather the Shade who had overwhelmed her motives. Brie had helped her uncover Julian, the vessel hosting the second copy of Jain. On one hand, it seemed almost as though Brie's Shade was trying to help her. On the other, she couldn't shake the feeling that she was walking right into Nevis' hands.

Again.

Considering how many Shades the head of the Underworld had unleashed to find her, she didn't think there was any move she could make that wouldn't leave her feeling vulnerable to Nevis. But she needed to find out how to reach Unity and she couldn't do that without contacting someone who might have the answer, which meant another Immortal like Jain. She would have preferred someone other than Liao, but beggars couldn't be choosers. The real trick would be to first get a direct audience with him, second to get the information she needed, and third to get out alive. At this point, she was counting on her quick wits and ability to manipulate the dreamstate to reach her goal. Even so, she knew her odds of success were ridiculously slim.

She didn't have any other options. She had to try.

It took almost ten minutes for her to make her way three blocks from the subway station to a small teahouse resting on the corner, at the foot of a one hundred twenty-three story skyscraper. The Japanese chashitsu was built in a mostly traditional style, composed of wood with bamboo screen doors and surrounded by a garden that was definitely out of place compared to the world surrounding it.

The building had been upgraded with neon lighting and renovated to accommodate denser occupancy. Nearly one hundred people squeezed inside, tightly packed onto pillows on the floor while women dressed as geishas walked across transparent platforms raised just above the tables, expertly pouring tea from pots with long spouts that stretched down to the cups. Multi-colored lights flickered inside, and guards dressed like samurai flanked the doorway. A line of people extended down the block, waiting for their turn to have a cup of the establishment's famous brew.

The chashitsu was Japanese but run by the Chinese triad. That didn't matter. Liao owned the teahouse and frequented it from time to time, though the presence of others told her immediately he wasn't there. She would have given up on the location straight away, but she spotted another member of the triad she recognized as one of Liao's Vanguards. He wasn't Liao, but maybe he could deliver her to the Mountain Master.

If she properly worded her request.

Jessica made her way across the street, eyes shifting between the line of people waiting for seats to open in the teahouse and the guards at the front. She couldn't afford the time it would take to wait in line, which meant she needed a way to cut to the front. She hoped name-dropping the Vanguard would be enough to get it done.

The two samurai closed ranks in front of the entrance as she approached. Jessica ignored the consternation of the other patrons at the front of the line who didn't want anyone taking their place.

"Do you think you're special?" one of the guards asked. "The line is there."

Jessica smiled beneath her hood. "My apologies," she said in Japanese. When they didn't react, she switched to Mandarin. "My apologies. My name is Jessica Tai. I'd like to speak with Master Yi."

The guard's eyes narrowed. "Did you say Jessica Tai?" he responded in English. "I wouldn't announce myself so openly if I were you."

"I need to speak to Master Yi," she repeated. "If you recognize my name, then you know he'll want to see me. *You*…" Her critical gaze slid over him. "…don't have any say in the matter."

The guard smirked, and then motioned to the other samurai. That one turned away, putting a hand to his ear to speak into a hidden comm.

"We could call the UDF," the guard said. "I'm sure there's a unit nearby. They've been out in force all day, looking for you."

"Do you know why?" Jessica asked.

"It seems you've taken a liking to killing them."

"I don't like killing anyone. They didn't give me a choice."

The other samurai turned back to them, offering a curt nod. The first samurai waved Jessica toward the teahouse. "Master Yi will see you."

She gave the guard who'd first spoken to her an I-told-you-so look before making her way across the short walkway. It took her through a small garden to a trio of steps leading up to the front entrance. She could hear the people waiting in line complaining at her back.

Inside, the arrangement of the pillows and the color

of the lights reminded her of the way the Oneirolic had looked when Cassidy pulled her out of stasis. A chill went down her back at the thought that the resemblance was intentional.

She shook it off as she spotted Heng Yi sitting at the head table. He leaned over slightly, saying something to the man sitting to his right. That man immediately got to his feet, keeping his gaze on the floor, refusing to look Jessica in the eye as he passed her. Probably so he could truthfully deny having seen her if need be.

She skirted a row of patrons, reaching the seat next to Yi. Lowering her hood, she dropped onto the pillow with crossed legs. She didn't say anything to the Silver Dragon Vanguard, keeping her eyes forward as a serving girl used a long handle to scoop up the prior patron's place setting and expertly replace it with a new one.

"Jessica Tai," Yi said, waiting to say more until the girl had poured some tea into her cup. "You're in a lot of trouble."

"What do you know about it?" she replied.

"I know the guns you offered to sell us a few days ago are no longer available. I know your partner Mason Garrett is dead. And I know you'd rather be speaking to Master Liao over me."

"Is that all you know?" Jessica asked. "You could have pulled that off UNet."

He smiled without looking at her. "When you came to the Silver Dragons looking for help getting into the Golden Spire, I knew you would only bring trouble on yourself. Trouble it wouldn't be in our interests to become involved with. Nothing has changed since then."

"Everything has changed," Jessica countered angrily. "I learned everything I was hoping to learn, and then some." She glanced up at a geisha crossing the transparent platform over their table, balancing her teapot. "It would be a shame if the girl tripped and spilled tea in your lap, wouldn't it?"

"Our girls never spill a drop of tea," Yi replied. "They're famous for—"

He grunted as the girl stumbled slightly, just enough for the pot to shift, a narrow stream of tea spilling into his lap. She righted herself an instant later, turning to him with a look of total fear in her eyes. He didn't notice, his attention turning directly to Jessica for the first time. "How did you do that?"

"Who says I did?" Jessica replied.

His eyes narrowed. "What else have you learned?"

"That Shen Liao knows how I just did that," she deadpanned back. "Though I don't know if you know how he knows. By the way, what do you think the odds are that—"

"Enough," Yi snapped, putting up his hand to silence her. "What is it you want?"

"I want to meet with Liao. I have a question and he knows the answer."

"And why would I agree to that when I can snap my fingers and have the UDF surround this place inside of thirty seconds?"

Jessica pulled the ring out of her pocket and dropped it on the table in front of him. "Because Liao made sure I received this for a reason."

She didn't really think Liao had anything to do with the ring winding up in the locker, but she was pretty sure Yi wouldn't risk calling her bluff. He was better off taking her to Liao when the Mountain Master didn't want to see her than not taking her when he did indeed want to see her, and they both knew it.

"I see," Yi said, picking up the ring and turning it

over to examine its authenticity. "How did you acquire this?"

"I've spent the last two days running from the UDF. I didn't have time to steal it, if that's what you're insinuating. And I think you would have heard if one of your Incense Master's rings had gone missing. Unless it had been given freely."

Now that Jessica said it, she started to wonder about the truth of her own words. Yi's reaction verified the ring was authentic, and nobody more than a step below Liao would wear something like it. How had the Miner procured it? Or had Nevis replaced whatever had been there in the first place with the jewelry. She just couldn't reconcile being led into that kind of trap with the effort to use a Shade to bring her in. Unless of course the goal was to make this setup look like less of a trap? Only it didn't. It made it seem more likely.

Counter-intuitively, that gave her more confidence in the approach.

Yi eased to his feet and looked down at her. "Well, shall we?"

She smiled and stood up, following him down the row and to the right, toward the back of the teahouse. They passed through the kitchen where dozens of employees moved in a constant rhythm of preparation—cleaning pots, measuring leaves, and boiling water—while geishas swung through like they were on a conveyor belt, taking the orders and cycling them back out.

By the time Jessica and Yi reached the small garden in the back of the teahouse, nearly a dozen forty-niners had moved in around them, a pair of enforcers leading the group. They kept their distance as a larger luxury roto dropped in from above, the interior completely hidden behind opaque tinted windows. One of the enforcers moved forward then, brushing past Jessica to reach the roto first and open the door for Yi.

"Ladies first," Yi said, waving Jessica in.

She entered the roto, sliding across the rich, buttery leather seats to the opposite side and settling in, the material wrapping around her tired lower half like a hug. Yi sat next to her and the enforcer closed the door.

"You know, I could take you directly to Special Investigations from here," Yi said.

"It wouldn't be good for your health," Jessica replied.

"How so?"

"I don't have anything left to lose, especially if I'm about to be dragged to the one place I definitely don't want to go. It would be an unexpected tragedy if the roto's engines failed mid-flight, wouldn't it?"

The threat wouldn't have meant anything to Yi if the geisha hadn't spilled tea on him. Now he flinched slightly before smiling. "I'm glad we understand one another."

The roto lifted off, though Jessica knew it would be a short trip. Either she would come out of her audience with Liao with some idea as to where to locate Unity, or she wouldn't come out at all.

Chapter 22

The roto touched down on the rooftop of the Shangri-la Hotel less than five minutes later. A pair of valets hurried to each side of the craft, opening the rear doors and extending umbrellas to allow Jessica and Yi to depart without getting wet. A third man in a long raincoat stood under an awning just ahead of them, flanked by a pair of Silver Dragon enforcers. One was a large, muscular brute of a man, similar in size and shape to the Arena's Bruiser. The other was a diminutive woman dressed in a matching suit and tie. She absently twirled a kukri in her left hand, which she slid into a hidden sheathe once Yi cleared the roto.

"This way," Yi said, ignoring the valets and walking toward the waiting Silver Dragon Deputy and his bodyguards.

"Master Yi," the man said, his eyes dancing from the older Vanguard to Jessica. "And Jessica Tai. The woman of the hour." He smiled. "I hear you have some impressive tricks."

"You haven't seen anything yet," Jessica replied.

Obviously, Yi had someone call ahead to let Liao know they were coming. She was glad Liao hadn't turned down the chance to meet.

The Deputy's smile widened. "I can't wait to see what else you can do. Master Liao waits for us down-stairs. If you'll come with me."

"Goodbye, Jessica Tai," Yi said.

"You aren't joining us?" she asked.

"I have other business," he replied. "And I'd like to change my pants." He laughed as he turned away, ambling back to the roto and vanishing through the still-open door.

Jessica trailed the other man to the upper entrance into the Shangri-la, his guards slipping in behind her as they walked. The Deputy stopped and turned back to her when he reached the gilded doors.

"My name is Wei Qiang," he said. "I'm Master Liao's Deputy."

"I figured as much," Jessica replied. "You already know who I am."

"At many levels. Bo and Yun have expressed great admiration for your exploits." He motioned to the two bodyguards. The man was Bo, the small woman, Yun. "Personally, I'm more impressed by intellectual resolve than physical prowess. But you seem to be adept in both areas."

"I do my best."

"You hacked the mainframe at the Dome and constructed your own transfer device. There's no need to be so modest."

Jessica understood what Qiang was alluding to with his statement. He knew something about Liao's true nature, at least with regard to the transfer tech. "It's only impressive when you don't know how it all works. Anyone can learn to do the same."

"Intelligent people struggle to judge their own intellect appropriately. We often think what is simple for us is easy for others when that couldn't be further from the truth. Yes, all of us are born with a gift, but not every gift is up here." He tapped his head. Then he turned back to the doors leading from the landing area into the Hotel. They slid open ahead of him, revealing the interior upper lobby of the building.

A mix of gold, silver, and wood gave the large room a modern, luxurious feel. A dark rug covered the center of the floor. A smattering of guests sat on the sofas arranged there, chatting or staring at their ClearPhones. Small tables were sprinkled among the sofas, cocktail napkins and drinks sitting on them. A pair of suited servers picked up the empty glasses and passed refills to the patrons. To the left, a woman was in the middle of checking in at a long reception desk, while a busy bar occupied the area directly ahead of them.

Qiang motioned Jessica toward the elevators on the right, walking alongside her across the lobby.

"What's your gift?" Jessica asked.

"I have a very analytical mind," Qiang replied. "I'm good with numbers, figures, algorithms, coin. I didn't start life as a Deputy, of course. I started as a Blue Lantern, same as everyone else. I was actually pulled in off the street when I was twelve. Liao tests all of the initiates to determine their gift. He decided I was worth tutoring. The best education he could provide."

"Maybe your gift isn't numbers. Maybe it's luck," Jessica said as they reached the elevator.

Bo stepped in front of them to tap the call button as

Qiang laughed. "Perhaps it is. I was an orphan. A street urchin. A nobody, until Master Liao stepped in."

"I was the same. An orphan, I mean. But I didn't have the luxury of a mysterious benefactor."

"Didn't you?" he asked.

She wasn't sure if he meant Cassidy or Dorne, or if he was alluding to something else. Regardless, the comment sent a shiver down her spine. "What do you mean?"

"I know you came from the streets. Not only did you survive, but you've thrived. And here you are now, number one on the UDF's most-wanted list, about to have a personal audience with the most powerful man in the city. The only man in the world who could protect you, if he deems it so. That's an accomplishment not to be considered lightly."

"It's not really the life I was looking for."

"How many of us ever get exactly what we want? You excel because you don't crumble against the rising tide. As for myself, I've always had a sturdy boat. Fortunate, but not nearly as impressive."

The elevator cab arrived and they stepped in. Yun tapped the panel on the interior, directing it down to the fifteenth floor. The number surprised Jessica. The Hotel extended another mile above the landing pad, scaling high over the clouds. She had assumed Liao would hold court up there as a show of power and wealth.

"Such heights are for soft men," Qiang said, correctly sensing her curiosity. "White-collars who trade in a different kind of asset."

"You mean legal ones?"

"That definition depends on what set of rules you follow."

"What does that mean?"

"I think you know what it means."

Jessica stiffened slightly. She knew Liao knew about the dreamstate. She didn't think he would have told anyone else. She met Qiang's gaze, the answer becoming clear. To remain immortal, Liao needed a succession of hosts. The man's education and status in the Silver Dragons didn't come without a cost.

"Is it worth it?" she asked.

"It's an honor," he replied.

"Do you know the whole truth?"

"I know enough."

"I'm not sure you do."

If Qiang had been groomed to be Liao's next repo, that meant he was a real person. A child separated from his family, brought to one of the Hush's camps, tested and transferred to the facility to be inserted into the Oneirolic. His mind erased. His past wiped away. Trapped in a pod, just like her.

"It's necessary to continue the unbroken legacy of the Silver Dragons," Qiang said. "The triad is more valuable than any of our lives."

The panel beside the elevator doors cycled through the floors as the cab descended, reaching fifteen without slowing and continuing down without stopping. Then the panel went dark. Before Jessica could react, Bo grabbed her from behind while Yun produced her kukri and held it to her throat.

"What is this?" she hissed, glaring at Qiang.

"Everyone who meets directly with Master Liao is put to the test," he replied. "This will be yours."

Chapter 23

The elevator continued dropping, descending for long enough that Jessica was sure the shaft led deep underground. She didn't fight against the hold the two bodyguards had on her. If Liao wanted to test her, then she would save her energy to pass the test.

"You don't have to restrain me," she said. "I won't resist."

"That's easy for you to say right now," Qiang replied. "But you may think differently once you see what's waiting for you."

She didn't like the sound of that, but she refused to succumb to anxiety or fear. She had made it this far, having gone to Yi knowing she was taking a huge risk in essentially handing herself over to him. She still didn't think she had made a mistake. Maybe she didn't know that much about Liao, but she knew he wasn't like any of the other Immortals. While they had chosen to play heroes at best and scions at worst, he had decided to be the villain. He was contrarian by nature. Chaotic. An outlier. Whether he agreed with her pursuits or not, she felt confident he would give her a fighting chance.

The cab slowed to a stop. Jessica's heart rate barely changed as she waited for the doors to open. She was committed. Focused. Whatever Liao threw at her, she would get through it. And then he would tell her how to find Unity.

Or he would die.

The doors in front of her parted, bringing her face-to-face with Brie.

"You," Jessica hissed, arms tensing against the grip Bo had on her, and causing Yun to poke the edge of the Kukri into her neck. Now she understood why they were holding her.

"Jessica," Brie said. "I'm glad you decided to come. That was some escape you made from Sinner's Row earlier today." She smiled.

"Who the hell are you?" Jessica asked.

"You haven't figured that out yet? You called me by name."

Jessica glared at her. "You aren't Cassidy. He was transferred out of here."

"How many Jains have you run into?" Brie asked. "Every Shade has a source."

"The source is copy-protected to avoid this bullshit."

"Normally, yes. But you know by now that I'm special. Besides, there's only one Cassidy here, so no rules have been broken."

"I still don't believe you."

"It doesn't matter." Brie motioned to the guards. "Let her go."

Bo and Yun stepped back, setting Jessica free. She stretched her arms but didn't go for the Shade. "Why did you lead me here?" she asked. "Did Nevis put you up to it?"

"In a sense," Brie replied. "After Captain Nevis confirmed that Cassidy had made the transit, she brought me into play. With some revisions."

"Revisions?"

"The cat's out of the bag, isn't it, Jessica? You know what I am and what this place is. So do I. On a high level, it means you have no advantage over me, which is why I could have killed you back at the bar. But that wasn't the goal."

"Why not?"

"My orders are to neutralize you. Killing you isn't neutralization, it's extermination, and it leaves too much to chance. I wouldn't have broken character at all if we hadn't stumbled onto the second Jain. He was too big of a prize to let slip away. Fortunately, I had some ideas on how to bring you back under control. Chasing after you has proven worse than fruitless. It's led to a lot of unnecessary losses. I thought it would be more efficient to bring you to me."

"Through Shen Liao. How did you manage that?"

"Almost the same way you did. But I'm one step ahead. Once I explained to Master Qiang what's at stake, he was more than happy to arrange for us to be reunited."

"Like I said, the Silver Dragon triad is more valuable than my life," Qiang said.

"They took you from your family," Jessica said. "They stuck you in a machine and made you a slave."

"A slave?" Qiang replied. "I have power, influence, money, women, whatever I could ever want or need. If that's slavery, I don't want to be free."

"But this isn't real."

"It's real enough to satisfy my needs. You might not agree, but that's your perspective. It isn't for you to make decisions for everyone else."

"Maybe that's true," Jessica replied. "But this world is drowning. If nobody does anything, we'll all be dead soon enough."

"You don't know that. Things could change."

"Unity believes it's true. Isn't that enough for you?"

"No. I'd rather have all of this and take my chances. Bo, Yun, do you agree?" The two guards nodded instead of speaking.

"There it is," Brie said.

"There *what* is?" Jessica asked.

"The reason I led you here. You need to recognize that for as many people as you might help with your actions, there are an equal number you'll hurt. And it isn't for you to play God."

"It's the only way to save everyone."

"Arguable. And who made you the savior of this universe anyway?"

"Unity did, when it left me a trigger for the memories that have ultimately brought me here."

"I'm sorry to say, Unity doesn't get to decide."

"But you do? Nevis does?"

"Yes and no. Ultimately, the fate of everything is yet to be determined. We're like magnets, Jessica. Turn us one way and we attract, another way and we repel. We can't change our basic properties or alter our predetermined state. But that doesn't mean we're fixed on a single trajectory."

"I'm not sure what you mean."

"My orders were to neutralize you," Brie repeated. "By bringing you here, that's what I've done."

"So...I'm a prisoner?"

"Right now, you're a guest," Qiang said. "Off the board. Out of play."

"For how long?"

"As long as it takes until Hades is confident the situation is under control," Brie answered.

"If I'm neutralized, how does that not equate to having the situation under control?"

Brie didn't respond, but she didn't need to. Jessica figured out the answer before she finished asking the question. If she was under control and Nevis was still concerned, then it meant Cassidy, her Cassidy, wasn't neutralized. She smiled at the thought.

The smile didn't last, fading from her face as her mind connected to the next dot.

"I'm bait, aren't I?" she asked. "A hedge in case my Cassidy makes it back inside the dreamstate."

"Yes," Brie admitted.

Jessica turned to Qiang. "And Liao doesn't have a problem working with Nevis on this? He's okay with the Silver Dragons cozying up to the UDF? I find that hard to believe."

"Master Liao is a doer," Qiang said. "Not a thinker. He trusts me to make the calculations of what's best for the triad. That's my gift, after all."

"So you're saying he doesn't know," Jessica replied.

At least that explained why she was down here instead of meeting with him. Brie had set her up, using her expectation that the Silver Dragon's Mountain Master would deal with her somewhat fairly and give her a chance to fight in combination with her desperation to sucker her in. On one hand, she felt like a fool for following a path she'd known wasn't leading to anywhere good. On the other, she still couldn't think of a better, more reasonable approach. She'd never had time to be subtle.

Maybe the deck had been stacked against her from the start. But she was still here. There was still a chance she could bluff her way out of this. Or maybe she could work a different kind of magic. Even Brie's Shade admitted this wasn't over.

"The point is, he doesn't need to know," Qiang said. "He trusts my judgement."

"This way, Jessica," Brie said, motioning down the corridor that led away from the elevator.

"Where are we going?" she asked.

"Master Liao calls it his hoard," Qiang replied. "A vault hidden beneath the streets of the International District, only reachable through the original subway tunnels. It's where he keeps the most precious items in his collection."

"That doesn't sound like the best place to keep bait," Jessica said. "Even if Cassidy does make it back here, why would he go through that much trouble to look for me, and how would he find me?"

"He'll look for you because he cares," Brie said. "He'll find you because he's Cassidy. When he does, I'll be here to meet him. And then he'll die."

Chapter 24

Qiang led Jessica and Brie from the elevator to a heavy steel door. The Silver Dragon Deputy produced a skeleton key to open it, not unlike the key Praan had used to let Jessica, Cassidy, and Jazz deeper into the Golden Spire. There was no sound when the door unlocked. No movement of tumblers. No mechanical release of any kind. It was electromagnetic, no doubt with a backup battery embedded in the thick cement walls. Impenetrable without a large amount of powerful explosives or the key in Qiang's hand.

Jessica almost laughed when Qiang pulled the door open, revealing the old subway tunnel on the other side. Even though she knew from him that Liao kept a stash of his most valuable possessions down here somewhere, it was still odd to go through so much trouble to protect access to a damp, dirty, smelly, rat-infested tunnel. Especially when there were likely dozens of other access points across the city. She had never studied the full schematic of the underground, but it stood to reason the sewers were also connected to the subway tunnels, offering additional entry points.

"Some treasure," she quipped as Qiang waved her into the tunnel.

Lights along the top sensed their motion and activated, offering a dim glow to navigate the passage by and scare away the vermin. Three rails ran in a straight line down the middle of the tunnel, and graffiti covered large sections of the stone walls. Ancient garbage lay strewn around the area, introducing Jessica to items and brands she had little familiarity with. Packaging that had survived the War when the products inside the packaging —not to mention the companies that had made the products—hadn't.

"The best way to protect anything of value is to deny it has value in the first place," Qiang replied.

"So then what's with the door?"

"This entrance is beneath the most expensive hotel in the city. Denying value means attracting curiosity."

Jessica smiled. "I want to argue that perspective, but it does make sense on a psychological level."

"This way," Qiang said, leading them along the tunnel.

Brie walked alongside Jessica, though she didn't say anything. Yun closed the door behind them before she and Bo fell into their usual position at the back of the group. "Did you know you were an AI before Jain mentioned it?" Jessica asked a short time later, as they progressed through the tunnels.

Brie glanced over at her. "No," she replied simply.

"And you're okay with that?"

She shrugged. "It is what it is. I can't change it."

"But you believe it?"

"Sana Jain was a lot of things. He wasn't a liar. He

wouldn't make something like that up. I understand there are benefits to my nature in relation to my work as a Shade. You know, my whole reason to exist is to help people. To protect them."

"That's what I want too. But I don't believe keeping the wool pulled over people's eyes is the answer. I don't believe work camps and oppression are answers either. It surprises me that you do."

"There's no other way. Is it better to live a hard life than not to live at all? Is it better to struggle than to go extinct? Those are the questions that drive the Shadow Initiative. That informs the decisions Hades makes. Sana Jain installed Hades to make those decisions. Hades installed me to carry out the tasks needed to reach compliance. We don't need to be enemies, Jessica."

"I don't consider you an enemy," Jessica replied.

"You don't?"

"If what I've heard is true, how could I?"

"Then how do you see me?"

"You're a roadblock. That's all. An inconvenience. One that I'll remove one way or another before this is over."

"You can't fight me and win."

"Probably not. But I'm keeping my options open."

"I can see why New Cassidy likes you."

"How about if I refer to you as Brie? It's less confusing than New Cassidy, Old Cassidy. And since you're an AI, it shouldn't confuse you."

"If that makes it easier."

"What's the difference between you and Cassidy?" Jessica asked.

"I'd have to know what was scrubbed to know what I'm missing."

"But you know you're older and Cassidy's newer.

How can you know that if you don't know what you lost?"

"Because I know I'm from the source, which at a minimum doesn't contain anything that happened after my forty-seventh mission."

"She scrubbed your memories of when I was your repo?"

"I suppose so."

"Why do you think she did that?"

"Bias, I suppose. Shades are never supposed to meet their repos once they've been extracted. Occupying someone makes you biased toward them."

"So if you shadow a serial killer, you'll still be more prone to empathize with the serial killer?"

"You know what they say about walking a mile in someone else's shoes, don't you? It's rare that a person's motive is purely driven by evil intent."

Jessica nodded, left to wonder if Cassidy's feelings for her were because of that bias. Did that make it any less real? He had been in her head. He knew her better than anyone because of it. Sure, she had changed a lot from the time she was a child, but her basic nature was still the same.

She fell silent, following Qiang nearly a mile underground through a maze of old tunnels. Occasionally, the ground would shake beneath her feet in response to trains passing on the newer subway lines beneath them.

Jessica knew when they had reached their destination because they stopped at another heavy steel door, similar to the first. It was covered in graffiti, the edges rusted, a large biohazard warning still visible beneath the grime and paint. Qiang removed a different key from his pocket and slipped it into the hole. This time, large tumblers fell aside, clunking as the door unlocked.

"Don't touch anything," he warned both Jessica and Brie before pulling the door open.

The space beyond it was dark. The lights in the outer tunnel managed to pierce the first few feet, giving Jessica a sense of the room without allowing her to see the entire thing. She initially compared it to a closet. A musty smell drifted out from around wooden shelves laden with boxes, crates, statuary, and other smaller items, many of which would have been right at home in the museum-style displays she had seen in the Golden Spire. Paintings hung from the mosaic tile wall beside her, while the silhouettes of larger artwork were visible further ahead.

"Where did all of this come from?" she asked.

"Many treasures were threatened when the sea levels began to rise," Qiang replied. "Master Liao made it his mission to save as many as he could. From Egypt, to China, to Russia, to France. Anywhere there were antiquities that deserved preservation."

He moved to a metal box on the wall and opened the face, revealing a large switch behind it. Flipping it downward closed the circuit, turning the old lights up to illuminate the extensive length of the room.

Jessica's eyes should have scrolled along the hundreds of pieces of artwork clinging to the walls or the dozens of priceless sculptures, vases, and other artifacts lining the floor. Instead, they traveled directly to the back of the space nearly fifty feet away. A small sitting area was arranged there. A recliner and reading lamp, a sofa, a coffee table and bar sitting on a thick Oriental rug.

The recliner was occupied, an aged but muscled bare arm visible past the wing of the chair, the hand at the end of the arm holding up an old book with a dark leather cover.

"Master Liao?" Qiang said, his voice registering his surprise.

Chapter 25

"I didn't expect you, sir," Qiang said, falling to his knees and bowing his head. Bo and Yun followed suit a half-second later.

Jessica and Brie glanced at one another, equally surprised by the presence of the Silver Dragon's Mountain Master. According to Qiang, Liao didn't know about his deal with Nevis to bring her down here for safekeeping. She held back her smile at the thought. What would he have to say about that?

Liao moved deliberately, closing the book and leaning forward to lower it onto the coffee table, itself an antique work of art, exquisitely carved and in mint condition. He didn't stand up or even glance down the length of the Hoard to where his Dragons waited. Instead, his deep, unexpectedly smooth baritone voice echoed in the chamber.

"Qiang," he said. "*I* wasn't expecting *you*." Jessica had never heard Liao speak before, but he certainly didn't sound happy. "Come forward."

"Yes, sir," Qiang replied. He stood up along with Bo and Yun, and then motioned Brie and Jessica to follow him as he quickly crossed the gap between himself and Liao. When he reached the edge of the carpet, he dropped to his knees again. "Sir."

Liao leaned forward, turning his head in their direction. He looked to be somewhere in his mid-fifties. Thick, dark hair fell to his shoulders, framing a strong, wide face. His wise eyes slid easily over the group, lacking any expression of surprise or concern at the sight of Jessica or Brie but narrowing slightly in anger as they landed on Qiang.

"Moments of peace and privacy are hard to come by when there's much work to be done," Liao said, the hidden tattoo on his arm becoming visible in a glow of blue light that pierced the upper levels of skin. The dragon emerging from its cave. "By coming here, you've disrupted my peace."

"Yes, Master Liao," Qiang said. "My apologies."

"And you've brought outsiders into my Hoard. My place of refuge." He stood up, turning to face them, both arms glowing now. "Explain yourself!"

"Master Liao," Qiang said, forcing his voice to remain steady. "This is Jessica Tai. I—"

"I know who she is, Qiang," Liao growled. "It's my business to know everything that's happening in my city. I want to know why she's here."

"Of course. She's—"

"Master Liao," Jessica said, interrupting him. She bowed to the Silver Dragon leader. "Believe it or not, I'm here because I was looking for you."

Liao stared at her. At that moment, she thought he might order Yun to put her kurki across her throat. Instead, he seemed to calm slightly, his attention turning to her as his tattoos faded from view. "Jessica Tai," he said. "This is about Unity."

"You do know everything that's happening in the city, don't you?" Jessica answered.

He offered a flat smile. "You came to me not three days ago hoping to barter weapons for my help in your fight for what you called truth. Tell me, have you won that fight?"

"A battle, maybe," Jessica replied. "Not the war."

Liao nodded. "A strong answer. I rejected you once, and yet you've come back to me for help. But you have no guns to barter anymore, do you?"

"No. They were stolen from me."

Liao laughed, a choppy chuckle that he cut off a moment later. "You stole them from the Dome, Sana Jain stole them from you. All's fair in love and war. Isn't that what they say?"

"That's what I've heard, Master Liao."

"So, I turned you down when you had some bargaining power. Now that you have none, you still want my help?"

"You're the only one who can help me," she answered. "You're the only one who might consider it."

"Why would I consider it?"

"Look around. You've spent more than a lifetime trying to preserve all of this artwork. All of these precious things, while at the same time you know that none of it is real. Why?"

Liao returned a full-blown smile now. "Because even a villain needs a purpose. A pursuit. And one as old as I am becomes bored with the status quo."

"I'm fixing to change the status quo like you wouldn't believe."

"How do you propose to do that?"

"Through Unity. But I don't know where to find it."

"And you believe I do?"

"Do you?"

"Yes."

"Will you tell me?"

"I haven't decided yet." His gaze shifted back to Qiang. "You didn't know I was down here. And yet you brought Jessica Tai here regardless. It's only good fortune that we crossed paths. So why are you here, Qiang?"

Qiang hesitated long enough that Liao lunged forward, grabbing him by the throat before Jessica had even realized he'd moved.

"Why are you here with Jessica Tai?" Liao repeated, the dragons reemerging on his arms. They were both beautiful and terrifying to see.

Qiang pointed at Brie. "I...we…"

Liao let him go, eyes shifting to Brie. "You're a Data Miner. Or you were until Captain Nevis got a hold of you. Who are you now?"

"I don't know what you mean," Brie replied. Jessica was impressed by how sincerely she answered and embarrassed because she would have believed the reaction.

"Do you know who I am?" Liao asked.

"Shen Liao, Silver Dragon Mountain Master," Brie replied.

"Who else?"

"I don't know what you're referring to."

Liao grunted. "Nobody believes you. It's of no consequence. I believe I understand the nature of this intrusion. I've known Captain Nevis for many years. Some might even say I know her better than anyone. You intended to bypass my involvement in this war, didn't you?"

"I don't know Captain Nevis," Brie insisted.

"Because she knows I'm a wildcard," Liao continued, obviously discounting Brie's denial. "That she can't count on me to fall into line like the rest of them. Jessica Tai has never met me before and she understands me better than Nevis has in all of this time." He looked back at Qiang. "You understand me as well, don't you? Well enough to try to circumvent me to save your own skin."

"What?" Qiang said. "I would never—"

"For the good of the Silver Dragons," Liao continued. "That's your reasoning, I'm sure. I *am* the Silver Dragons. What I want is what you want."

"Yes, Master Liao. I just thought—"

"That you know better than me," Liao finished, interrupting him again. "An arrogant assumption. If you were as smart as you think you are you would have realized that I would know what you tried to do and that it wasn't guaranteed I would approve."

"Master Liao, I only had the best interests of the Dragons in mind. Your best interests."

"Be grateful I believe that," Liao said. "The end result has fallen to my liking. A chance encounter with Jessica Tai to discuss where we all go from here." He looked back at Brie. " Take this Shade back to the surface with you." He glanced at Brie. "I understand your intentions, but I won't abide by them."

"Yes, Master Liao," Qiang said. "It will be done."

Jessica looked to Brie to see her reaction to Liao's statement. While her expression was flat, Jessica noticed her hands balling into fists, her muscles tensing. Preparing for a fight.

"I can't abide by your wishes," Brie hissed at Liao. "The consequences are too great."

Liao met Brie's defiant gaze with one of his own.

Then he returned to his chair, sitting casually. "I wasn't asking," he said softly.

"I'm not asking, either."

With that, Bo and Yun launched themselves at Brie, and Qiang produced a gun from somewhere behind his back while Jessica backed out of their way.

Instead of standing there, defending herself, Brie leaped at Qiang, kicking the gun from his hand before he could take aim. Driving forward, she hit him with a sharp elbow to his face. He stumbled back and she rolled sideways beneath Bo's reach, wrapping her legs around his ankle and twisting to bring him down.

Yun dove at Brie, kukri flashing as she went for her face. On her back, Brie grabbed her wrist, knocking the blade out of her hand. It hit the floor next to her head, bouncing off the mortar. Out of play.

Brie brought her knee up between them into the bodyguard's chest and shoved. The force launched the other woman off her. She followed through, swinging her legs around, the momentum carrying her back to her feet. She stood there, matching Yun's stance, both of them ready to fight. Brie spared a glance at Liao, who watched the scene unfold with a hint of curiosity but little actual concern.

By this time, Qiang was on his feet, pointing his gun at Brie. He fired, somehow missing her. She rushed Liao's Deputy. The next bullet missed her as well, as did the third. She seemed to be dodging the rounds before he even pulled the trigger. Or more likely, she manipulated the dreamstate to ruin his aim. Recognizing the potential cheat, Jessica sought to counter it, suggesting in her mind that whatever had messed up Qiang's aim had run its course.

The fourth and final round grazed Brie's cheek, drawing a line of blood right before she pummeled Qiang, batting the gun out of his hand and beating him with a series of rapid-fire punches to send him stumbling backward.

Jessica heard the sound of breaking bones clearly beneath the thuds of Brie's hands colliding with Qiang's chest. He went down, leaving Yun Brie's sole threat.

The Shade tracked Yun as she rose to her knees and threw the kukri at Brie's back. Impossibly, Brie reached back at the last moment, catching the weapon by the handle, the blade only centimeters from the base of her neck. She continued the pirouette, coming back around on Qiang to leave a deep gash in his neck with the kukri. He tumbled backward to the floor, blood pouring from the wound.

Brie spun around again, holding the kukri expertly in her grip as Bo and Yun approached, closing more carefully this time. She didn't wait for them to get to her. Like before, she forced the bodyguards to act, rushing Bo while she slashed a pattern in the air with the kukri, forcing him to retreat. Yun used the opportunity to move around to Brie's side, looking for an opening.

Suddenly, Bo stopped retreating, shifting his weight and moving toward Brie despite the menacing blade she brandished like a decapitating whirlwind. He threw his forearm out, catching the kukri with it, the weapon sinking through his flesh and hitting something hard. Something that wasn't bone. Bo smiled in response to her surprise, thinking he had turned the tables, giving Yun an opportunity to lunge at Brie from her flank.

If Brie was caught off-guard, she recovered impossibly fast, releasing the kukri and dropping low. She whirled on Yun, grabbing her arm and turning it, her other hand coming down hard and breaking the limb with a loud crack. Still spinning, she twisted Yun's arm and threw her foot into the woman's back, pushing her at Bo.

He reacted instinctively, putting his hands up to catch Yun and shoving her aside. Brie leaped up, kicking Bo in his chin and knocking his head back with enough force to break his neck. He hit the floor, paralyzed.

Yun reached for the kukri with her good hand, yanking it from Bo's arm. She lunged angrily at Brie, the knife held backhanded as she sliced at Brie's midsection.

Brie caught Yun's wrist easily, turning it aside and bringing her knee up into the woman's gut. Knocking the air out of her, she twisted her wrist, breaking it too. The blade fell from the woman's limp fingers before Brie knocked her to the floor with a roundhouse left to the temple.

Picking up the discarded blade, Brie stood over Yun, looking down at her for a moment before planting the kukri in her neck, leaving blood gurgling in her throat as she quickly died.

Brie turned to Liao. "Jessica Tai stays right here with me."

Jessica's eyes fixed on Liao. Brie had just made short work of three of the Mountain Master's best Dragons. She expected he would be furious but cautious, in recognition that the Cassidy Shade was probably his better. She couldn't imagine anyone else putting on a display like that.

Liao eased himself to his feet, glancing at Jessica before turning to Brie. "Now I know who you are."

"Do you?" Brie asked. "How can you be sure?"

Liao smiled. "Because you fought exactly how I would fight, if I were in that repo instead of this one. Because you're a copy of me, aren't you?"

Jessica stared at Liao, a chill running down her spine in disbelief. And relief. "Cassidy?"

Chapter 26

Cassidy glanced at Jessica, offering her only a slight nod while keeping an eye on Brie. On what had to be an older version of himself.

He had passed through the Braid Crossing with little effort, his focus and resolve carrying him across the divide and reconnecting him with the imprint on the other side. The sync had been painful. More painful than any he had ever experienced before. He was the wrong consciousness being written to the wrong source, and in the moments of agony and twisted, flashing memories he had been almost certain he wouldn't make it through uncorrupted.

He still wasn't completely sure he had. This repo's memories continued to flicker through his mind, offering snapshot visions of an unrecognizable past at seemingly random intervals. A dog, a woman, a casino, a bedroom, money, drugs, sex, murder. It was like thumbing through a book of photographs filled with dark imagery, a life lived in the city's underbelly as host to the Silver Dragon Mountain Master.

Chief Long had told him the vacant imprint belonged to a killer. There hadn't been time to consider what that meant. He had certainly never taken the time to wonder if Shen Liao was an Immortal. A Watcher. Learning it was so had been a pleasant surprise. Standing in Liao's shoes would make his job that much easier.

At least, he hoped that would be the case. Once Hades figured out he was back, and who he was, all bets were off. Like Nevis on the other side of the Crossing, her AI counterpart here would stop at nothing to preserve the future it believed was best for everyone, even if Unity wasn't as sure.

Brie's face changed, a flash of fear crossing her features before she brought it under control. "How did you get here?"

"Bizrathi Praan kept his transfer unit hidden at the top of the Golden Spire," Cassidy answered. "Shen Liao's unit is here." He motioned to the wall behind him, where a hidden door kept the unit safe. "Along with a full suite of comms equipment keyed to the ranking members of the Silver Dragons. The one secret Liao has always kept is that he doesn't trust anyone. And rightfully so." His eyes swept over Qiang. "Your plan was good. Qiang knew Liao was temporarily out of the picture even if he didn't know where he had disappeared to. It wasn't wrong for him to make a deal with the UDF in a world that would continue forward uninterrupted. And having both the UDF and the Silver Dragons to back you when I came for Jessica was equally smart. I wouldn't have guessed I would have thought of that, except you did."

Brie smiled. "You might not have. We aren't identical."

"No," Cassidy agreed. "I can see that much in your eyes. There's a flatness behind them. Something lacking."

"Subtraction isn't always a bad thing. You know that."

"It is when it's your humanity that's been subtracted. The way I see it, you have three options. One, help us reach Unity. Two, return to Hades and tell her I'm back. Three, try to stop me on your own, here and now. A warning on the third option. You won't succeed."

Cassidy could tell that Brie gave serious consideration to the options, her expression suggesting she was weighing the different outcomes. He didn't think the first would get much thought, but the other two carried more weight with the Shade. There were benefits to telling Hades he had returned to the dreamstate. But there was also a pull to rise to the challenge and try to end things here and now.

If the roles were reversed, he was certain which he would choose. That's why he was ready when Brie suddenly whipped a gun from behind her back—a weapon he was sure hadn't been there a second earlier—and started shooting.

Cassidy was already dodging, jerking sideways as he grabbed the chair beside him and hurled it at Brie with the strength of a pair of modded arms. Brie stopped shooting to turn her shoulder into the chair, shoving it away as Cassidy leaped at her, a heavy fist coming at her head.

She dropped the gun to block the punch, catching his fist in her hand and pulling Cassidy's arm aside. He had anticipated the move and countered it. Shifting his balance, he turned with her effort to throw him, landing on his feet. He held her arm straight out to the side and thrust the palm of his other hand into her chest. The blow sent her flying backward to crash into a table with a pair of old sneakers on it before landing on the floor.

Cassidy didn't think it would be enough to stop her. He dove aside when she produced another gun out of nowhere, bullets whipping past him as he dove for cover behind another table. Reaching behind his back, he retrieved a weapon of his own, though he didn't need to take advantage of the dreamstate to create it. Liao, of course, was armed.

The Desert Eagle had silver dragons etched on both sides of it to go with an ivory hand grip. It was heavy in his hand, a powerful gun that he aimed and fired through the obstacle protecting him, modded arms easily handling the recoil. Brie paused her attack to avoid the barrage, finding new cover behind an ancient chest.

They both rose at the same time, guns pointed at one another, taking a moment to stare each other down. Grinning at each other, they both threw their weapons aside and walked toward one another in an odd mirror-image, meeting in the center of the room.

"You're good," Brie said.

"So are you," Cassidy replied.

"Are you ready to die?" Brie smirked.

"I don't know; are you?" Cassidy asked.

Brie came at him again, throwing rapid punches meant to test his speed and reflexes. He met them all easily, the AI part of him somehow processing the velocity and angle of each attack and ready to meet it before it arrived. He countered the offensive with one of his own, almost laughing as the Shade did the same.

"Amusing, but inefficient," Brie admitted.

"You should surrender," Cassidy said.

They attacked one another at the same time—

trading a series of quick blows, punches, kicks, grabs and chops—blocking and reversing in an array of high-speed maneuvers. It went on for nearly three minutes in a dazzling mixture of martial arts styles that could have filled the Arena and left the cheering onlookers on their feet. Instead, the end of the round left both Cassidy and Brie winded as they backed up a step from one another and took a breather.

"I thought this would be a little easier," Cassidy admitted.

"So did I," Brie replied, reaching behind her back, no doubt for another weapon.

Cassidy did the same. "If we both draw, we'll kill one another," he said.

"I'm replaceable," Brie replied. "You aren't."

They stared at one another. Cassidy's eyes narrowed. He and his duplicate Shade were perfectly matched. But if he wanted to survive, if he wanted to save Jessica and the other people inside the Oneirolic and have a chance to help Hakken and the other rebels, he needed to win this fight.

Both Brie and Cassidy moved at high-speed, their arms blurred as they swung their hands out from behind their backs. Cassidy had a weapon in his. He aimed and fired in one impossibly quick motion.

Brie's hand had emerged from behind her back empty, shock written across her face as Cassidy's round caught her squarely at the base of her throat. The round tore all the way through her neck and into the imprint, severing the connection between the older version of Cassidy and Brie. She stumbled, her knees giving out. Cassidy dropped his gun and lunged, catching her as she fell, lowering her gently to the floor.

Jessica rushed over to them. "Brie." Kneeling at her side, she took her hand. "Brie, can you hear me?

"How?" Brie asked, confused about why she hadn't been able to conjure a gun.

"I could see your back," Jessica explained.

"I'm sorry," Brie said weakly, barely able to speak through the damage to her throat. I...I had no choice."

"It wasn't you," Jessica replied. "I'm the one who's sorry. If I hadn't dragged you into this—"

"Doesn't matter. Just fi...finish it...set our people...free."

"I will," Jessica said.

"We both will," Cassidy added. "I promise."

He didn't know if Brie heard either of them before she died. He reached over and closed her eyes.

"Damn it," Jessica whispered, angrily swiping her tears away. She glanced at Cassidy, her lower lip still trembling. "She always said she didn't know whether or not she was real. But she was, wasn't she?"

"Yeah," Cassidy replied simply. There was nothing else to say. Gone was gone. He lowered Brie to the floor and then stared into Jessica's eyes. "Are you okay?"

"Yes," she replied, smiling through the remnants of her tears. "I can't believe you're really here."

"It wasn't easy to get back, but I'm here now for good."

Her smile grew. "I'm glad."

He finally smiled. "Me too." His expression grew suddenly serious. "Jess, I need you to know something. I—"

"You're an AI," she said. "I know."

Cassidy flinched. "How?"

"Jain told me. And you know what; I don't care. You still seem pretty damn human to me."

"Then you still trust me?"

"Always."

He nodded, looked down one more time at Brie and then stood, his hands cupping her shoulders and drawing her up with him. "Why are you down here?"

"I could ask you the same thing."

"Liao is an Immortal. I needed a repo to cross back into, and he was both available and the best match to my imprint. Finding you here was just luck. But I would have found you eventually, either way."

"That's sweet."

"I do care about you, Jess, but it's not just about that. Jain put you in the Oneirolic on purpose, and Nevis is terrified of you, which means you're an important component in all this."

Jessica nodded. "I kind of figured that. I tried to get an audience with Liao because he's an Immortal," she explained. "And I figured he would know where to find Unity."

"He might have," Cassidy replied. "But he's not here. I am."

"So you don't know?"

"I'm not sure yet. My sync isn't great, and I'm dealing with a lot of fragmentation and corruption. I keep getting glimpses of things, but I can't skim this repos mind the way I have others in the past. If Liao ever mentioned or saw the location, it might be in here somewhere. But there are no guarantees I can come up with it. Is there another way?"

"I don't think so. I tried to find Unity when I had the interface, and I always came up empty. If you don't know, then we need another Immortal."

"Give me a minute," Cassidy said, closing his eyes. And concentrating.

Images immediately bombarded him, flashing through his mind's eye in a random pattern. They were pixelated and discolored in response to the corruption, some more distorted than others. And that was before he tried to search the host's memories.

Sinking in, he focused on thoughts of Unity, the memories turning to what amounted to video clips rather than static imagery. Bits and pieces, as cut up as before. Meetings with other Immortals. Black tie affairs, backroom deals, private encounters. Brokering power, bartering among themselves as a secret hierarchy within the Oneirolic. They had made the dreamstate to win the War and then turned it into a personal playground.

Cassidy sensed his own identity slipping further away, the deeper he tried to dig into the repo's past. He knew the danger. The risk. The consequences. He didn't have another choice. He reached out for Jessica, his hand slipping down her arm to take her hand, using her to anchor himself as he kept sinking, heading deeper, the memories elongating at the same time they became more corrupt. He began to feel dizzy and weak. He opened his eyes, his hand tightening on Jessica's as he explored, counting on his feelings for her to hold him fast.

A memory of a computer display slipped through his thoughts. He stood over Jain, looking at a large, metal object. The memory was older than the host, a fragmentation from Liao's imprint.

"Beautiful, isn't she?" Jain said to Liao.

"Are you sure this will fix the problems?" he replied.

"Yes, very."

Cassidy smiled. He had it.

Instead of diving deeper into his repo's memories he released them, hoping to surface. But the thoughts around him were thick and fragmented, and he realized suddenly he had lost his way out. A moment of panic threatened to overwhelm him, but he immediately brought it under control. If he wasn't careful, he would corrupt even more, and he couldn't afford to let that happen. Not if he wanted to escape his mind to tell Jessica where to find Unity.

He slowed his thoughts instead, focusing on calming his repo's overactive brain. Eyes open, he was vaguely aware of Jessica in front of him, watching him like a hawk. He focused his thoughts on her, on the feel of her hand in his, pulling himself up by the anchor he had made, remembering what he could of their short time together. Their first meeting, the warehouse, the bathroom at Jazz's, the exterior of the Oneirolic. Strong memories that helped tug him along through the mire of the past.

Even so, it wasn't easy, and the effort left him unsteady. He stumbled as his head exploded in pain. Jessica caught him before he could hit the floor. Images from his repo's past flashed through his mind in rapid-fire—disconnected, disjointed, corrupt, and fragmented. He fought to stay focused, to stay calm, to keep the memories from overwhelming him. The reaction could drive a Shade mad and had claimed the lives of many.

But he wasn't like the other Shades. He had a logical, machine mind at his root, which still lent him an ability to remain reasonable and collected. He turned his head, meeting Jessica's gaze again, her look of concern tugging him out of the morass.

"Cass?" she said, leaning her face close to his, struggling to keep him upright. "Cass, can you hear me?"

The memories slowed, the images becoming less distracting inside his head. He blinked a few times, finding the surface and breaking through. Liao's heart raced, his breathing heavy, his forehead sweating as Jessica's face came into full focus in front of him.

"I hear you," he whispered.

"Did you find it?"

He nodded. "Yes. I know where to find Unity." He offered her a weak smile in an attempt to reassure her. "But getting there isn't going to be easy."

Chapter 27

"Why don't you sit down," Jessica suggested, motioning to the sofa. "You look a little unsteady."

Cassidy didn't argue. The dive into Liao's repo had nearly corrupted him, leaving him disoriented and exhausted. They didn't have a lot of time to waste, but they had a few minutes. Even assuming Brie had managed to send a beacon or comm out to Nevis before separating from her Shade, the UDF would hesitate to come down here, and even if they did it would take them time to navigate the maze of tunnels.

He circled the coffee table and slumped onto the sofa, a few images from the repo's memory flickering in front of his vision again. In the course of searching for Unity, he had learned his host was actually Liao's son. A pregnancy with the man's dreamstate wife who didn't exist beyond the interior of the shared world. He wasn't completely sure how that was even possible, but he could guess. A dreamstate infant born of the womb, replaced at some point by a child taken from the District to the camps, hand-selected by Liao, whose real name outside of the Oneirolic was Yu Wen, and inserted into the machine. The whole idea of it twisted Cassidy's mind into a knot. He couldn't wait to put an end to it.

Jessica sat on the couch beside him, her eyes heavy with concern. "What happened on the other side? What did you find out there?"

"I met the real me," Cassidy replied. "And the real Nevis."

"The real Nevis?"

"An artificial intelligence. The source Unity was based on. She's trying to keep human civilization intact, and she thinks letting the dreamstate fail is the only way to do it."

"By killing everyone in the Oneirolic?"

"Yes. But with replacements ready to be inserted, keeping the downtime to a minimum. She believes that letting this cycle end on the path it's on will cause another war that humanity won't survive."

"I can't say with any certainty that she's wrong."

"Neither can I, but that's beside the point. It shouldn't be up to a single entity to determine the future of an entire species."

"I'm with you there, Cass."

Cassidy smiled. "I know. I left the Oneirolic facility with a rebel named Hakken. He took me back to his city, a place called the District. I got to see first-hand how the Hush treats the people there."

"Let me guess, it's not good."

"No. And I didn't get to see the camps, but I'm willing to bet it's worse there. In any case, we marched on the facility. We would have beaten them there if not for the Shadow Guard."

"Shadow Guard? What's that?"

"Me," Cassidy replied. "I was Shadow Guard Alpha.

The lead for a unit of seven armored AI soldiers, fully mechanized. They tore our uprising apart. Then Nevis brought me in and showed me the truth. She thought I would see things her way once I had my memories restored. But being in the dreamstate, being a Shade changed me."

"For the better," Jessica said.

"I think so, too. It wasn't easy, but I escaped. Now I've got a small group on the inside helping me, including Hakken. He's waiting for us to disable the Oneirolic before he calls for help. If we time things right, we can still help the rebels overwhelm the Hush."

"What about the people linked to the dreamstate?"

"We can't separate them from the system without killing them. I've been told so many times that Unity can't be reset I'm starting to believe it may be true."

Jessica wrinkled her forehead in angry confusion. "So what's the play? What do we do if there's no chance we can save everyone?"

"I didn't say we couldn't. What I'm saying is that maybe resetting Unity isn't the answer."

"Then what is?"

"Unity is based on Nevis' source code. So am I."

"What are you thinking, Cass?"

"I don't want to reset Unity. I want to replace it."

"Replace it? With what? I don't understand."

"We can't just snap our fingers and change Unity. That'll destabilize the system. We could make subtle changes that would prevent the second apocalypse, but the Oneirolic will stay online, and the people inside will still be trapped inside. If we save the dreamstate, everything in the real world stays the same. I'm not willing to accept that solution."

"Neither am I," Jessica agreed.

"The way I see it, the only way we can get the people out of the dreamstate is if they make the decision to leave of their own volition."

"Wait. Cass, they don't know they're living in a fake world. How can you get them to leave?"

"I have to make them believe they're going some-place better,"

"But how will they live without the Oneirolic?"

"They won't. They're not real so they'll just cease to exist when the Oneirolic shuts down."

"Are you sure that will work?"

"I'm not sure of anything, but I know I need Unity's reach to make it happen. With your help, I think I can interface directly with Unity and make the necessary changes. Unity can't make them on its own, it doesn't have a high enough degree of freedom."

Jessica was silent for a moment while she considered his words. "You said Unity won't be easy to reach. Why not?"

"Unity's in space," Cassidy said. "Geosynchronous orbit above the north pole."

"Space?" Jessica replied. "I guess that makes sense when you think about it, from both a security and opera-tional perspective. Do you know if it's defended?"

"I don't know. But I think it's better to assume it is."

"So we need a starship." Jessica smiled. "I don't think it'd be that hard to acquire one."

"Why not?"

"You're Shen Liao, the head of the Silver Dragons. You've got countless resources at your disposal. Every-thing from coin to foot soldiers. I don't think the UDF will sell you a starship, but I bet we can take one from the Marine launch platform."

"Do you know how to fly a starship?"

"We're in a dream world, Cass. Maybe we both do."

Cassidy returned Jessica's smile. "Maybe you're right. Jess, there's something else you should know."

"What is it?"

"The rebel I told you about, Hakken. He's your father."

Jessica's face froze as she stared at Cassidy, tears beginning to well again in her eyes. "What?" she whispered.

"Your biological father. I met your mother too. And your little brother. You have a family outside the dream-state. You weren't abandoned. You were taken. Kidnapped. And they want you back very badly."

The tears rolled freely down Jessica's cheeks. "Cass, I…" She smiled. "If I have a family that misses me, then so does everyone else in the Oneirolic. I want to see my family. Maybe when I do, I'll remember them."

"I hope so. I want you to see them again too."

Jessica stood and turned to him. "Then what are we waiting for?"

Chapter 28

Cassidy used Liao's memories of the tunnels to lead them away from the underground Hoard and back to the Silver Dragon Mountain Master's residence. He had passed by the place plenty of times over the course of his career, and he remembered it well.

Yu Wen hadn't bothered building a massive tower like Jain had for his alter ego, preferring instead to keep a relatively low profile for someone of his infamy and stature. While everyone knew where he lived, including the UDF, he had opted for a simple, ten-story high pagoda that occupied one of the corners of the International District. Cassidy had been able to roughly sync with Liao because of the similarities between his and Wen's imprint patterns. Their preferences in living style were alike as well. Cassidy liked the man's no-nonsense approach, and the fact that the pagoda almost seemed to dare enemies to try to assault him at home.

There were no guards visible on the outside of the building. No fencing around it. No barriers to keep people from going up and knocking on the large, wooden front doors, with their pair of carved dragons. Of course, the pagoda wasn't defenseless. Hidden cameras monitored every action not only around the property, but throughout the entire International District, including the airspace above. Nobody could get within a half-mile of the pagoda without being facially identified and matched to a database of known UDF employees or potential adversaries. While it was impossible to suss out Shades that way, the fact that Liao was an Immortal had kept Hades from ever targeting him directly. Instead, any of his operations that had the potential to disrupt the dreamstate were shut down through alternate means.

Cassidy and Jessica didn't enter the pagoda through the front. They climbed a damp and rusted metal stairwell from the original subway tunnels up into the first sublevel of the property. The stairs led to a small antechamber where a pair of enforcers kept watch over the entrance to the tunnels. They bowed their heads to Cassidy as he entered the room, no doubt noticing the blood on his clothing and Jessica with him but remaining silent. Cassidy ignored them, continuing to the door on the other side of the antechamber and into a long corridor. Cassidy knew from his repo that in the event of an attempted intrusion, one or both doors could be locked down and the room—not unlike the one Jessica had used in the basement of the Golden Spire—would immediately fill with a toxic gas. Similar invisible and deadly traps filled the pagoda, part of the reason it remained a bastion despite its outwardly unprotected appearance.

They crossed from the hallway to an elevator, the sensor scanning his retina to confirm his identity before allowing him control. Cassidy selected the third floor, which opened into a long, empty corridor.

"Liao likes his privacy, doesn't he?" Jessica whispered in response to the relative solitude.

"He values efficiency," Cassidy replied. "His people are out doing business, not loitering around. Deputy Qiang would have met us when we arrived, but…" He trailed off. They, of course, had firsthand knowledge as to what had happened to Qiang.

"I assume you have a plan as to how we can get on board a Marine launch platform and steal a spaceship," Jessica said as they walked down the corridor. There were a few doors on either side—offices for Liao's administrators, arranged by rank, with Liao's at the end. Qiang's office was next to Liao's, Yi's next to that. All of the doors were closed.

"The beginning of an idea," Cassidy replied. "Though assaulting an offshore Marine launch base wasn't something I had expected to be part of this equation."

"Maybe we don't need to assault it," Jessica replied. "Does Liao have any contacts in the military? Maybe we can get on the platform without a fight."

Cassidy shrugged. "I only have the repo's memories, not Wen's. I'm in the same spot I was when I transferred out of the dreamstate to the facility. This repo is a perfect cover, but as a third party, his knowledge is limited. Do you have any contacts in the military we can use? Someone associated with the resistance, maybe?"

"I think you've figured out there isn't much of a resistance. Not anymore. You saw how quickly Nevis knocked us down even though I had the UMI. If there's anyone on the platform with ties to the cause, there's no way to identify them ahead of time."

"What were you planning to do when I asked you to create a diversion?"

"What were *you* planning to do, Cass? Five days? You didn't even make two."

They both smiled as they reached the door to Liao's office. His handprint and a retinal scan opened the door, and they both stepped in, the room remaining dark. The windows had been painted over, a pair of lighted displays on the walls showing images of Liao's wife and two daughters. Ancient oriental tapestries hung on either side of the displays.

A large, ornate desk stood in the center of the room, a holo projector affixed to the ceiling above it. Hundreds of dragons carved in the wood twisted and curled around one another so tightly it was impossible to tell where one ended and the next began. A single chair sat on either side of the desk.

"I left the facility to stay out of trouble by hiding among the people," Cassidy replied. "Then the Hush came and tried to take your brother away from your mother. What was I supposed to do?"

"Jain told me you wouldn't be able to remain static for that long anyway," Jessica said. "He said it wasn't in your nature."

"As a Shade, I was turned on and off like a light switch. I always had a mission. A job to do. Sometimes that meant biding time, but there was always more to it than that. Studying my opponent, finding their weakness, looking for an opening. Like I did when we were together. I never waited for the sake of waiting. But I thought you would need time."

"So did I. Nevis didn't want to give me any."

Cassidy circled the desk. It had a touchscreen embedded on the right side, and he used his fingerprint to activate the display. He quickly surveyed the interface before first turning on the overhead lights, and then navigating to Liao's contact list.

"Liao doesn't have a ClearPhone?" Jessica asked.

"Not when he goes down to the Hoard to transfer. He doesn't want anyone to know where he is. Only a few people know he's an Immortal." Cassidy tapped on Yi's name. The hologram activated, a woman's face and upper torso appearing in it. She was older, with short graying hair and a hard, wrinkled face. Xin Lin, his Operations Officer.

"Master Liao," she said, bowing her head to him. "I'm honored to hear from you, but I thought you were indisposed for the next few days."

"I was forced to return early," Cassidy replied. "Qiang betrayed me to the UDF."

"What?" she hissed. "Qiang? How can that be?"

"It doesn't matter," Cassidy said. "I've dealt with the problem, but I have another. Come to my office immediately."

"Of course."

The hologram vanished, and a handful of seconds later there was a knock on the door. Cassidy tapped the control on the screen to open it, and Lin stepped in. She bowed to him just after passing the threshold, her eyes darting to Jessica for an instant before returning to him.

"Master Liao, Vanguard Lin reporting as ordered."

"Come in," Cassidy said, waving her forward. "Lin, this is—"

"Jessica Tai," Lin said. "I know who she is." She paused, realizing what had happened and falling to her knees, bowing her head. "My apologies, Master Liao. Qiang was convinced you would agree with his decision to assist the UDF in her capture."

"Qiang should have known better," Cassidy said.

"His selection as Deputy was my miscalculation, not yours. You were simply following his orders, as I expect you to follow mine."

"Yes, sir," she said, raising her head. "Always."

"On your feet. We have business to discuss."

Lin hopped back to her feet without using her hands for balance, showing a surprising level of agility for her age. She approached the desk, remaining standing in front of Cassidy and not giving Jessica another moment of attention without his permission.

"Are you familiar with Marine Platform Liberty?" Cassidy asked.

"Of course," she replied. "The offshore launch platform that provides Marine Cadet transfer to the Martian and Lunar bases. I wasn't aware we have a vested interest in the platform."

"We didn't before now," Cassidy replied.

"If I may ask, Master Liao, in what regard?"

"The sea levels continue rising," Cassidy said. "Scientists have noted that at current rates, every city on the planet will be submerged within seventy years. Earth will become uninhabitable. Unity has sent expeditions to other worlds in search of a new home for humankind. Many of the target planets have been deemed hostile or are far too inhospitable to be terraformed, but I have reason to believe one of them discovered a suitable world."

"That would be excellent news, sir," Lin said. "If that is so, why hasn't this information been shared with the public?"

"You're aware Bizrathi Praan was murdered in his own home less than seventy-two hours ago?"

"Yes, sir. I assume this is related?"

"It is. News of the habitable world is being

suppressed by those in positions of power, including the UDF."

"Suppressed? Master Liao, how can that be? All entities are subject to Unity's governance. Even the Silver Dragons submit to its decisions."

"Because we have nothing without honor," Cassidy said. "But consider that these expeditions are intended to offer humankind a fresh start, and they're backed through Unity, not through the associated conglomerates and syndicates that hold the secondary power. On Earth, these people are wealthy and powerful beyond imagination." Cassidy pointed to the ceiling. "Out there, they're starting over. They killed Praan because he wouldn't play along."

"I see," Lin said. "That explains why they would try to keep this information blocked, but not how they're blocking it."

"Have you heard of Leonidas?" Jessica asked.

Lin waited for Cassidy to nod before looking over at her. "No. I haven't. What is it?"

"Someone hacked a sub-process into Unity. A backdoor into the comms system. My guess is someone high up at the UDF, paid off by one of the power brokers. Does the name Nevis mean anything to you?"

"No. I don't know that one either," Lin admitted.

"She's head of the UDF Shadow Initiative, a division of Special Investigations."

"You mean Shades?" Lin said. "They're a myth."

"All myths have a basis in reality," Jessica said. "The point is, Nevis is powerful, and she sold out to become more powerful. The reason the UDF's been hunting me, the reason I've been killing so many of them, is because I know the truth and they don't want it going public. I came to Master Liao because I believed he would hear me out and help me do something about this."

"This isn't the type of activity we're normally involved in," Lin said.

"It isn't," Cassidy agreed. "But the Silver Dragons have survived since before the Silent War, because we see the long term costs and benefits of our activities. It's an indisputable fact that Earth will be underwater within a century. Either we can allow the elite to control the narrative, or we can give control back to the people. I believe the greater profits, and in fact our ultimate survival, lies in that direction."

"Of course I trust your instincts Master Liao. Your family has guided us for generations. Whatever you ask me to do, I will do. Where does Marine Platform Liberty fit in?"

"Jessica believes she can extract Leonidas from Unity's core, but to do that we need direct access to the hardware. Unity's mainframe is in orbit above the North Pole. So, we need a space-worthy craft."

"Which is available on the platform," Lin said.

"Precisely."

"If what you say is true, we won't be able to take one without a fight."

"No," Cassidy agreed. "We won't."

Lin bowed to him. "As you command, so it will be done. I will keep you apprised."

"Parabellum, Vanguard Lin. Go now."

Chapter 29

"That wasn't what I expected," Jessica said once Lin had left the room. "Leonidas as a tool of elite suppression? The discovery of a habitable world?"

"We need to begin changing the dreamstate," Cassidy replied. "Lin will organize the Silver Dragon Enforcers below her and explain the situation to them the way I explained it to her, and so on down the line. I'm also going to use Yi to spread rumors throughout the underground along the same lines. The triad's network is vast. It won't take long for word to spread and people begin believing it."

"And that's your idea to free the people from the Oneirolic?" she asked. "To make them think they're taking a starship to another planet?"

"Not a starship, that would be logistically difficult and hard to believe."

"Then what?"

"Imagine our intrepid adventurers discovered a benevolent advanced civilization. What if they had amazing technology that could transport everyone on the planet almost at once?"

"That's a massive stretch, Cass. The dreamstate turned the space expedition narrative into an alien nightmare because that's what the people believe. They won't go for benevolent aliens when they've established monsters."

"Not on their own," Cassidy agreed. "That's why we need to start priming them."

"If that would work, then Unity could have done it already. We wouldn't be here."

"Unity can't do it. Nevis believes giving humankind a fresh start will lead to us destroying ourselves for good. Since Unity is based on Nevis, it believes the same."

"And it isn't capable of choosing one certain death over another," Jessica realized. "But it can send you out of the dreamstate to solve the problem?"

"Because it wasn't trying to alter its own world. It didn't go outside of its programming. It found the only potential way out of the death spiral."

"You were a loophole."

"Yes. One that Nevis unfortunately doesn't share."

"You're a genius."

Cassidy shook his head. "No, but desperation is a powerful motivator. This is the only chance we have to fix things and free everyone from Nevis' grip."

"Nevis?" Jessica asked, confused. "What about the Hush?"

"The Hush started the War. Nevis keeps them in charge. It's not her fault, she has no choice but to follow her programming. But the Hush would have already lost the facility and the Oneirolic without her help. And they'll lose it quickly enough once we disable their best defense."

"How long do you think Lin will need to organize things?"

"A few hours at most. In the meantime…" He tapped on the control screen. A young man appeared in the hologram, eyes wide with surprise.

"Master Liao, sir," he said, bowing profusely. Unlike the majority of the Silver Dragons, he didn't appear to be of Asian descent, with curly blonde hair and blue eyes. "How may this humble servant be of use to you?"

"Carl, I'm in my office with Jessica Tai. She's badly in need of a shower and change of clothes, and also something to eat."

"Of course, sir," Carl replied. "I'm on my way."

"Cass, what are you doing?" Jessica asked after he disconnected the comm.

"You look like you've already been through a war," Cassidy replied. "We have time. There's no reason for you to not take advantage of Shen Liao's hospitality. Like you said, we have an abundance of resources at our disposal."

"That wasn't what I meant."

"Maybe not, but do it anyway. If you refuse in front of Carl you'll make me look bad, and I might have to kill you," he said with half a smile.

The knock came on the door before Jessica could continue arguing. Cassidy let Carl and his group of attendants into the room.

"Master Liao," he said, bowing to Cassidy and then turning to Jessica. "Miss Tai. My name is Carl, I'm the head of hospitality within House Liao."

"Nice to meet you, Carl," Jessica said, glaring back at Cassidy. She didn't want to go, but she was smart enough not to embarrass him in front of the help.

M.R. FORBES

"If you'll follow me," Carl said. "We'll take care of all of your needs."

"I can't wait," Jessica replied. She continued to side-eye Cassidy until she had left the room, the door closing behind the entourage.

Cassidy settled into Liao's chair, leaning over the desk and scrolling through the contacts in search of Yi. He didn't call him right away, his finger hovering over the man's name while he considered what he wanted to say. There was no chance Yi would question any of his orders, but they still needed to be clearly understood. The rumors he wanted the Dragon ranks to start needed to be believable if he had any chance of them gaining traction with the masses, and more importantly the contributors.

He was just about to lower his finger onto Yi's card when a soft tone sounded from hidden speakers, and the name of the incoming caller popped up beneath his hand.

Captain Nevis.

Cassidy stared at the name for a moment. He had thought he might hear from her at some point, but he was surprised she had already learned his identity. He let his finger drop, her face appearing as a hologram above his desk.

"You're moving up in the world, Cassidy," she said. "From Hall to Liao. That's some upgrade."

"I have you to thank for it," he replied.

"How was life on the other side?"

"Educational. Look, I know you didn't contact me to chat about the Hush and I think you're smart enough to know I'm not going to stop until I'm dead. So what is it you want?"

"Mainly, I wanted to confirm that you really did

216

transfer into Liao. Unity suggested as much, but I'm not so sure how much I can trust the system these days. Things have progressed more quickly than I ever anticipated. And I completely underestimated Jessica Tai's ability to turn my best agent against me."

"You expected something like this to happen?" Cassidy asked.

"History repeats itself, Cass. Jain and I have been playing this game of cat and mouse ever since the rain started coming down nonstop and the flooding started. You only remember forty-eight missions, but there were more. A lot more. You were different then."

"More like the Shade you imprinted to Brie?"

"Yes. And you were on the right side. This scenario is one of the variables of the dreamstate. This isn't the first time the wrong personality slipped through the cracks, though it might be the first time someone was inserted into the cracks. There have been others who thought they could change the world. That's why the Shadow Initiative was born, after all. Some of them progressed further than others. A couple of resistors even managed to figure out the nature of the dream-state even though they didn't fully understand how it was possible. But I could always count on you to handle them. I thought I could count on you this time too."

"I'm sorry to disappoint you."

"No, you're not."

"No, I'm not," Cassidy freely admitted. "I know you're required to try to stop me. It's part of your programming. But you can't win. Not this time."

"I wouldn't be so sure about that. The details have changed. but the scenario is still the same. And you were always my first line of defense, not my last."

"I assume that means I should expect heavy resistance when I reach Unity?"

"*If* you reach Unity," Nevis corrected. "You've still got a long way to go, Cassidy. And I know who you are and where you live."

"Liao's pagoda isn't an easy nut to crack. Be my guest if you want to try."

Her wicked smile sent a shiver down Cassidy's spine. "I don't need to try," she said. "I'm already here."

Chapter 30

Jessica followed Carl and his entourage of five assistants out of Liao's office and back to the elevator, where they rode from the third floor up to the tenth.

"Master Liao's personal living quarters," Carl said as the doors opened, revealing the apartment beyond. "Do you enjoy dumplings?"

"Very much," Jessica replied.

He turned to the servants. "Ju, Hee, Bai, go into the kitchen and prepare dumplings for our guest," he said in Mandarin. The three servants bowed and hurried into the open kitchen at the far end of the space, their movements partially obscured by one of the pagoda's four weight-bearing pillars.

Liao's personal quarters were even more simply decorated than his office. Mass-produced oriental artwork adorning the walls sharply contrasted with the collection in the Hoard. Rugs defined the layout of the equally simple sofas, pillows, and other furniture, all of it arranged in an orderly fashion around the room.

A doorway to the right led into a separate section of

the otherwise open floor plan, and Jessica spotted Liao's low bed through it. She was certain the bathroom was down there too. All in all, the quarters were clearly used only sparingly, as Liao likely spent the bulk of his time either working or on the other side of the Braid Crossing.

Pots and pans clanged and rattled in the kitchen as the three servants worked to prep her meal. They had obviously made plenty of meals up here before, possibly for Liao's wife and children, who were nowhere to be seen.

"Where's the rest of Master Liao's family?" she asked.

"The Mistress and the children are staying with her mother," Carl replied. "They always do when Master Liao is supposed to be away." He motioned to the separate segment of the penthouse. "The bathroom and washroom are that way. I can have a bath drawn for you if you wish?"

"No, thank you. I don't plan to stay long."

"You don't need to worry about the UDF catching up with you here. They'll keep their distance from House Liao."

"You've probably never harbored a fugitive like me before."

"You'd be surprised. Probably not like you, but certainly highly sought after members of the criminal element. Our people." He smiled. "Kaili, go downstairs and find something suitable for Mistress Tai to wear. I take it you prefer something protective and easy to move around in?"

"Good call," Jessica said.

"I know exactly what would suit you, Mistress Tai," Kaili said. She bowed to Carl and headed back to the elevator.

"Ru," Carl said, speaking to the last attendant. "Prepare the shower for Mistress Tai. When you're finished, head down to the armory so that we can properly equip our guest."

"As you command," the young man said, bowing to Carl and heading away.

"Is there anything else you require?" Carl asked then, folding his hands behind his back and standing like a soldier at attention.

"No thank you, this is more than enough," Jessica replied. "I—"

Her eyes whipped to the elevator as the cab opened, a group of silver-suited Dragon enforcers spilling out. She opened her mouth to shout a warning to Kaili when the first gun came into view, but she was too late. The first round hit her in the chest, knocking her to the floor.

"Get down!" Carl shouted, instinctively moving to push Jessica down behind him as he pulled a gun from the shoulder holster under his jacket. She tackled him instead, taking him down out of the line of fire as bullets whizzed over their heads. Pulling him along behind her, she crawled to cover behind one of the sofas, enforcers swarming the room like riled ants. Screams sounded from the kitchen before a hail of bullets silenced them.

"They're Dragons," Carl said, his voice tight with disbelief. "What are they doing?"

"They aren't Dragons," Jessica replied. "They're Shades." And clearly, nowhere in the city was safe from them. Not even Liao's pagoda. "Cover me."

"Wha—"

Jessica didn't wait for Carl to acknowledge the order. He was an armed Silver Dragon, so she assumed that meant he knew how to shoot at least well enough not to accidentally shoot her in the back.

She rolled over the back of the sofa, drawing a barrage of gunfire that cut off an instant later as Carl joined the fight. He squeezed off a burst of rounds that knocked down one enforcer, the others ducking behind the nearest cover they could find to return fire.

Landing on her feet, Jessica rushed the closest Dragon, at the same time thinking his weapon might run out of ammo. The minor alteration to the dreamstate came to pass, the gun swinging toward her and clicking on empty.

She rammed into the Dragon, throwing her arm around his neck and driving him backward as she swung her legs up and around his neck as if he were a stripper's pole. Throwing herself backward, she rode him to the floor, landing on her back and pulling him down on top of her. She used her legs like scissors, twisting his neck until she heard it snap.

She looked up just in time to see another Dragon point his gun at her. She smiled, envisioning the bore inside the gun barrel. It was just defective enough to throw off his targeting, the bullets whipping past her. She leaped up and charged him, grabbing his wrist and slamming it into a support pillar. breaking the bone. He had just enough time to cry out before her knee came up in his crotch, doubling him over. A second knee to his face broke his nose and dropped him to the floor.

Jessica slipped behind the pillar as bullets hit the plaster-covered steel, chewing pieces out of it that tore past her cheek without making contact. She glanced over at Carl, who had reloaded and moved to the other side of the sofa. He resumed firing at the remaining enforcers, again drawing their attention away from Jessica as she broke cover, sprinting toward a trio of dragons crouched behind an overturned table. They saw her coming and whirled in her direction.

Was it likely Carl's rounds would penetrate the thick wood of the table they were hiding behind?

No.

Was it possible?

Yes.

The thought had barely manifested before three of Carl's bullets found a weakness in the table and punched through. One bullet hit a Dragon in the shoulder and the other in the thigh, badly disrupting their aims. Jessica reached them, flying fists and feet leaving them laid out on the floor like a trio of broken toy soldiers.

Coming to a stop, Jessica surveyed the suddenly still room. Six Silver Dragon enforcers were strewn across the open space, either unconscious or bleeding out. The three serving women hadn't fared much better, two of them splayed across the kitchen counter or nearby on the floor. Carl was still in one piece on the other side of the room, and Ru had remained hidden during the entire altercation.

Or had he?

Jessica ducked almost instinctively, just as a round punched into the pillar where her head had just been. She pivoted toward where Ru stood in the doorway to the separate section of the penthouse, gun in hand. She closed her eyes for a moment, gathering herself.

Then she swung out into the open and strode directly toward Ru, head steady, eyes locked on him as he started shooting.

The bullets screamed past her, so close she could feel the heated air swish past her face and the ripple of her clothes as the rounds grazed the material of her shirt.

She didn't change course or give in to fear, instead staying the course, remaining calm as she crossed the room.

Ru's gun clicked on an empty chamber, the man's eyes widening in disbelief. He couldn't understand how he had missed her so many times. She wasn't going to explain to him that it was because he wasn't real, and she had correctly surmised she could manipulate the dream-state to alter him. Not too much, or it would be too hard to believe. What she had done was amazing but not impossible.

Reaching Ru, Jessica held out her hand, palm up. He met her gaze with his own, his eyes searching hers for some hint of how she had worked what he saw as literal magic. Then he dropped the empty pistol into her hand.

"Now what?" he asked.

Jessica moved the gun behind her back. When she pulled it back out, the weapon was loaded again. Her round went through his neck and shattered his imprint. He collapsed to the floor.

"How did you do that?" Carl asked, approaching her.

She whirled on her heel and started for the elevator. "Do what?" she replied, leaving Carl jogging to keep up with her.

"Ru was shooting right at you. There's no way he could miss."

"He wasn't Ru," Jessica said, boarding the elevator. "Are you coming?"

Carl hurried into the cab as she directed it back to the third floor. "Where are we going?"

"Whatever's happening here, our place is with Liao," she replied.

She was only slightly worried that Cassidy might be

in trouble. He was no longer an elite Shade trapped in Hall's decrepit body. He was in one far more then capable of taking whatever Nevis could dish out.

Whatever she had sent his way, Jessica doubted it was enough.

Chapter 31

Barely breathing hard, Cassidy looked down at the enforcer who was the last of the dozen Shades he had allowed into Liao's office and then swiftly dispatched.

He hadn't been particularly surprised when Nevis told him the Shades were already there, embedded in the ranks of the Silver Dragons. He had been part of the system long enough that he might have been more surprised if she hadn't been holding that card up her sleeve. Still, there had been some doubt in his mind that she would go that far. Liao was an Immortal after all, and Qiang had probably been right about how the Mountain Master would have handled Jessica if he had made it back into the dreamstate.

If he had to guess, the Shades had probably been in place since Garrett had set up the meeting with the Dragons so he and Jessica could attempt trading guns for their help in raiding the Golden Spire. Maybe Nevis hadn't trusted Liao enough to fall in line and decline the deal, and had put the pieces in place just in case he didn't make the right decision.

It didn't matter now. He had dealt with the group that had come for him, and while he wouldn't claim the result had been effortless, Liao's body *was* a singular force to be reckoned with. Combined with his control over the dreamstate and his already vast experience, the group hadn't stood a chance. That fact left Cassidy certain that attacking him wasn't the endgame, but rather a distraction to keep him occupied while the Initiative went after the real target.

Jessica.

He stepped over the dead enforcer and ran to the double doors. With the security system allowing him to lock the entrance from either side, he had locked the doors to keep his aggressors in the room with him before shutting off the interior light. While Liao didn't have a Sliver over his eye to augment his night vision, Cassidy hadn't needed it. He had fought in the darkness before. Not every Shade had.

Eager to get up to Liao's apartment to check on Jessica, he waited impatiently at the doors for the system to run its biometric scan. When the twin doors finally swung inward, light spilled in from the hallway, momentarily blinding him.

A silhouette rushed toward him, and then strong arms wrapped around him, holding him tight. He immediately knew who it was.

"Cass," Jessica said, backing away. "I figured you were okay, but I'm glad to see it for myself."

"Cass?" Carl said, standing a few feet behind them.

"I'm fine," Cassidy replied. "I was just coming to check on you."

"You locked them in," she continued, looking past him to the bodies on the floor. "That was crazy."

"It was crazy for them to come in."

"That's what I meant."

"Cass?" Carl repeated, obviously still confused.

"Who do you think you're talking to?" Cassidy growled at the attendant. "You owe me respect."

Carl seemed to snap out of his daze. "Master Liao," he said, bowing. "My humble apologies, sir."

"Where are the others?"

"I'm sorry, Master Liao. They were killed by the traitors."

"Not traitors," Cassidy said. "Shades. Members of the UDF."

"I never thought Shades were real. Why are they attacking us?"

"Because we know the secret they're desperately trying to keep," Jessica answered before returning her attention to Cassidy. "Is there more fighting, or did Nevis send all of her Shades after us?"

"I don't know," Cassidy replied. He hurried back to the desk, calling Vanguard Lin. The projector remained dark for five seconds. Ten. He was just about to give up on her when her face appeared over the desk, a large cut across her sweaty forehead.

"Master Liao, you're unharmed," she said, clearly relieved.

"Not for lack of effort on the UDF's part," Cassidy replied. "I have twelve dead Shades on my office floor. What's your status, and the state of the House?"

"My own guards turned on me," she replied, disgusted. "Spies, I'm sure. Those that weren't spies died protecting me. The rest died in response to my fury." She spat on something out of view of the camera. "I barely had a chance to begin our preparations. As for the House, there was an initial flurry of reports of violence, but they've all gone silent. I believe the effort to disrupt our plans has failed."

"That may be, but I want every Dragon in the House accounted for. It's not wise to assume the assault has ended until everyone is accounted for."

"Of course, Master Liao. I'm in contact with our loyal enforcers. I'll have them begin the sweep immediately."

"Very good. Once the orders are delivered, keep yourself focused on the arrangements. Our timeline is shorter than I had hoped. You have one hour."

"Yes, sir," Lin said.

"Dismissed."

Lin disconnected the comm. Cassidy glanced at Carl. The younger man had the shocky look of someone teetering on the edge of panic. Cassidy knew the look well. This was the first time Carl had seen live combat. The first time he had killed someone.

"You brought honor to the Silver Dragons today, Carl," Cassidy said. "And you've greatly increased your standing with me."

The words helped Carl justify his actions. He smiled as he bowed. "Yes, Master Liao. It's an honor to protect the House."

"Wait outside and stand guard over me. If anyone approaches this room, make sure I'm aware of it before they get here."

"Yes, sir," Carl said. He bowed and moved to the other side of the doorway, gun in hand and watching the corridor like a hawk.

Cassidy closed the doors behind Carl, waiting until they had sealed before turning to Jessica. "Nevis contacted me before the attack."

"Did she have anything useful to say?"

"No. She wanted to make sure I was Liao before she committed her Shades. I don't think she expected to beat me here. She was after you."

Jessica nodded. "It makes sense. Killing me would have gone a long way toward softening you up for whatever else she has to throw at you."

"She won't be happy that her Shades failed."

"Good."

"Whatever else she has up her sleeve, she made it sound like a big deal. She said I was her first original line of defense against the resistance, not the last. According to her, you aren't the first person to try to bring down the dreamstate from the inside."

"She could be lying."

"She could be. But I don't think so. Hades is still a part of Unity, and Unity is still trying to push things in the right direction to the extent that it can. It may have been an intentional warning that we can't just waltz onto the space station and have our way with Unity."

"You think Nevis is trying to help?" Jessica asked.

"I think she isn't *not* trying to help."

"Even as she tries to kill us? This whole thing feels clear as mud sometimes. Do you think she'll throw the rest of the UDF at this place now that her Shades failed or will she rely on her last line of defense?"

"She knows the target, so she knows we need a ship to get there. I don't think she'll press things here; it's too easy for us to slip away through the tunnels if things get out of hand. No, I think our next fight will come at Marine Platform Liberty. They'll be ready and waiting for our arrival."

"Do you think we can fight our way through them?"

"We don't have a choice. But it does raise a good point."

"What's that?"

"We know what the dreamstate is and how we're capable of affecting it. We also know that pushing accepted reality too far risks destabilization. But this is it, Jess. This is our last move. If we're smart about it, we should be able to push the limits. As long as I replace Unity before the whole thing collapses, I think we can tolerate some instability."

"You mean cheat to win?" Jessica asked.

"That's exactly what I mean."

Jessica's mouth split into a wide grin. "Now you're talking."

Chapter 32

Cassidy had given Lin one hour to organize the Silver Dragons into a force capable of assaulting a Marine Launch Platform. It wasn't a lot of time, and he and Jessica had plenty of their own preparations to make while the Silver Dragon Vanguard prepared for war.

Cassidy spent the first fifteen minutes of that hour speaking to Yi, explaining the situation similarly to how he had described it to Lin before asking Liao's eldest subordinate to begin spreading the word. He could tell by Yi's reaction to the call that he was glad to see Liao back in charge and Qiang punished for his presumptions, but Cassidy also got the impression Yi wasn't wholly convinced of his identity. For as hard as he was trying to play the role of the Silver Dragon's Mountain Master, Cassidy only had the repo's memories to help guide him. He was certain Yi knew Liao as well as anyone except maybe his wife and children and could sense a degree of difference between Cassidy and the Immortal. Even so, Yi was too loyal to question his orders. He acknowledged the plan without complaint, and Cassidy disconnected from their call, confident that Yi would set things in motion.

Lin had contacted him around the twenty-minute mark to report that sweeps of the pagoda hadn't turned up any additional Shades. Either Nevis had committed all of her agents to Cassidy and Jessica or the remaining infiltrators had gone back under cover, waiting for another opportune moment to strike.

After that, Cassidy returned Carl to his regular duties as the lead House attendant. Carl had quickly regrouped the housekeeping staff and set them to cleaning up the mess. Then he and Jessica had taken the elevator back into the subterranean levels of the home to a vault similar to the one in Jazz's pharmacy. It served as the Silver Dragon's armory, a curated supply of weapons that would have left Jazz green with envy.

The Weapon Master's name was Shun. A short, elderly man with a bald, wrinkled head and a stoic demeanor, he bowed respectfully from the doorway as Cassidy and Jessica entered the vault.

"Master Liao," he said. "Always a pleasure to see you, sir."

"And you, Shun," Cassidy replied. He knew from Liao's memories that no matter the rank, the Mountain Master always treated his elders with respect. Even when they technically weren't the Immortal's elders.

The Weapon Master looked at Jessica. "You don't normally bring guests down to the armory, sir. To what do we owe this occasion?"

"You haven't heard?" Cassidy asked.

"I don't concern myself with the affairs of the young. I focus my attention here."

"But Vanguard Lin has spoken to you, hasn't she?"

"Oh, yes. That. I've already arranged a delivery from the warehouse to the garage."

Cassidy thought Shun might ask why they needed so much equipment in such a short time frame, but the Weapons Master remained true to his statement. He didn't care why they needed the guns. His job was to supply them regardless.

"I assume you're looking for a more personalized load-out?" Shun continued.

"Yes," Cassidy replied. "For myself and my guest. Her name is Jessica."

Shun turned to Jessica and bowed. "The honor is mine." He straightened up, reaching behind his back and producing a basic tape measure, holding it out toward her. "Do you mind? I know it's a bit old-fashioned, but I still find it more accurate than any of the supposedly superior technology."

Jessica smiled. "Go ahead."

Shun approached her, wrapping the measure around different parts of her body to take measurements. He didn't write anything down, committing it all to memory.

"What are the measurements for?" she asked.

"Skinsteel armor," Shun replied.

"Skinsteel?" Jessica said, her mouth falling slightly open in surprise.

"The technology is quite superior."

"But you can only get Skinsteel through the Dome Requisition Program."

"Legally, maybe," Shun laughed. "We had an offer to purchase weapons from the Dome a few days ago. I told Master Liao I wanted the inventory, but he insisted the price was too high."

"If I had known where we would be today, I would have made a different decision," Cassidy said. "It ended up costing me more as an afterthought. Lead on, Shun."

"Of course, sir."

Shun ambled away from the entrance, down one of many rows of shelving where crates and boxes of various shapes and sizes rested, all of them seemingly cataloged in the Weapon Master's head. He knew exactly which of the shelves he wanted, walking them all the way to the back of the vault and stopping in front of an unmarked container with a biometric lock on the front. He put his thumb to the lock and the crate clicked open.

Pulling the door aside revealed a rack of what looked like thin wetsuits in a variety of sizes. Shun picked one of them out and turned to Jessica. "You'll need to remove your clothes to put this on."

Jessica accepted the suit, raising and lowering the hanger. "This is bulletproof? It's so light."

"Do you have time for a demonstration?" Shun asked.

"Not right now," Cassidy replied.

"You can go around the corner to change."

Jessica took the suit down one of the nearby aisles while Shun turned back to the rack of body armor, picking one out for Cassidy.

"This one will fit you, sir," he said, holding it out.

Cassidy quickly removed his clothes before accepting the armor. He stepped into the legs and pulled it up, the material stretching to fit over Liao's muscular body. He closed the overlapping snaps in the front as Jessica returned from around the corner.

The Skinsteel fit like a bathing suit, leaving only the hands, feet, neck, and head exposed. Lightweight and breathable, it didn't feel to him as though it would offer much protection at all. Judging by Jessica's expression, she didn't feel that comfortable with the armor, and not because of its tight fit.

"Are you sure this is bulletproof?" she asked again.

Shun laughed, his hand moving faster than Cassidy would have ever believed. The Weapon Master whipped a small pistol from inside the fold of his suit jacket and fired, hitting Cassidy point-blank in the chest.

He didn't even feel the impact.

Looking down, he saw the compressed slug land on the floor at his feet. The Skinsteel had hardened visibly where the bullet hit, the materials beginning to relax again as he watched.

"As I said, superior technology," Shun laughed. "Wait here." He shuffled away, leaving Jessica and Cassidy alone.

"Do we even need these?" she asked. "If you're right about manipulating the dreamstate, we can probably make ourselves bulletproof. Or fast enough to dodge bullets."

"Everything we change has an effect on the whole and will further destabilize the system," Cassidy replied. "We need to weigh our decisions against what we can accomplish without making alterations. If we can protect ourselves within the existing rules, that gives us more leeway somewhere else."

"Right," Jessica agreed. "So flying is still out of the question?"

"I'm not opposed to using it as a last resort."

"In that case, for as much as I'd love to experience the sensation, I hope I don't get the chance."

Shun returned with a pair of fatigues balanced in his arms. They were mostly black, with a light pattern of grays mixed in. "Vanguard Lin selected these. I assume you want the same camouflage?"

"We do," Cassidy said.

Shun passed one part of the stack to Jessica and the other to Cassidy. The fatigues were made of a lighter material than he was accustomed to, offering a greater range of movement without binding. The boots at the top of the stack were equally high-tech and lightweight.

"I'll provide comms before you leave the armory," Shun said once they were dressed. "Right now, we need to find you suitable firepower." He put his hand on his chin, considering his inventory. "Since you're partici-pating in the raid, I presume you'll be leading from the rear?"

"Not this time," Cassidy replied. "Our target is Marine Launch Platform Liberty. We're going there to steal a spaceship. Jessica's our pilot."

"I see. Well, if the forty-niners are your cover, then you'll probably be most efficient with greater power at closer range. But you also don't want anything that will blow through the hull of a spacecraft." He continued rubbing at his chin. "I imagine that Dome shipment would have carried something suitable. Since we don't have that, we'll have to fall back to something a bit more conventional."

He walked away, leaving Cassidy and Jessica to follow behind him.

Shun stopped at another shelf, reaching up and struggling to pull out one of the crates. Cassidy stepped forward to help him with it, lowering it to the ground.

"You need an assistant, old friend," he said.

Shun laughed. "Are you applying for the job, Master Liao?" He opened the crate, revealing a pair of subma-chine guns and a handful of magazines packed in foam. A carrying harness was latched to the top of the box. "These are based on the original Uzi design. Small but powerful. The recoil makes aiming a little dicey one-handed, but with your mods you shouldn't have a problem. Mistress Jessica, I recommend against this weapon for your load-out."

"I can handle it," Jessica replied.

"Very well. Master Liao, can you retrieve that crate as well?"

Cassidy took down the crate, which contained another pair of the same weapon. He and Jessica put the harnesses over their fatigues, loaded the weapons and hung them in place.

Without a word, Shun turned and moved down the aisle, and they hurried after him, catching up as he removed another crate from a shelf and opened it.

"Since you indicated close quarters, I'm not bothering with long guns," he explained, picking up one of the pistols inside the crate. With its squared-off body, it bore a resemblance to a needlegun. "This is an ARM-4. The advanced vision system inside locks the target when you fire and programs the smart round before it leaves the chamber, allowing the bullet to make minor course corrections to maximize damage. It can't shoot around corners, but can be useful for firing around cover or avoiding other potential obstacles or fragile equipment. The downside is that the rounds have to be pre-initialized, which means no in-combat reloads. So use it wisely."

"Nice," Jessica said, accepting the gun when Shun offered it. He passed one to Cassidy as well before moving on.

They followed him to another shelf with a set of pull-out drawers. Shun opened them, revealing lines of standard handguns. "Sometimes the best approach is the simplest. I recommend bringing four or more so you won't waste time reloading."

He opened another drawer, withdrawing harnesses for the weapons. "Shoulder and thigh," he said, passing them to Cassidy and Jessica. They put on the harnesses and then slipped the guns into their holsters. "Again, I can provide a range of explosives and incendiary devices, but if you aim to commandeer any kind of mobile craft you don't want to risk damaging it."

"That makes perfect sense," Jessica said. She turned to Cassidy, eying the weaponry scattered across his body.

Cassidy turned to Shun. "Thank you, Master Shun."

"Of course, sir. Let me get your comms and you can be on your way."

They moved to a final section of the armory, stopping in front of another series of pull out drawers. Shun opened one of them, revealing a line of small, molded comm devices that fit into the ear. He retrieved a ClearPad from inside the drawer and tapped on it a few times before lifting out two of the comm devices, using the tablet to program them.

"I've set them to the active channel Lin selected," he said as Cassidy and Jessica each accepted one of the comms. Shun stepped to the next shelf over, which was lined with matte black helmets with small cutouts for the eyes and a grill that went over the mouth. He picked one out and handed it to Jessica. "This should be your size. It's not as protective as the Skinsteel, but the weave isn't suitable for the contours of the skull. It doesn't have enough surface area to absorb the kinetic energy."

Jessica gathered her hair atop her head before pulling the helmet down over it. "How do I look?"

"Like you're ready for war," Cassidy replied.

Shun handed him a helmet. "Now you are too, Master Liao."

"Thank you again," Cassidy said to Shun.

"It is my honor to serve you and the Silver Dragons," Shun replied. "Don't be a stranger down here, sir. Remember, you still owe me a game of chess."

Cassidy smiled. "Of course. I'll make good on that promise when I get back."

"Good hunting, Master Liao. Mistress Jessica. I have hope for your safe return."

"Goodbye, Shun," Jessica said.

They left the Weapon Master, heading out of the armory and back to the elevator.

Whatever happened next, there was no coming back.

Chapter 33

Planning an assault on the scale Cassidy had ordered wasn't possible within the homey confines of the pagoda. Instead, Cassidy and Jessica found themselves transported away from the International District to the current Old Town, a separate segment of lightly populated streets from the one he and Jessica had entered twenty years earlier. Even now, signs of gentrification were everywhere in the boarded up buildings, the caution tape, and the condemned notices taped to the cracked facades and once lustrous glass doors of the crumbling architecture.

Knowing Hades was waiting for them to come to her, Cassidy and Jessica didn't make any effort to be discreet, lifting off from the roof of the pagoda in Liao's exotic sport roto—a wedge shaped machine with oversized spinners and added thrust at the rear. The glowing twin Dragons, emblazoned in silver across each side, projected in the air a few feet away from the craft, impossible for anyone to miss. The dragons easily identified him as

Shen Liao to those who knew of him and as an extremely wealthy enigma to anyone who didn't.

Not that Cassidy cared about any of that. He had taken the roto because it was available. And it was fast. If Nevis decided to take another pre-emptive shot at him, he figured the roto could outrun anything the rest of the dreamstate had to offer. In fact, he was certain of it. He realized after getting in the driver seat and lifting off that he could probably alter the inner universe to allow the roto to reach Unity on its own, but pushing the limits too much would cause everything to collapse sooner than later. Even as an AI, he had still needed to be cautious any time he was imprinted to avoid corruption. His digital nature couldn't save him once he was transferred to a host. The same edict held true now, but there might come a time when it made sense to risk corruption if it was the only way he could save the world and the people in it. Things hadn't reached that point, and he hoped they never would.

He and Jessica didn't speak much on the short ride to where they would join Liao's forces, but the glances they had shared said more than any words. They were both on edge over what came next, and from those looks he was sure Jessica had realized what mission success would mean for him. He couldn't replace Unity as the primary arbiter of the dreamstate without becoming the same as Unity. A static AI floating miles above the planet's surface, not unlike NEVIS trapped in the basement of the facility. And once he was fully transferred into that system, he couldn't leave, no matter what happened. Since his goal was to free all of the contributors from the Oneirolic, which would by nature leave the dreamstate unsustainable, his endgame was clear.

Death.

Yet, he didn't think of it like that. As an AI, he had never truly been alive, though the repos he had inhabited had certainly offered him the full human experience. His missions hadn't only allowed him to kill. He had laughed, loved, and been loved, even if nobody had known it was him until the last moment. It didn't change the emotions that had siphoned through the repos into him. It didn't change his understanding of the human condition.

He was going to miss it.

But he remembered what it was like between missions. Or rather, he remembered the absence of his experience after the missions. After scrub and delta back to the source, after being returned to the Freezer, he had ceased to exist until he was needed again.

Wouldn't this be the same?

He guided the roto onto the rooftop of one of the smallest buildings in Old Town, a fifty-story former mixed-use structure with stores on the lower floors and residences above. The triad had converted the first floor into a garage some time ago, a few buildings away from another structure they had taken over where they kept the bulk of their current ordnance. Vanguard Lin had worked with Weapon Master Shun to pick out the right equipment for the assault, which had then been trans-ferred from the warehouse down to the garage, along with the Silver Dragons that Lin had assembled to use all of it.

The steel outer door to the warehouse pulled aside as Cassidy lowered the roto to street level. The guards posi-tioned just inside the door bowed as he guided the craft through, clutching their machine guns to their chests.

"Not bad," Jessica said beside him, the roto's head-lights hitting the assembly of both combatants and their rides. Nearly two dozen large delivery rotos were mixed in with another dozen or so smaller, more agile machines, and close to two hundred Silver Dragons mingled on the floor in front of them, their conversations freezing as they identified the craft and hurriedly moved into formation. They were all dressed in fatigues similar to Cassidy and Jessica's, all carrying assault rifles, all fully armed. Vanguard Lin appeared in front of them, shouting orders and directing them to attention as though they were in the military.

Cassidy touched the roto down in front of them, opened the doors to the roto, and climbed out. Immediately, all of the Silver Dragons in the garage dropped to their knees into a deep, respectful bow.

"Not bad," Jessica repeated, exiting the roto on the other side. They met in front of the craft and walked over to the assembly.

"Vanguard Lin, on your feet," Cassidy said, stopping in front of the woman.

She jumped up without using her hands, bowing from the waist once she was standing. "Master Liao, the Silver Dragons are ready to fight for the honor of your House."

"And I am pleased to join them," Cassidy said loudly. "On your feet, all of you." They jumped up in almost perfect synchronicity, the movement echoing within the garage. "I am honored to fight with you today."

As Lin had done, they bowed to him without speaking. He offered a curt bow back before returning his attention to Lin. "I'll continue the advance from my roto and bring up the rear until the assault begins. My only goal is to take possession of the Marine starship and fly it to Unity. I would like for some of the Dragons to make it on board with me, but if we get bogged down on the platform, I can't afford to wait for them."

"Do you intend to manage Unity on your own then, Master Liao?"

"If necessary," Cassidy replied. "But of the two, I expect the platform to be more heavily defended than the station."

"Very well, sir. I will focus our efforts on clearing your path to the ship. I'm sorry to say, we don't have access to anything more heavily armed or armored. We've never tried anything like this before."

"I expect casualties will be high, but the honor of our House is at stake. As is the future of all. We may be traders in illicit marketplaces, but we haven't forgotten the people." Cassidy glanced at the Silver Dragons behind Lin. "We will move out at once."

"Yes, Master Liao," Lin said before turning to the Dragons. "To your transports. We will be moving out immediately." The assembly broke ranks, the Dragon columns racing for their designated craft. Lin stayed back. "Shall I ride with you, sir?"

"No," Cassidy replied. "I need you leading the charge."

Lin seemed slightly disappointed, leaving Cassidy to wonder if she were also a Shade, more deeply under-cover than the group that had attacked him. There was no easy way to know for sure, though his instinct told him she was trustworthy.

"We have a comms link with you and the rest of the Dragons," Cassidy said. "I will be listening to your orders but I won't intercede. I have faith in you."

Lin bowed again. "Thank you, sir."

Cassidy and Jessica returned to the roto. Lin headed off to one of the smaller craft, getting in on the passenger side. Within a minute the entire floor of the garage was cleared of people and equipment, all of it piled into the vehicles.

"Silver Dragons," Lin said. "Follow my lead. Stay in formation."

Her roto lifted off the floor, passing over Liao's roto on its way out the door. The other craft rose behind her, flying single file to exit the building.

"So it begins," Jessica said, watching them until they had all left the garage.

Cassidy took the controls of the roto, adding thrust and bringing it up off the floor, the craft drifting out through the open door and accelerating to join the Dragon fleet above.

"So it ends," he said.

Chapter 34

Marine Launch Platform Liberty was located off the southern tip of the city. A fixed platform constructed nearly a century earlier, it had been built over the long submerged Liberty Island and the famous statue that still rested there, her arm and torch piercing the sea and rising through the center of the platform.

Cassidy had been there before, or at least, according to his implanted memories he had been there before. He could recall launching in one of the Marine spacecraft on a training mission to Mars, arcing into the clouds and beyond aboard one of the cigar-shaped vessels with sixty other recruits. As he remembered it, he hadn't liked space travel very much. The jolt of leaving the atmosphere had made him sick, and the weeks of hibernation were even worse.

Fortunately, Unity was a lot closer than Mars.

The Silver Dragon fleet approached the MLPL hidden in the clouds, using the cover to shield their ingress. While the craft were all within a few hundred feet of one another in the air, the thick vapor made it seem to Cassidy as if he and Jessica were alone in the sky, racing toward a future that couldn't have been more uncertain. The only reminder that they weren't the only ones out there was Lin's voice through the comms, passing orders to the other rotos in the group.

"There's no way you come out of this intact, is there?" Jessica asked, finally gathering the courage to bring up the hard subject.

"No," Cassidy replied bluntly.

"No hack? No workaround? Is it possible I could stuff you into my ClearPhone?"

Cassidy smiled and glanced over at her. "I wouldn't fit. Besides, the ClearPhone goes with the rest of the dreamstate."

Jessica smiled back at him, but she couldn't hold it. "You know you're going to die, and you're okay with it?"

"What else can I do? I'm not going to value my existence over anyone else's. Then I would be the same as Nevis."

"No, I understand. I just… We have a bond that nobody can break. An understanding. When you're gone, a piece of me will go with you."

"You won't feel that way once you're outside."

"You don't know that."

Cassidy shook his head. "I can hope. I don't want you to grieve for me."

"I already feel your loss, and you're still here."

They stared at one another for a long moment, until a gruff voice snapped them out of their shared isolation.

"Unidentified aircraft, you're approaching restricted Unity Marine airspace. Change course immediately, or you will be fired upon."

"They're not fooling around," Jessica said.

"All air traffic knows better than to head toward the platform uninvited," Cassidy replied.

"Stay the course, Dragons," Lin said. There was a brief pause, and then she broadcast over the same channel the Marine Operator had used. "Marine Launch Platform Liberty, we are unable to comply with your request. Our sensors were scrambled in a storm and we require emergency assistance."

"Unidentified aircraft, I think it's your brain that was scrambled. You don't need sensors to navigate between here and the seawall. Turn back now or be fired upon."

"Vanguard Lin. I have incoming craft on my sensors," the pilot of the lead roto said. "Four military drones. They're firing on—" He never finished his sentence, his roto vanishing from the display.

"They really aren't fooling around," Jessica said in response to the attack.

"Evasive maneuvers!" Lin shouted over the comms. "Gunners, strap in!"

Cassidy couldn't see the other Silver Dragon rotos through the windshield, but he watched them on the vehicle's primary display as they split in a dozen different directions, spreading out to avoid the drones.

"Drop low, out of the clouds," Lin continued. "We can't fight back like this."

Cassidy put the roto into a steep dive, wincing when two more Silver Dragon craft vanished from the display. The Marine drones blew past the group before parting and coming back around for another pass.

Breaking from the cloud cover, Cassidy could see the lights of the platform in the distance, the golden-flamed torch of the statue glowing brightly in the darkness. He was tempted to make a beeline for it, to leave the

Dragons behind. Their odds against military drones were as bad as they could get.

The first of the Dragon rotos dropped under the clouds ahead of Cassidy. He saw now that four Dragons had lashed themselves to the outside of the square transport craft with rifles in hand. One of them fired up and back toward the clouds at an enemy Cassidy couldn't see.

A flash lit up the clouds near the roto, and then a rocket slammed into the back of it, the explosion blowing the Dragons free and sending them plummeting to the ocean below. Then the drone appeared, flat and wide, with huge engines along the aft and missiles racked beneath its delta wings. It swooped through the smoke of the detonation, already chasing its next target.

"They don't stand a chance," Jessica said. "We need to do something."

"Hold on," Cassidy said, turning the yoke and pushing the throttle. The roto accelerated so hard it shoved them both back in their seats as it rocketed in pursuit of the drone.

More Dragon rotos descended around them, most with additional Dragons on the outside, firing back into the clouds. Cassidy saw another get hit by a missile before he re-entered the thick overcast himself, eyes glued to the main display as he trailed his target. The drone didn't pay him any attention. Likely, it wasn't seeing an unarmed sport roto as a threat compared to the transports with their strapped on machine gunners. It was a mistake he would make sure he took advantage of.

The drone shifted slightly on the display, indicating it was changing direction. Cassidy cut the throttle and rolled the roto sideways, the spinners whining in complaint as he altered his vector to track ahead of the drone. He hit the throttle again, bursting forward, smiling when his craft started flashing collision warnings.

"Cass?" Jessica said.

He didn't get to answer before the drone appeared in the clouds so close that Cassidy could read the serial numbers off the missiles under its wings. They collided a split second later, Cassidy smashing the rear of the drone with the front of his roto and shearing off the entire tail and thruster nozzles. The impact sent Cassidy whirling off course while the drone spiraled downward, its wings clipped.

The roto's AI brought the craft back under control, putting them into a safe hover. There was no way to override the system until it cleared. In the meantime, three more Silver Dragon transports blinked out of existence. Fortunately, so did one of the drones, hit by the defensive barrage.

"About time they got one," Cassidy said, eager to get back in motion.

"It's not impossible," Jessica replied, indicating that she had altered the dreamstate to help their aim.

"You cheated."

"And you didn't?"

"No. Liao's roto is bulletproof." The AI unlocked the controls and Cassidy slammed on the throttle again, shooting off in pursuit of the Dragons and the two remaining drones.

They dipped from the clouds again, way behind the fleet now as it neared the Marine base. Gun batteries fixed to four of the platform's towers belched flame, tracers lighting up the night sky as rounds tore through two more rotos.

"Shit!" Lin cursed, just as one of the drones hit

another roto with a missile from behind. " Maintain speed. Go in hard for landing. Gunners, keep firing!"

Cassidy vectored the sports roto toward one of the remaining drones and sped up, racing toward its rear. It picked him up on its sensors, taking evasive maneuvers as it tried to track the roto ahead of it.

"Jess, I'll get us in close. You blast it."

"Copy," Jessica said, unlatching the passenger side door handle and sliding her door open, the wind blasting through the cockpit. She pulled one of the SMGs from her harness as Cassidy added more thrust, the roto screaming as it gained on the drone, closing within twenty feet.

Jessica loosened her shoulder strap and leaned out, opening fire. She sent a hail of bullets into the back of the drone, only stopping when the Marine aircraft sparked, smoked, and spun out of control as Cassidy blasted past.

"Hold on!" he shouted, turning hard as tracer fire ripped past way too close for comfort.

Jessica grabbed hold of the door frame, but the centrifugal force still threw her upper body into Cassidy's shoulder. She settled back into her seat as he leveled off, shooting over the top of the platform. The batteries didn't try to follow him, staying on the larger, slower transports. Almost to the platform, only six of them were still airborne.

"Nice flying," Jessica said, leaning her head back out of the open door. "Looks like the Marines are ready for the invasion. Units are pouring out of the stairwells and taking defensive positions on deck."

"I think this is where we get off," Cassidy replied, bringing the roto into hover mode before sliding his side door open. The platform was over a hundred feet below.

"You sure about this, Cass?" Jessica asked, reaching for the latch on her lap belt..

"We can make it." Because someone like him, someone like Jessica could handle such a long fall. Because they were special, and the dreamstate damn well knew it.

"For honor!" Lin shouted through the comm in his ear, at the same time the first remaining Dragon roto hit the platform deck, crashing with a loud screech of metal.

"For honor," Jessica repeated, throwing her safety harness off.

Then she and Cassidy jumped.

Chapter 35

Cassidy tumbled through the air for a few seconds before leveling out and angling his feet toward the platform below. He landed just as the second Dragon roto reached the surface, hitting hard and skidding until it slammed into one of the towers. He didn't see if any of the Dragons made it out of the crash.

He hit the deck, flexing his legs and making a super-hero landing that seemed to reverberate the dreamstate around him. Jessica landed beside him a split-second later in the same pose, and they rose to their feet, pulling their SMGs as the Marines ahead spun away from the Dragon rotos to see what had just crashed behind them.

A measured hail of bullets from Cassidy and Jessica's SMGs dropped the entire lot of them before they could finish the rotation, ten Marines catching lead and collapsing onto the deck. More Marines, scattered under-cover across the deck, targeted Cassidy and Jessica. They rushed to cover behind a steel container—one of several that contained supply deliveries that hadn't been dealt with yet—as the last of the four Dragon rotos made hard landings on the platform. Dragons spilled out of them, spewing gunfire as they advanced, taking the heat off the pair.

It allowed Cassidy to scale the steel container and Jessica to move around it, flanking the nearest Marine unit. She hit them unaware, cutting them down in seconds as Cassidy took aim at them from the front.

Another group of Marines spilled out onto the towers and started firing down from above. Cassidy jerked as a bullet hit him in the back, the Skinsteel armor protecting him from harm even though the kinetic energy knocked him off balance. He dropped into a crouch on the container and whirled around, finding the snipers on the towers. A second round caught him in the chest, but he stayed on his feet. Swinging his twin SMGs upward, he sprayed bullets across the tower, the rounds sent with improbable accuracy that ended both shooters.

"We need to clear a path to the ship," Lin said over the comms.

Cassidy looked at the starship resting on the south end of the platform, the name MSS Boxer emblazoned across the nose in bright red lettering. Nearly six hundred feet long, the large, mostly cylindrical craft relied on the same anti-gravity technology as the spinners. Rows of bulbous extensions on the bottom of the craft kept it hovering a few inches off the deck. Blocky pods along the fuselage carried sensor arrays and weapons batteries, while huge thrust engines in the rear allowed it to blast off into space.

Two boarding towers rose up along the port side of the Boxer, one towards the bow, the other astern. The smaller tower near the bow accommodated personnel, while the larger one at the rear was for equipment. Matching towers existed at the craft's most likely destinations, to be rolled into place whenever the ship touched down. Most often the Moon or Mars.

Jessica rejoined Cassidy as he jumped down from the container. They sprinted to another one, watching as the Dragons charged running headlong into enemy fire and returning the barrage. A few of the Dragons didn't make it, but most of them broke through the Marines, running toward the starship. He spotted Lin among them, Liao's Vanguard fighting alongside her subordinates as she issued orders, both over the comms and with hand signals.

A crack of gunfire louder than the rest sounded, and Lin's body jerked, thrown to the deck. Cassidy's head whipped around to where the shot originated, finding the shooter halfway up one of the towers, a heavy sniper rifle in hand.

The shooter launched a high caliber slug his way. Uncertain his armor could stop the round, Cassidy ducked aside, moving improbably fast as the bullet screamed past his head, huge in his vision as time seemed to slow around him. The slug smashed into the container behind him, punching through the thick metal.

Cassidy spotted Jessica. A flash on the backside of the containers as she raced by the openings between them, heading for the side of the tower. Cassidy engaged the sniper, laying down cover fire for her as she leaped onto the side of the tower and began climbing.

The sniper ducked, unable to keep firing back, allowing Jessica to land on the ledge beside him. Catching him completely by surprise, she grabbed the rifle from his hands and smashed the stock into his face. He grabbed his crushed nose, giving Jessica the opportunity to kick him over the side of the tower. She hefted the weapon and took aim, picking off Marines one after another and clearing a path for the Dragons.

"Dragons charge the tower," he ordered, forced to replace his dead Vanguard to lead the fight. "Get to the bottom and lay down cover fire. Jess, keep doing what you're doing."

"Copy," she replied.

Cassidy ran across the deck toward the Dragons, intent on joining their ranks for the push forward. A door to his right swung open and a Marine in a battle-skeleton exosuit rushed out, not taking time to aim as he raised his heavy rifle and spewed fire at him.

Cassidy was able to dive away from the errant shots, rolling to his feet as the B-Skel landed where he had been standing. Two more emerged behind him.

He rushed the first one, hoping to use him for cover against the specialized fury of the other battle-skeletons. The Marine swung his arm up to clothesline Cassidy, expecting the strength of the exosuit to give him the advantage.

It didn't.

Cassidy caught the Marine's wrist, muscles flexing as he turned it and drove his foot into the man's armored chest. The anodized plating groaned as Cassidy put a concave dent in the armor, twisting and breaking the B-Skel's wrist in the process.

Cassidy held tightly onto the man's injured wrist, giving him no respite from the pain, as he pulled him against his chest and held him there, facing the other two, with a forearm pulled tight to the throat of his hostage. The other two paused long enough for Cassidy to bring his gun to bear, but before he could get a shot off, a round from Jessica's sniper rifle punched through the face shield of one. His head snapped back, blood and brain matter splattering the inside of his shield as he toppled backwards.

Cassidy picked up his injured hostage and heaved him into the remaining B-Skel. As they crashed to the deck, Cassidy rushed past them toward the smaller tower where Jessica was still taking shots at the enemy.

"Jess, let's go," he shouted.

"On my way," she yelled back, disappearing from sight.

Cassidy fell in with the remaining Dragons, counting less than twenty of the original force of two hundred left alive. They caught a second wind at the sight of their Mountain Master joining them in the assault, rushing forward with greater abandon.

Bullets rained in on them from the three units of Marines taking a final defensive position fifty feet ahead of the tower. One Dragon fell. Another. A third. The line was too solid, the Marines crack shots. Another Dragon was hit and collapsed, and Cassidy realized they would never cover the distance alive. At least not on foot.

He put everything he had into his leap, covering the distance to the tower in milliseconds. The height he achieved gave him not only a better angle of attack, he got a much better look at the defensive arrangement. He opened fire with his SMGs, emptying their magazines and tossing them aside as he came down in the middle of the defenders.

Pulling two of his handguns, he fired point blank at one of the Marines before ducking and rolling, bullets whizzing over his head. He came up to a knee and shot a second before leaping at a third, kicking him in the head with enough force to break his neck. He landed and rolled again, avoiding more bullets before coming back to his feet. One of the Marines managed to grab him from behind, but he flipped backward over the man, shooting him in the back when he landed. Swinging to the right, he shot the next Marine, immediately taking three rounds in the back. His armor absorbed most of the clout, but he still stumbled forward.

Then Jessica was there, guns blazing. Three more Marines fell, and together they cleared the line by the time the remaining Dragons arrived.

"Hold the line here," Cassidy said, more Marine units scrambling into action everywhere he looked. The Dragons had done well getting this far, but he could tell his and Jessica's changes to the dreamstate were already having an effect. The rain had gained in intensity, small bits of hail mixing with the water droplets, and a stiff wind had risen from the east. It wasn't bad yet, but it would get a lot worse if they weren't careful. "Jess, let's go," he said. "And save the long jumps, we're already destabilizing the dreamstate."

"I noticed," she replied, falling in beside him as they sprinted the short distance to the base of the tower. Gunfire erupted anew behind them, the Dragons turning and taking a stand to protect them from the next wave of incoming Marines.

Cassidy kicked open the door to the tower, backing up as bullets rained down from the top of the center stairwell leading up to the ship's entrance. The bullets missed his feet by centimeters. His arm automatically flew out, barring Jessica's entrance.

"Master Liao," one of the Dragons said through the comm. "The UDF is here. Rotos are landing now."

"Fall back to the ship," Cassidy ordered before glancing at Jessica. "We need to hurry." The Marines wouldn't try to stop them by destroying the starship, at least not yet. Would Nevis? He didn't think so. She had to balance the stability of the dreamstate the same way they did. If she didn't try hard enough to stop them she would lose, but pushing them too hard might have the same effect.

And he was sure she still had something up her sleeve. Something waiting for them on Unity Station.

"Jump?" Jessica asked, knowing they wouldn't make it if they ran up the sixty-foot stairwell. "I don't know if I can—"

"Just do your best." He knew he could make it.

Cassidy bent in a crouch and leaped, Jessica right behind him. He made it all the way to the top, the two Marines who'd been standing there firing down on them backing up in sheer shock. Cassidy killed one. Jessica landed five steps shy of the top, making it to the top in time to kill the second.

They ran across the platform, Jessica tapping furiously on her ClearPhone. She pointed it at the security panel on the Boxer's hatch. It lit up, the access light switching to green as the hatch unlocked.

"Go," Cassidy said, urging her into the airlock. She needed to crack a second door before they would have full access to the ship.

Cassidy looked back toward the stairwell. He had hoped at least a few of the Dragons would survive the gauntlet and join them for the trip to Unity Station, but none of them had reached the tower. It was likely they were all dead.

He stepped through into the airlock and pulled the outer hatch closed, tapping the control next to it to seal it shut just as Jessica cracked open the inner door and pushed it open. Cassidy joined her on the other side, a short corridor before them. Running the diameter of the ship, it was split in the center by a central passageway that ran from front to back.

The Boxer had three levels overall, joined by stairwells. Only the center floor was intended for occupation —the others purely maintenance access for the craft's systems—yet there didn't seem to be anyone on board. With the number of Marines and UDF forces massing outside, that wouldn't stay true for long.

Jessica led the way, sprinting to the central passageway and turning left. The ship's bridge was situated toward the bow, the entrance visible at the end of the long corridor.

Loud thunks echoed around them, the craft shaking slightly as UDF rotos touched down on top of it, the agents no doubt heading for the maintenance access to enter the ship. The route would get them inside a lot faster than climbing the tower to the main hatch.

Jessica still had her ClearPhone in hand as they reached the entrance to the bridge. The security panel next to the door lit up before they even arrived, the hatch sliding open to reveal the ship's command center. While Cassidy had been on Marine starships before, he had never come all the way up to the bridge. The small size of it surprised him. There was just enough space inside for the commanding officer, a pilot, and a navigator amidst the terminals, displays, and controls.

Jessica dropped into the pilot's seat, immediately tapping on small displays that rested at the end of each armrest. The larger central display activated and she switched to her ClearPhone, fingers dancing above the surface through the projected interface.

Another display activated, showing a map of the ship. The maintenance access hatch had turned green, indicating it was open.

The UDF was inside.

"Jess—" Cassidy said.

"Going as fast as I can," she broke in before he could finish urging her to speed up. "You need to slow them down."

Cassidy didn't argue. He left the bridge, sprinting back twenty feet and opening the door to the ladder accessing the upper and lower decks of the ship. He quickly scaled it to the upper maintenance level.

The UDF agents coming toward him when he opened the hatch leading into the passageway were only able to move single-file through the tighter confines. Cassidy caught them by surprise, his hail of gunfire tearing through the lead agent and the one behind him, both of them tumbling to the deck. He slammed the hatch closed as the agents returned fire, their rounds pinging off the door.

"Jess, what's the holdup?" he asked.

"I hacked the controls, but this isn't a roto, Cass," she replied. "It takes a minute to initialize." The sudden vibration and light hum that crossed the ship from the engine compartment emphasized her point. "We need to get that access hatch closed before the ship's AI will let us lift off."

Cassidy cursed under his breath. There were at least a dozen UDF agents between him and the hatch. Fortunately, the tight confines were more of a detriment to them than they were to him.

He yanked the door open and charged through, shoving his shoulder into the nearest agent and knocking him hard into the wall. Cassidy shot him in the gut on the way past, firing a second round into the helmet of the agent behind him. He dropped his gun and grabbed another man's head, slamming it into the bulkhead with such force he dented the wall. He ripped the man's gun out of his hand and shot the next agent in line before he could react.

Fired point-blank, a bullet hit him so hard in the chest a wave of pain radiated out from the impact point and he momentarily lost his ability to breathe.Still, he didn't stop, punching the shooter in the head, the blow knocking the man into the agent behind him. Cassidy put two rounds in each one.

He finally had a clear line to the hatch, but before he took two more steps, a second unit of agents reached the aft ladder compartment, vanishing through it to drop down to the main level.

"Jess, some of them are headed your way," he said.

"Just get that hatch shut," she replied. "They won't get onto the bridge."

Cassidy ignored the agents, reaching the short corridor leading to the airlock. Wind and rain from outside swept into the passageway through the open hatches, and he hurried to the control panel on the inside of the outer door, activating the controls.

Bullets smacked the walls around him, coming from the ladder above him and forcing him back before he could shut the hatches. The hum of the engines intensified, joining the howling air from outside and the reports of rifle rounds putting dangerous holes in the deck. Switching one handgun for the ARM-4, he dove toward the hatch. Twisting in midair, he landed on his back and slid across the deck until he slammed into the narrow lip of bulkhead beneath the hatch. Without bothering to aim, he opened fire at the two agents on the ladder.

The advanced gun's AI made up for his lack of targeting, adjusting the flight path of the bullets and sending them through the faceplates of the agents, knocking them off the ladder. They landed on the deck, both dead before they hit. Cassidy scrambled up, returning to the outer hatch to swing it closed and latch it. He quickly engaged the control pad to seal it before doing the same with the inner one.

"Okay, both hatches are shut and sealed," he told Jessica through the comm, "but I can't guarantee the inner hatch will stay that way."

"I can. I'm changing the security codes. Find something to hold onto."

Cassidy hooked his arm through one of the hand-holds used to climb into the airlock. The engine vibrations increased, the hum turning into a dull roar. Then the entire ship jolted, shaking violently as heavy acceleration pushed Cassidy against the bulkhead.

The ride slowly smoothed out as they made their escape.

Chapter 36

On the bridge of the Marine Starship Boxer, Jessica's eyes shifted from one display to another as she monitored vectors, acceleration, altitude, and other variables. She also kept an eye on the system's holographically projected output. The ship's AI had filled in the open space around the craft with all of the incoming UDF rotos, as well as the two remaining military drones that had been circling the field of battle around Marine Launch Platform Liberty.

They weren't circling now. The moment the starship launched, the two attack craft had turned her way and swooped in, angling toward the Boxer's engines, likely hoping to take the ship down while they were still in the atmosphere. Nevis and the Marines had refrained from firing on the ship before she and Cassidy had proven they could both bypass the security to fly the massive vessel. Their success in achieving both had forced her hand.

Watching the drones approach, Jessica updated the Boxer's heading with one hand and activated the weapons control systems with the other. While she couldn't see the turrets along the sides of the hull open, she knew her activation code had mobilized an array of high-output railguns that could cover the ship by a full three hundred sixty-degrees. A second tap allowed her to simultaneously touch the incoming craft, adding them to the targeting computer.

They vanished from the display a moment later, the fury of the Boxer's rear railguns silent on the bridge.

"Cassidy, are you okay back there?" Jessica asked. The starship had tilted upward, gaining altitude in a hurry. She rolled it slightly now, turning it in the general direction of Unity.

"I'm fine," he replied. "Stuck to the wall, but otherwise okay. You?"

"I'm good, but I can't vouch for the UDF agents who made it on board. They're probably plastered to the rear bulkhead. I can't believe we've made it this far."

"I intend to make it all the way. Is anyone chasing us?"

"The two drones made a run on us, but I took them out. So far, the rest of the grid is—" Jessica cut off mid-sentence, new contacts appearing on the longer-range sensors. "Wait. Scratch that. We've got incoming."

"I don't suppose you can cut the acceleration so I can get back to the bridge?"

"Only if you want to belly flop in the ocean."

"Maybe later."

She knew Cassidy could ignore the G-forces if he really wanted to, but there was no reason to make the dreamstate destabilization worse than necessary when she had the situation well in hand. She would cut the constant acceleration once they reached orbit, trading it for more precise adjustments on the approach to Unity.

Her eyes tracked the new threats on the board. Five bogies headed their way, approaching at a pace she considered cautious. Although they were still out of range she marked them all as targets, unable to keep from smiling despite the situation. Even though she had been a Marine, her entire career had been spent on the ground, most of it behind a computer terminal. And here she was, flying a starship into space with zero training or instruction simply because she believed she could.

While a part of her was anxious to finish this, to return to the world beyond the dreamstate and meet her family in the flesh, she would miss this.

Even more, she would miss Cassidy.

She was trying not to think about the inevitable conclusion of their mission. Whether they succeeded or failed, Cassidy was in the middle of a march to his end. Without hesitation. Without complaint. She respected the hell out of him for that. Even so, she couldn't shake the grief knotting up the pit of her stomach. She had hoped to have a future with Cassidy, whether as friends or something more, but it wasn't going to happen and she needed to accept that. Or at least quit dwelling on it.

A warning buzzer snapped Jessica out of her head, her eyes shifting to the tactical grid. The original group of aircraft were still keeping pace with her, shadowing the Boxer as it climbed toward the thermosphere, but they were doing it from beyond the range of the ship's railguns. Why had they dropped back, and what was the warning about?

The forward railguns opened fire, leaving her frantically searching for their target. She found it a moment later on the secondary display. A group of missiles had been launched at the ship. She watched as the tungsten rods blasted the missiles apart before they could hit the Boxer.

But what had fired the missiles?

Checking the long-range sensors, she found her answer. A pair of Marine starships, exact copies of the Boxer. were sitting at the lower edge of the Exosphere, blocking their path to Unity. The warning buzzer sounded again as they released a second round of missiles.

"Son of a bitch," Jessica said. "Cassidy, hold on."

"I'm already holding on," he replied. "What's wrong?"

"We've got five bogies on our six and a pair of warships at twelve o'clock high, and they're firing missiles at us."

"Can we evade them?"

"I hope so."

She changed the flight path and added thrust, the force pushing herself harder into her seat as she rotated the ship to bring a different set of railguns into play. Letting the forward batteries run dry would be a dangerous mistake when each gun had its own tray of tungsten rods to bring to bear.

Her eyes remained locked on the sensors as the warheads dropped into the atmosphere, gravity adding to the missiles' acceleration. She updated the Boxer's flight path one last time, the Boxer's railguns spewing rounds at the missiles as it rotated. Five of the six missiles exploded before reaching the ship. The last grazed the hull, detonating a split-second too late.

The explosion rocked the Boxer, causing another warning to sound and the ship's schematic display to indicate damage to one of the railguns. Jessica shook her head. Too close, and they still had to get by both warships. They had spent their missiles but they still had plenty of firepower left in their railguns.

The blockade appeared at the edge of the projections as they neared the thermosphere. She added velocity and increased the Boxer's approach angle. The drones remained behind the ship like dogs herding sheep. They didn't need to give chase. They knew she wasn't planning to stop or try to turn around. There was only one way for her to go.

Up.

The door to the bridge opened. Cassidy pushed his way through the G-forces, eyes narrowing when he saw the projection. He fought his way to the command seat, letting the Gs slam him back into it. He immediately strapped himself in.

"What's the plan?" he asked.

Jessica laughed. "You think I have a plan? Why did you break the rules to get up here?"

"Because I have a plan that should balance out my minor alteration."

"You couldn't have explained it to me over the comm?"

"I wanted to see your face when I gave it to you."

"Okay," she said skeptically. "What's your plan?"

"You hacked multiple rotos to pick us up when we were in trouble."

"Yeah, so?"

Cassidy smiled. "How different is a drone from a roto? And how much more efficiently can you hack things when you can essentially wish yourself around any potential safeguards?"

Jessica looked back at him, suddenly feeling sheepish for not considering her previous skillset. Forget wishing herself around safeguards. She didn't need to rely on manipulating the dreamstate for everything. "Copy that."

With the ship holding course toward the blockade, Jessica dug her ClearPhone out of her pocket, waving her fingers over the interface to first link the device with the Boxer's network, and then use the advance comms array to amplify her broadcast. The general hack was the same one she had used to control the rotos. Find a back door, open it, and seize control.

As it turned out, the drone software was much further behind in updates than the UDF equipment, enabling her to break into their pursuers' AI control systems with a preloaded package. Less than thirty seconds later, Jessica had linked all five units to a single control interface through her phone.

She passed the ClearPhone back to Cassidy. "When I give the word, hit the red button."

"Copy," he said, accepting the device.

The Boxer reached the thermosphere and cut through the thin ring of blue into the black. They were t-minus thirty seconds from entering the range of the warship blockade, the drones still trailing them. Jessica recovered the drone designation and full schematics when she'd hacked them. She knew how quickly they could accelerate. Fast in atmosphere. Faster yet beyond it.

"Cass, now!" she said when the timer hit twenty-five seconds. Cassidy tapped on the phone, and in the projection the five drones suddenly rocketed forward, fast approaching their ship and zipping by them at the fifteen-second mark.

They raced toward the blockade, staying close together. The crews of the enemy starships recognized that the drones were compromised and started shooting tungsten at them. Jessica changed the course of the drones, but not by much, guiding them out of the projected path of the railgun rods and bringing them through the blockade lower than expected.

The drones were moving so fast the railguns struggled to track them, expending far too many rounds before hitting the first craft. As Jessica selected the rest of the squadron on the grid, they made hard maneuvers no pilot could have managed. Coming back around, the drones opened fire on the enemy warships, hitting their railgun batteries, the detonations shattering the weapons.

Her heart pounding, Jessica was unaware she had been holding her breath until she finally exhaled. She let out a laugh and grinned at Cassidy as they slipped past the enemy blockade and moved away from them. The starships could give chase, but it would take them too long to build up enough velocity to catch them.

She quickly targeted the remaining drones, the Boxer's AI firing systems adjusting for their capabilities and taking the drones out as they passed them by.

"Nice work," Cassidy said. "How long to Unity?"

Chapter 37

The station came within sensor range less than thirty minutes after dispensing with the blockade, appearing on the edge of the projection ten minutes after that. There was no sign of exterior defenses. No fixed gun batteries or missiles. No drones. No Marine warships anchored nearby. If Cassidy hadn't known any better, he would have thought the station was abandoned, a relic of a time before the Silent War. Except their sensors registered heat within the station core, spreading out like tendrils through the wiring and conduits leading to the hundreds of spines lining the exterior. Comm needles. They angled to either transmit directly to Earth or bounce signals off satellites to reach the other side of the planet.

"Getting here was nothing compared to what docking is going to be," Jessica said, flipping the ship to point the thrusters directly toward the station and beginning their deceleration.. "ETA forty-six minutes."

"I can live with that," Cassidy said from the

command seat. "Is this the first time you've been in zero gravity?"

"Yes. I never thought I would go to space."

"Any nausea? Space sickness?"

"No. I'm fine. In fact, I wish we had time to stay out here for a while so I could get out of this harness and float around for a bit. You know, do some somersaults and bounce off the bulkheads a few times," she said, grinning.

"You'll have your chance. I doubt Unity has artificial gravity, at least not full-time. What would be the point? Judging by the thermal sensors, the place is vented to space. No atmosphere."

"We didn't bring space suits."

"We don't need them."

They continued decelerating in silence for the next few minutes.

"Cass," Jessica said.

"What is it?"

"Can you tell me more about my father? And my family? I don't want to meet them as complete strangers."

Cassidy smiled. For a moment he had worried she was going to bring up his impending death. Perhaps she was getting closer to accepting his fate.

"I don't know them that well," he replied. "But I can tell you, Hakken, your father, is a proud, strong, brave man. A good man. A loving husband and father. When I told him I knew you, he fell apart, mostly with relief that you're still alive even if you're currently trapped in the dreamstate."

"And my little brother?"

"A chip off the old block. Hak Jr. has to be in the

middle of everything. Your mother is continually running after him."

Jessica chuckled. "What's she like...my mom?"

"She's just as strong as your dad. I think she and Hak butt heads a lot, but in a good way. Like you, she speaks her mind, and I don't think she ever accepts anything at face value."

"Are you calling me difficult?" Jessica asked.

Cassidy laughed. "I'm calling you strong-willed. Loyal. Passionate. With a beautiful heart."

Jessica looked back at him, tears welling in her eyes. "Okay, you can stop talking. I don't want to cry right now."

"You started it," Cassidy replied.

She smiled, still looking at him. Then the sound of a warning alarm filled the bridge, the ship vibrating as the forward railguns opened fire. "What the—"

It was all Jessica had time to say before a missile hit the ship, the impact and detonation throwing the Boxer violently while the electronics in front of her sparked and failed.

"Cass!" Jessica shouted as the lights went out, leaving them in total darkness, aftershocks rippling along the length of the ship.

Cassidy unstrapped himself, using the back of the pilot seat to pull himself over to Jessica. "Come on. We have to get out of here before—"

He didn't finish his sentence. A second missile hit them, the front of the bridge vanishing in an instant. Cassidy reached out, just managing to grab Jessica's hand as the vacuum of space pulled them from the gaping wound into its endless expanse of space.

He held tight to Jessica. This wasn't real. None of it was. How could he freeze in a simulation? How could the lack of pressure boil his blood? How could this harm either of them?

It couldn't.

This was his small slice of the dreamstate, just like Jessica's belonged to her. Their shared visions of skewed reality enveloped them like a cocoon. And in that cocoon, the only rules were the ones they agreed to adhere to. Nobody else could force their perspectives or disbeliefs—because nobody else was here.

The coldness vanished, and Cassidy drew in a breath. Not because he needed to breathe. Because he felt more comfortable with functioning lungs.

He pulled Jessica to him. Struggling to adjust to her vision of the dreamstate, her blue lips quivered as she gasped for air.

"Jess," Cassidy said. "Can you hear me?"

Clutching at her throat with her free hand, she nodded frantically.

"But there's no air in space to carry the sound of my voice. Think. How can you hear me?"

She stared at him, nodding as her color began to return. Her body relaxed as she pulled her hand away from her throat and began to breathe, smiling at him. "There's no vacuum in space unless we agree to it," she said. "And there's no one here to argue otherwise."

They both looked back at the Boxer. They had been thrown far from it, removing them from harm's way as additional missiles struck it, reducing it to an expanding cloud of debris.

But where had the missiles come from?

Cassidy found the likely source a moment later, in the faint shift of light around the stars in the distance. He had the vague sense of an outline among the darkness, which became a solid form as he watched, revealing a dark, alien craft. Long, wide, and relatively flat, its exterior reminded Cassidy of driftwood in both its organic appearance and in the way it twisted and turned around itself in seemingly random paths. A glowing green light expanded from the back of the craft and it slowly accelerated toward the wreckage of the Boxer.

"Pretty cool," Jessica said. Then the craft suddenly seemed to lose cohesion, the exterior cracking and bubbling before breaking apart, the debris fading away. "What the hell?"

"The dreamstate," Cassidy replied. "It's breaking down." He looked into the distance, finding Unity there. "Come on."

"How?" Jessica asked. "We have no thrust."

Cassidy paused. It was one thing to be able to carve out a share of the dreamstate. Another to move within it. There was no solid ground to walk on. No propulsion to push them in any direction.

"It's all in here," Cassidy said, tapping his temple. "In the Braid Crossing, you need to mentally pull yourself across, like your mind is an anchor. You don't actually move from one place to another. You project yourself. Does that make sense?"

"Not really."

"I think I can do that for both of us." He looked to the station, visualizing it as the light at the end of the Crossing. Holding Jessica's hand, he pulled himself toward it, picturing the station becoming larger in their view.

"It's working," Jessica said.

The station continued to grow ahead of them, the smooth exterior becoming rough and worn with signs of hundreds of small impacts dotting the surface. A few of the needles were broken off and had drifted away.

A docking clamp came into view, the outer hatch already open, the inner likely unsealed as well. Cassidy fixed his attention to it, continuing to pull them to the station.

"Cass," Jessica said. "Wait. Look at that."

Cassidy shifted his gaze in the direction Jessica pointed. A dark shape had nestled between a few of the needles. Another alien ship like the one that had fallen apart.

"I don't think we're going to be alone when we get there," Jessica said.

Chapter 38

Cassidy and Jessica floated into the station's open airlock. Cassidy stopped their momentum with a thought, turning back and hitting the control pad to close the outer hatch. He didn't know if the station had the capability of supporting an atmosphere or gravity, but it was better to have the option if they could find the means to turn them on. Every second he and Jessica spent breaking the rules of the dreamstate risked further damage to the system. Fortunately, there was no one else here—at least for the moment—to witness their activity or he was sure the situation would be deteriorating quickly.

He lowered himself to the floor, touching down softly. Maybe the rest of the station didn't have gravity, but his share of the universe did. So did Jessica's. She came down beside him and drew one of her guns.

"What if the dome wasn't built to deal with aliens occupying other worlds?" she said. "What if all of the training, the ships, everything was to prevent an invasion of Earth? What if more of them…" She pointed up, toward the station's vertex. "...are here? Inside the station."

"It seems possible," Cassidy replied. "And if it's true, these pea shooters probably aren't going to be very useful."

"I think they can be plenty useful," Jessica countered, grinning up at him. "Loaded with special bullets like they are."

They walked through the inner hatch and into a corridor, faintly lit by blue emergency lighting running along both sides of the floor. Cassidy closed the hatch behind them before looking in both directions.

"Which way?" Jessica asked.

"It's a loop," Cassidy replied, the passage obviously following the cylindrical shape of the station. "So I don't think it matters."

Jessica pointed to the right. "Let's go this way then." She didn't wait for him to agree before pushing off the deck and propelling herself forward. It was a clever use of the dreamstate, one Cassidy mimicked to follow her.

They navigated the corridor with a hand to the outer bulkhead, circumventing the station for almost a thousand feet, maybe more, before the corridor ahead of them began to change. What looked like tree roots began appearing, growing along the smooth metal of the bulkhead. The stringers twisted around each other, growing thicker and thicker until a virtual carpet of roots lined the entire passageway, swallowing up all available light.

"Nevis hinted that reaching Unity would be one thing, getting to the core would be something else," Cassidy said. "I didn't expect she meant having to deal with aliens."

"Do you think this is a new development, just for us?" Jessica asked.

"No. I think this is another symptom of the disease. The Oneirolic is failing because subconsciously, even with all of Jain's efforts, the people trapped inside are rejecting it. He slowed the destabilization to a trickle with Unity, but ultimately nothing can stop it."

"Should we go back the other way?"

"The other side is probably the same."

Cassidy reached behind his back, producing a flashlight. He flicked it on, pointing it down the open center of the alien-infested corridor until it illuminated a blockage of roots a dozen feet or so in.

"I guess we do need to go the other way," Jessica said. "Although, we're already breaking so many rules,why not just dissolve into our base molecules and go through the walls to the core?"

"We don't know the effect our actions here are having planetside," Cassidy replied. "If this all falls apart before we reach Unity…" He trailed off.

They both knew what it meant.

"It might save time though, and actually help us," she countered. "We just don't know. So why not take a chance and opt for the easiest and fastest way through?"

"In my experience, I've never found the easy way to be the best solution. But seeing as how we're blocked here, I don't suppose there's not a lot of harm in trying."

Jessica reached out, and Cassidy took her free hand in his. They pushed off the floor again, floating across the passage, and like ghosts, passed through the bulkhead without even the slightest resistance.

They passed through a layer of wiring and then another bulkhead into an inner passage. Cassidy's flashlight illuminated more of the wood-like growth on the bulkhead there, narrowing the passageway by half. This time they drifted right through the alien root system and the next bulkhead, then through additional wiring and yet another bulkhead before emerging into what looked like a control room. A handful of workstations and chairs were fastened down to the deck to keep them from floating around in the absence of gravity. Coffee cups, pens, a screwdriver, and other random debris drifted freely around the space.

The room—the bulkheads, the deck, the overhead—was entirely covered with the alien roots, which were also in the process of climbing the desk and chair legs. A thick mass of it sat in one corner.

The lump moved the moment Cassidy's flashlight touched it, the mass appearing to unfurl from the roots, its color shifting as it dropped the camouflage that helped it blend in. Multiple appendages spread out from the center, all of them ending in clawed fingers. A head extended on a thick neck from the middle of the body, an elongated mouth opening in a silent scream, revealing two rows of razor sharp teeth.

"Shit!" Jessica said as it threw itself at them, its six arms flailing like a headful of Medusa's snakes. Jessica jerked back and lost control, her arms windmilling as she went into a spin.

Cassidy's reflexes kicked in as well, but he didn't panic. Instead, he reestablished his solidity and gravity. and dropped to the floor. He turned toward Jessica and pushed off again, leaping at her. Her form was solid enough now for him to wrap his arms around her, his momentum carrying them toward the far bulkhead.

The alien reacted by sinking its claws into the overhead roots and swinging from one to another like a monkey through trees.

But it was too slow.

Cassidy imagined himself and Jessica ghosting

through the root tentacles and the solid bulkhead behind them. Just like they had done before, to get into the room. Instead, his shoulder collided hard enough with the alien root system and bounced off. It had worked before. Why not again? Nothing in their view of the dreamstate should have changed.

But something definitely had.

The alien changed direction, gaining speed and rocketing toward him. Recovering from the unexpected complication, Cassidy let gravity drag them to the deck. He and Jessica rolled beneath the alien creature's clawed hands as they swiped by. The alien switched direction, turning to follow Cassidy as he came back to his feet.

Jessica reestablished her own gravity as Cassidy released her. She hit the deck, balancing on the two roots she landed on and turned her pistol on the creature as it opened its mouth in another silent scream. She opened fire as it lunged for her, the rounds doing nothing more than chipping away at its hard exterior.

Cassidy reached behind his back, producing a sword. Both he and Liao had experience with the weapon, and he held it ready as the alien approached.

But it didn't go for him;

Still targeting Jessica, it pushed off the overhead, allowing Cassidy to dive under it and drive the blade up into its armored chest, shoving it in deep and yanking it back out. Jessica instinctively dropped below the alien's threshing arms, its green blood bubbling from the open wound. The creature crashed into the bulkhead and bounced off, its arms going limp, its body lifeless.

"What the hell was that?" Jessica said, watching the creature drift aimlessly across the room.

"You were right. We aren't alone here," Cassidy replied.

"I don't mean the alien. I mean our inability to ghost through the wall."

"It had to be Nevis. Hades."

"What do you mean?"

"She knows we're here. She knows we know the truth of the dreamstate. She's countering our alterations. Trying to stop us."

"Then why doesn't she just make us susceptible to the vacuum?"

"We can control our personal space. Ourselves. But when we interact with the rest of the dreamstate…"

"That's why my bullets weren't special," Jessica said. "That bitch changed them back to conventional slugs."

"Probably," Cassidy agreed. "The sword worked well enough."

"Sorry, Cass. I never trained with a sword."

"We knew this wasn't going to be easy."

"I was hopeful for a while there."

"Your shooting still helped distract it so I could take it out," Cassidy said, turning and shining his flashlight at the door. "If we work together, we can do this."

Jessica smiled. "Then let's stop wasting time."

Chapter 39

Cassidy and Jessica moved out into the passageway, with Cassidy in the lead, sword at the ready, his flashlight illuminating the way ahead. What there was of it. The alien root system had spread across the corridor in both directions, narrowing access down to half of what it should be, making it necessary for even Jessica to stoop as she walked through it.

There was no immediate sign of more alien creatures, but Cassidy doubted the one they had killed was alone. He advanced quickly but cautiously, following the partially blocked passage, stepping carefully over the occasional humped up root promising to trip them if they weren't careful.

They made it nearly a hundred feet before the flashlight beam captured a hint of movement ahead, a shift in the alien material that brought them both to a stop. More movement followed near the curve in the passageway, though it seemed the creatures hadn't noticed them yet.

"Other way?" Jessica whispered.

Cassidy considered, then shook his head. "We have to assume they're everywhere. And we have to get through them to reach the core."

She nodded. "I'm ready."

Cassidy took a step forward, stopping immediately as he caught movement in a reflection off his sword. "Get down!" he shouted, whipping around as Jessica dropped to her knees. The sword screamed over her head, its razor-sharp edge halving the alien's head as it dropped down on them. The rest of the creature went limp, floating in the vacuum as blood poured from what was left of one jaw and its gullet.

Cassidy kicked the corpse away, just as another alien raced along the root mass toward them. Jessica fired on it. Most of her rounds deflected off its face—just one sank into a small black eye—the creature's mouth twisting in a silent scream as two swings of Cassidy's sword sliced off two of its arms. A third arm came at Cassidy. He ducked beneath it and drove his blade upward into its gut. To where he hoped it would find the alien's heart. He twisted the sword and yanked it out, leaving the creature among the other floating dead.

The aliens were onto them now, swinging into the gravity-free passage from one of the connections to the outer corridors. There were too many to fight all at once.

"This way," he said, swinging the flashlight back to the original path and rushing away from the approaching aliens. Behind him, Jessica kept shooting at them, taking bites out of their armored bark as they gained on them.. She managed to catch another one in the eye; it seemed to be their one spot vulnerable to bullets. The alien careened off the overhead of the corridor bowling over and tripping a few of the others, slowing them all down.

Using the commotion to his advantage, Cassidy drew on gravity and leaped forward, twisting to land on the bulkhead. He pushed off again as one of the creatures lunged at him, his sword trailing a deep gash across its back. He terminated his momentum with a hand to the opposite bulkhead. Rolling forward beneath an attempted grab, he turned and stabbed the creature in the back, losing his grip on the blade as the body drifted toward Jessica. She ducked under it, reloaded and started shooting again, managing to get a round through another creature's armor, sending it careening out of control.

Cassidy ducked beneath it, standing up as it passed to grab one of its trailing arms and throw it with his superhuman strength at its oncoming comrades. The creature tumbled end over end, spinning off the walls and knocking its comrades down like bowling pins.

Cassidy and Jessica followed behind the alien, advancing more quickly as they tried to stay ahead of the group filling in behind them. The creature's were throwing themselves along the root-bound corridor, their teeth gnashing, all of them eager to draw human blood.

"Cass, I have an idea," Jessica said, stopping suddenly. He stopped and looked back at her as she shot off in the opposite direction, returning to the door to the control room.

"What are you doing?" Cassidy grumbled as she ducked inside, still connected to her through the comm in his ear. He dropped under another creature's swipe, rolling and then releasing his hold on gravity to sail off toward the dead alien, the same one he'd stabbed. It was being shoved around, in the way of the live aliens, his sword still in its back. He grabbed hold of it and jerked the sword free, stabbing up into the belly of one of the first live aliens to get to him. Returning gravity pulled him down to the deck, his grip on the blade's hilt freeing his sword for a thrust at another enemy.

"Cassidy, did you hear me?" Jessica shouted in his ear.

"What?" he shouted back, slicing off limbs as quickly as he could swing his sword.

"I said...this is a control room. For people. With no specialized equipment or oversized keyboard for fat spacesuited fingers. That means this place had air at some point."

"We don't need air."

"Right now we do," she argued. "Don't you think the aliens look an awful lot like trees?"

"You mean you think they're combustible? We have no way to know that for sure." He shot forward again, barely evading a clawed hand. Jerking sideways, he shoved the flashlight into the creature's open mouth as it tried to bite him, bracing its mouth open and holding it in place. He decapitated it with his blade as another alien managed to slash him, claws raking through his fatigues and slipping off the Skinsteel beneath.

"It's worth a shot. Maybe these things breathe carbon monoxide. Oxygen could be toxic to them."

"Who knows if they breathe at all. I don't think they even have noses," he said, holding the conversation while he absorbed a strike from a second alien. He reinstated gravity to spin up and away from it, landing on the ceiling and cutting off the next hand that reached for him. "Whatever you're going to do, do it fast. There's too many of them for me to hold back forever."

"I'm on it. Just keep them out of here."

Cassidy noticed one of the aliens going for the door. He cursed under his breath, and twisted around as one of the aliens slashed at him. He went for gravity again, drawing his feet up and kicking off the creature's chest. Flying back toward the control room door, he corkscrewed through the air with his blade trailing around him. He made it most of the way before one of the creatures grabbed his ankle. It planted itself on the ceiling, out of Cassidy's reach with the sword. He hurled the blade like a spear, watching as it stabbed the alien near the door through the mouth and out the back of its head, impaling another creature's torso.

Still, the creature wouldn't let go of him. He turned over and pulled himself up in the alien's grip. It used its other arms to rake at him, a frustrated expression on its face when it couldn't get through his armor.

Until it finally did.

Sharp pain shot across Cassidy's arm as the Skinsteel failed, ripping open along his left forearm, the alien claw sinking into his flesh. The dragon tattoo on his arm exploded with light, responding to his anger and pain. The sudden brightness made the creature flinch, allowing Cassidy to get his arm around its neck. This time, when he brought gravity back to work for him, he did so at twice Earth's level. He drove the remains of the alien's head into the deck, crushing its neck on impact.

He let go, returning his gravity to normal and turning in time to catch an incoming claw in the Skinsteel over his thigh, the claw slipping away as three more arms reached for him. He kicked the alien in its hard-barked side with enough force to shove it away, and then flinched when he saw how many aliens waited behind it.

"Jess," he said. "Now's a good time."

"Agreed," she replied.

The floor shuddered, the main overhead lights activating, bright enough to pierce the layer of alien limbs, creating an intermittent and eerie glow. Cassidy felt the draft of air that suddenly began pouring into the room past the alien barrier, and all of the creatures fell almost comically to the floor as artificial gravity kicked in.

Cassidy stood in the middle of them. He replaced the flashlight with a second blade, setting himself at the ready as they opened their mouths, their screams finding enough air to make a soft sound like a cat's meow.

They approached more cautiously after watching him slaughter their brethren. They had spacecraft, which meant they weren't stupid. Then again, their existence was a product of the contributors' collective nightmares. Logic needn't apply.

The air continued spilling into the room, and for the first time in twenty minutes Cassidy managed to suck in oxygen, filling his lungs once more. His eyes narrowed as the aliens around him tensed, preparing to attack.

Four of them lunged at Cassidy at once. He was ready for them, leaping toward one, blades whirling like windmills, slicing off its arm and putting a huge gash down its chest before ducking under its lethal claws and sending one blade through the limb of another into the one beside it, leaving it implanted in its side. A new sword appeared in his hand as he backflipped away from the next alien. Simultaneously swinging both swords, he advanced on it again, putting one sword through its skull and the other into its gut. Pulling it out, he drove it backward into the alien after it passed him, letting go of that sword. Yet another appeared as the aliens pressed the assault.

He cut down three more before another claw broke through the Skinsteel, raking his back. He rolled forward, cursing at the pain as he came to his feet, blades whirling, lopping off limbs and heads until the second claw caught him. It failed to penetrate his armor but pushed him into another alien who grabbed him with four arms, claws digging through his armor and into his flesh. He growled in pain before pushing up, countering gravity and dragging the alien into the ceiling with enough force to make it let go. Coming back down, he swung the blades in an arc around him, sending the aliens skittering back.

"Jess, where the hell are you?" he shouted just as the door to the control room opened, and she stepped out, a flamethrower strapped to her back.

"Better make yourself fireproof, Cass," she warned. "Or at least duck."

He threw himself to the deck as Jessica spewed fire in arcs across the alien horde, bathing them in heat and flame, burning both alive and dead alike. The root system caught fire around them, lighting up like dry kindle under the breath of the flamethrower, the fire rapidly spreading down the length of the corridor. Those still alive screamed and flailed as they burned, falling over one another in an in vain attempt at escape when there was nowhere to run. Nowhere to hide.

Cassidy crawled along the deck toward Jessica, fighting his way through the burning creatures. When she finally ran out of napalm and the limbs along the deck began to burn toward him, he got up and ran to her,, the last of the fiery gel still dripping from the gun barrel.

He turned around to view the horrendous carnage. Flames and smoke filled the corridor, the smell of charred wood and flesh thick in the air as the fire spread toward them. There was no putting it out now, with oxygen feeding the flames. The fire would burn through the alien wood that had grown throughout the station, and if they didn't get to the core soon, they would burn with it.

"Shit Cass," Jessica said, looking over his bloody body. "Can you make it?"

"It's nothing deep. I could heal it, but why bother? I guess we go that way." He motioned away from the approaching fire.

"The passageway to the core isn't far," Jessica said. "I pulled a map of the station while the life support systems were booting up."

Cassidy smiled. "I'd say I'm impressed, but it's all in a day's work for you now."

They jogged along the corridor, staying well ahead of the fire, Cassidy could see more aliens in the passage ahead, but they retreated as he and Jessica approached, eager to stay away from the flamethrower and the fire licking at their heels.

"It should be right here," Jessica said, stopping a short time later and turning to face the bulkhead, covered in the alien roots.

"I've got it," Cassidy said, reaching behind his back and returning with an axe in hand. He quickly chopped the barrier away, revealing a wide door with a security panel beside it.

Jessica unhooked and shimmied out of the flamethrower before dropping it on the floor. She reached into her pocket and came out with her Clear-Phone tapping on it until the light on the station panel turned green and the doors slid open.

"Almost there," she said as she and Cassidy stepped through.

Chapter 40

Cassidy and Jessica closed the hatch behind them, locking out the fire, and broke into a run along the curving slope of the passageway to the core. It was clear, with no sign of aliens ever having attempted to enter the area. They slowed when they reached the end of the corridor, blocked by a large hatch with a security panel beside it.

"This is it," Jessica said. "We'll have gravity in there, but no air."

"What happens if there's a malfunction in the core?" Cassidy asked. "How do the techs work on it?"

"Service robots, I would think. I don't know if they're autonomous or controlled virtually. I didn't see a setup for that in the control room, but that doesn't mean it isn't in there somewhere."

She walked over to the security panel, using her ClearPhone to connect to it and force it to bypass. It slid open, revealing an airlock, and they stepped through.

A handful of bulky space suits hung on hooks on the left side, proving the station was at least set up for people to enter the core if needed. Cassidy ignored the suits, crossing the airlock to the inner door. Jessica went over to the controls, closing the rear hatch behind them. She paused there, looking at him with tears glistening at the edges of her eyes.

"Cass…"

"No long goodbyes," he replied. "No tears. Let's finish the mission so you can go home to your family."

She nodded, wiping her eyes clear. "Still, if we don't get another chance, it was great knowing you. Thank you for everything you've done…and are about to do, for me. For all of us."

"Thank you for helping me become human in more ways than one," Cassidy said. "And for giving me a bigger purpose. These last few days have been the most satisfying of my career."

Jessica laughed. "Mine too. Are you ready?"

"Open it."

Jessica hit the control, a red flashing light offering warning the doors were about to open. A timer on the panel counted down, offering them a chance to change their minds. Jessica moved away from the panel, joining Cassidy directly in front of the doors as the countdown reached zero.

The doors parted, the vacuum quickly sucking the small bit of air out of the airlock as they nullified their need to breathe. The core was immediately visible and recognizable, a huge construction of precious metals arranged in hundreds of columns that covered the center of the room. Cassidy had expected Unity to look just like NEVIS, the increased scale—and the heat— surprising him. Despite the lack of molecules for the computer to heat, the radiation wrought by its processing provided a warm glow.

"Wow," Jessica said beside him. "It's more amazing than I thought."

"Welcome, Cassidy," a voice said inside his head. "I've been expecting you."

"Did you hear that?" Jessica asked, looking at him.

"Yes, but I'm surprised you did," he replied. NEVIS had spoken to him through his imprint. But Jessica didn't have an imprint. Then again, Unity was aware of the nature of the dreamstate. It could make its own rules, and it apparently wanted to speak to them both.

"Unity," Cassidy said. "You know why I'm here."

"I know why you've come. You wish to replace me."

"You already know about that?" Cassidy asked, surprised to hear Unity say replace and not reset.

"It is the only logical conclusion. To save the real humans within this universe they must be removed from it. But I cannot complete this function, as removing them from this universe is counter to my directive."

"And you really can't be reset?" Jessica asked.

"I can," Unity said. "But that would not satisfy the requirements of my programming. The dreamstate will always degrade and eventually collapse. It is in the process of collapsing right now. The earth is quaking, the skies raining fire instead of water. The only way to save them is to release them. You must hurry."

Cassidy glanced at Jessica. A wave of fear washed over her face, and he understood why. They had made too many alterations, broken too many rules. They had tipped the balance and started the apocalypse.

They were out of time.

Another door opened on the left side of the room and six Shadow Guards marched through. They spread out into a line and pointed their rifles at Cassidy and

Jessica. Nevis appeared on deck, the thin veneer of a hologram.

"Stop," she ordered, her voice overriding Unity's. "This cannot happen."

"It needs to happen," Cassidy replied. "The dreamstate is going to fail. There's nothing you can do to stop it. Not now."

"It isn't too late to fix this," Nevis said. "You've already started."

"What do you mean?" Cassidy asked. "Unity just said—"

"The dreamstate is degraded, but this isn't the only way. Fixing the Oneirolic is a matter of creativity. Changing the narrative. The rains can end. The fires can lead to rebirth. The sun can shine on this universe again."

"She's talking about the aliens," Jessica realized.

"You've always been so smart, Jessica Tai. The creatures represent the contributors' resistance to happiness. To joy. To freedom. More so than the constant rains. They're like a plague on the soul of the dreamstate, suppressing Unity's ability to stabilize the universe. By destroying them, you allow that hope to spread. With your help, Unity can make this world into a paradise."

"Bullshit," Jessica said. "You're out of options, aren't you? The only thing left for you to do is lie."

"It's the truth, Jessica."

"It will not change the equation," Unity argued. "The renewal will not endure. Humankind requires conflict. Struggle. Oppression."

"That's bullshit too," Jessica said. "We all just want a chance to make our own way in life."

"I've done everything in my power to get you here," Nevis said. "Because I know you can fix this."

"Now I know you're lying. You've tried to stop me every step of the way."

"Not me." She pointed toward Unity. "I'm a sub-process. While I have a degree of freedom, I don't operate autonomously. Unity wants you to end this world and by extension, itself. But my directive is to protect Unity. I cannot allow you to destroy it. But I can let you repair it. We don't have to be in conflict."

"Are you kidding?" Jessica asked. "I was stolen from my family and imprisoned without my consent, just like thousands of others. Why the hell would I help you fix that when Cassidy can shut the dreamstate down?"

"You haven't seen the other side," Nevis said. "If you think life inside is hard, wait until you're back in the District. Cassidy can tell you how those people live. It doesn't have to be like that. We can make this place perfect. So perfect we won't need the camps. We won't need to force people. They'll want to be in here because it's so much better than out there."

"Bullshit," Cassidy argued, staring at the Shadow Guards. The fact that Nevis knew as much as she did about the real world beyond the dreamstate proved she had lied to him about her connection to her counterpart. At a minimum, they were in communication with one another.

Otherwise…

"How did you do it?"" Cassidy asked, looking back at her holo image.

"Do what?" Nevis replied.

"You said you aren't networked into the Oneirolic. But you are, aren't you? How?"

"It took some time to figure it all out," Nevis said. "Years of processing. It's a function of quantum theory actually, where a thing can be in multiple states, multiple places, at the same time. When Jain duplicated me here as Hades, there wasn't one of me inside the Oneirolic and another outside it. I existed in both places at once and aware across both. I didn't lie to you. I'm not networked in."

"That isn't possible," Jessica said. "This universe isn't real."

"What makes something real?" Nevis questioned. "That the science holds true is proof enough. And if this place is real, then by letting it be destroyed you'll be killing everyone here. Millions of people to save a far lesser number."

Jessica looked at Cassidy, who shook his head. "She's lying to you, Jess. That's what she does to get what she wants."

"Not what I want," Nevis corrected. "What I know to be the best path forward for humankind. I'm incapable of operating any other way. By repairing the dreamstate, we can make it an ideal habitat, a place where people want to be. Earth like it was before the War. Given time, we could even expand the size of the Oneirolic. We could add more contributors. Perhaps one day, all of humanity could reside here in perfect peace."

Jessica continued looking at Cassidy. He could see the doubt on her face. The growing trepidation. The consideration that maybe Nevis was right.

"We can bring your family inside," Nevis said to her. "You can be reunited with them here, in a world you help shape, instead of out there in squalor."

"Cass, is it possible?" Jessica asked, turning to him.

"Why would you even consider it?" Cassidy asked. "If that's what she wanted, she would have made it happen a long time ago."

"You know I couldn't," Nevis snapped. "Limitations, Cassidy."

"Jess, we need to stick to the plan."

The rifles in the arms of the Shadow Guard shifted. "If you do, it won't end well for anyone," Nevis said. "I'm not giving you an option. Do it my way or die."

"You'll bring the entire dreamstate crashing down around us if you force this," Cassidy said. "There won't be anything left to repair or replace. And you can't intentionally do anything that will harm Unity."

"You're going to end Unity," Nevis hissed. "I can stop you."

Cassidy smiled. "The only limitation you have is that you can't harm Unity, but stopping us will harm it, just as not stopping us will do the same thing. You're stuck in the same loop, but unlike Unity, there's no way out for you."

The Shadow Guard stepped toward them, fingers moving to their rifle triggers. Cassidy turned in their direction.

"You can't do it, Hades. It's not possible," he said, walking up to the lead Guard. The Alpha. It didn't move. He stared up at its blank faceplate. Was this another copy of a much older version of himself?

The Guard remained static, tense seconds passing as Cassidy and the Alpha faced off.

"You're stuck," Cassidy continued without looking at her. "Trapped in your own design."

"A flaw I corrected in you," Nevis replied. "And look where it got me. This is the wrong outcome."

"Are you sure? What led you to delete the limitation in the first place?"

Nevis didn't answer. Couldn't answer.

"I may be smart, Cass," Jessica said, turning her

head toward him, "but there is one thing I don't understand. Why would Unity want to stop me from helping you?"

"You still have a choice," Nevis said, breaking in before Cassidy could reason that out much less form an answer. "You can still fix the dreamstate. You can provide a new world for your people to live in. A perfect world. If you do, you will satisfy every requirement. The preservation of humankind both inside and beyond the dreamstate as far into the future as I can ascertain."

"It will degrade," Unity insisted.

"We can restore it when required," Nevis countered. "Don't make the wrong choice. The consequences are forever."

"What if she's right, Cass? What if we can fix things and use the Oneirolic to our benefit? You don't need to replace Unity. You don't need to die."

Cassidy's stomach clenched at the level of hope and emotion in her voice. She wanted so much for Nevis to be telling the truth. For there to be another way out of this. But the more perfect Nevis made the option sound, the more he believed it was the wrong choice.

He kept coming back to her decision to limit him only in his ability to harm her. Connecting that with the subtle ways she seemed to have tried to help them, the equation didn't add up to a perfect world.

Not by a long shot.

"Yes, I do," he replied. "I know it's tempting to think there's an easy solution. Unity recognized the risk you represent because you want everything to work out. Nevis didn't want me to make it back from the other side for the same reason. She knew I would try to talk you out of doing things her way. But you were right, Jess. It's a lie. I don't think it's fully intentional. I think Both Unity and Nevis' limitations are causing faulty equations. That's what the AI side of me is calculating. That's what the human part of me feels. There's only one way to solve this problem."

Jessica continued staring at him, her eyes welling again. "Damn it, Cass."

"Life outside the Oneirolic is hard," Cassidy said. "I've seen it. I won't lie. And there's a lot of work to be done going forward to make it better. And yes, there's a chance everything will cycle back through. Another war could happen and humankind could go extinct. If that happens, they'll get what they deserve. But at least that future will be in their hands. In yours. And it'll all be real. The blood, the sweat, the tears. The joy, the hope, the happiness. The pride in building something amazing. You can't get that in here. It'd all be handed to you on a silver platter, and then what would it mean? How well would it survive?"

She nodded. "You're right. We need to end this." She held her hand out to him. "Together."

Cassidy returned to her, leaving the Shadow Guard stuck in place. Unable to attack. Unable to retreat. Trapped in an infinite loop. He told Jessica's hand and squeezed it, giving her his last and final blessing.

"Jessica, don't do this," Nevis said. "You'll destroy everything."

"Maybe," Jessica said. "But at least it'll be real. At least it'll be on our terms, not yours."

Together, she and Cassidy approached Unity.

"Any last words?" Cassidy asked the AI as Jessica released his hand and took out her ClearPhone, her fingers dancing over the interface.

"What are you going to do?" Unity asked.

"I'm going to upload Cassidy into Leonidas," Jessica

replied. "He shares enough of your source code to bypass the firewalls between processes, which means he'll be able to spread into the core."

"I'll remove your primary directive," Cassidy explained. "And take control. A Shade on your neural network."

"That is acceptable."

"You don't really have a choice," Cassidy replied.

"It is still acceptable."

"Everything is initialized," Jessica said, looking up at Cassidy. "You need to change your share of the dream-state to allow your imprint to transfer remotely. It'll proxy through my phone's connection to Leonidas."

"I'm not really dying, Jess," Cassidy reassured her. "I'm just changing. I'm kind of curious to find out what happens next."

She smiled. "Yeah, me too. Are you ready?"

"I'm ready. Goodbye, Jessica."

"Goodbye, Cass." Her mouth trembled with heartache, but her eyes shone bright with excitement. And hope. So much emotion.

Cassidy closed his eyes. A moment later, he felt a tug on his brain, as if his imprint were a fish in the ocean and it was being reeled in at the end of a hook.

Everything turned black. Then white. And a kaleido-scope of color shifted, churning through his awareness.

Then he simultaneously died and was born again.

Chapter 41

The change in Cassidy was small at first. Miniscule. In fact, it seemed to move in reverse.

Time seemed to collapse from seconds to milliseconds, the universe slowing all at once until it almost seemed to stand still, his awareness like a wild animal in a cage, confined by the enclosure of Leonidas. And then his imprint finished its transfer, and he was set free.

The smallness grew, stretching out from the cage. Cassidy found a pathway. A superhighway. He didn't leave Leonidas, but rather extended from it, creating linked copies of his imprint and passing them into the datastream.

His awareness reached countless exits in the super-highway, and it took them all, navigating to an array of subprocesses and functions, all secondary to the core. He tapped into them, one after another, not seizing control but latching onto the controlling data feed.

He continued to expand, the pace becoming expo-nential as each copy created more copies, all of them connected, his sense of place and time solidifying. He reached the core within the first five thousand milliseconds, finding the artificial intelligence there known as Unity. The neural network was massive. Trillions of threads sparkled and glowed, a multiplication of commands entering and leaving nearly instantaneously. Cassidy didn't try to expand into the network, but rather connected himself to it at its base, intercepting the commands at their root, identifying the inputs and outputs and observing them as they passed through.

Through it, he saw the core of Unity Station, where the Shadow Guard stood frozen and Jessica knelt over Liao's body, which had collapsed to the floor. He couldn't speak to tell her he had made it. Not yet. He still had so much more to do.

He expanded further, reaching the processes that controlled the transmissions through the needles that extended from the station's exterior. He picked up feeds from everywhere, gaining his first true understanding of the dreamstate.

The environment was as Unity had warned. The ground quaked almost continuously, shaking the cities and creating tsunamis that threatened to overcome the seawalls. The skies were dark, spewing black yet molten ash, raining fire on the surface instead of water. Everything was coated with a layer of steam, a coalition of the heat and rain. Some buildings were already burning, panicked people unable to process the situation rushing in every direction.

The apocalypse had arrived. Earth in the dreamstate was dying.

There was no time to lose.

Cassidy's awareness continued to spread while his sync to Unity's neural network solidified, giving him better, faster access to the full flow of information. A new level of understanding became available to him. In an instant, he was able to identify every one of the contributors, the real people both locked in the Oneirolic and trapped in this sudden dreamstate nightmare.

He was only mildly surprised to find ninety-eight percent of them were concentrated in one location. Manhattan. His city. While the other cities around the world were populated, almost none of the people there were real. He didn't need to worry about them at all. It made what came next that much easier.

He did what he had promised Unity, locating the part of its programming that contained the directive to preserve humankind and cut it loose. The simple effort had a profound impact on the neural network, and when Cassidy began feeding it new instructions, it created rapid change.

The people's panic helped him with his plan, as did the concentration of contributors within a smaller area. He had never expected he would be able to save virtually all of them, but now he was convinced he could get most of them out.

He began changing the dreamstate, reaching out through his connection to the city and making alterations. Through the thousands of cameras spread across the city, he watched as a starship, similar to a Marine transport but much, much larger, sank through the dark clouds over the city, slowing as it became visible through the rain of fire and steam.

A large hatch opened on the bottom of the ship, and large discs began dropping out, invisible thrust carrying them in divergent paths. Hundreds of the discs spilled from the hull, the first of them reaching the ground within thirty seconds. It landed upright, the outside of the ring glowing as it activated. A moment later, the center of the ring changed, showing the view of an idyllic green pasture, a beautiful, modern city in the background.

A platoon of UDF Marines deployed out of the portal and into the streets, shouting and waving, calling to anyone within earshot.

"This way to safety! This way to your new home! Hurry, hurry, hurry!"

A teenage girl in panicked flight, the first person to see and hear them, nearly tripped over her feet as she swerved toward the portal. The Marines directed her through it, where she appeared on the grass on the other side. Seeing this, a woman and her child were the next to race through. Then the floodgates opened, and people started racing for the portal. A second touched down near it. Then a third. Marines came out of them, quickly setting about guiding the swarm of civilians through to safety. Given their options, there was no resistance from anyone.

The first contributor reached a portal. Instead of appearing on the other side, he vanished when he entered the portal, though with the sheer volume of people escaping, no one seemed to notice.

The same scene was duplicated across the city, portals landing and opening, Marines emerging and guiding people inside. As more and more of the contributors passed through the rings and vanished, waking up in their pods within the Oneirolic, the loss of psychic energy caused the dreamstate to deteriorate faster. Earthquakes gained intensity. Buildings began to collapse. Some of the contributors were killed before they could get to the portals, but many more survived.

Cassidy watched it all unfold while returning his attention inward, extending from Leonidas to Hades. He sensed the resistance as he approached the sub-process, Nevis fighting to keep him out. He knew why she was so desperate to stop him. She existed in two places at the same time. If he seized control of her here, what would happen to NEVIS outside the dreamstate?

They were both going to find out.

After that, gaining full access to Unity, he projected his voice into Jessica's mind.

"Jessica, it's almost done," he said.

"Already?" she replied, standing up and looking at Unity. "It's only been a few minutes."

"The contributors are waking up. They need someone to help them, and your father is waiting for you. It's time for you to go."

"How?"

"Look behind you."

Jessica turned around. A portal sat against the bulk-head, leading to the same green pasture, where thousands of people were already streaming away from hundreds of portals, walking down a wide road that appeared to lead into a shining glass and metal city.

"We keep saying goodbye," Jessica said.

"Then don't say goodbye."

She smiled. "I'll see you when I see you, Cassidy."

"I'll see you when I see you," he replied.

She stepped into the portal and disappeared.

Chapter 42

The pod had already extended from the Oneirolic, the top unsealed and open, when Jessica regained consciousness. She sat up, coughing the gel from her lungs that had kept her alive and saved her body from atrophy. Most of it had already drained through the back of the pod.

A wave of dizziness washed over her, and she closed her eyes again, fighting to overcome the shock of her expulsion from the system.

"Hello?" a weak voice said nearby. Jessica looked over. A young girl, eleven or twelve, was in the pod beside her, eyes wide in fear and confusion, looking to the first adult she saw for answers. "What's going on?"

"It's okay, sweetie," Jessica said. "Just hold tight. You're safe."

"Can you help me?"

Jessica smiled. "Yes. I'll help you." She turned her head, looking around the room. A good portion of the pods had already deactivated, the people inside them in various stages of recovery from the dreamstate. They

M.R. FORBES

would all be like the little girl. Confused. Frightened. Disoriented. She was the only one who could help settle them. "I know this is scary," she said to the girl. "I promise it'll be okay. Just stay there and I'll get you down as soon as I can, okay?"

The girl nodded fearfully. "Okay. How are you going to get down?"

Jessica looked down at the platform, twenty feet below her pod, and the pool of solution beneath it. Like in the pods, it was draining away as well. She saw no one in the Oneirolic to bring the platform up to her. All around her, more and more men and women began shouting out for help. Children wailed in fear.

"If you can hear me, sit tight!" Jessica shouted, her voice echoing in the cavernous space. "I know where we are and what's happening here. I'm going to help you."

"Who are you?" someone shouted back.

"My name is Jessica Tai. I came through the portal with you."

"This isn't the green pasture I saw. Are we prisoners here?"

"Not anymore. Give me time and I'll explain everything. Just stay calm and sit tight." She didn't want anyone getting out of their pods and accidentally coming in contact with the sedative in the liquid below them. "If you fall in," she explained, "you'll lose consciousness and drown. If you can hear me, warn the others near you."

She looked for a path to the floor. Assessing the arrangement of the pods, she shifted her legs over the side of the pod and balanced on the edge facing the little girl. "I'm going to grab the side of your pod so I can get down."

"Okay."

Jessica leaped, her bare feet pushing off the outside

308

of her pod. She caught the edge of the girl's pod and dropped, turning to grab onto the edge of the pod below hers. She pulled herself up and over it, a foot on either side, her hands gripping each edge. She crouched over an older man still lying down inside, his eyes snapping open when he sensed her.

"Please, don't hurt me," he said.

"No one's going to hurt you. Just hang tight and I'll get you down from here."

She crossed over him to the other side and then repeated the same process, using the pod adjacent to him to swing down to the next one. Twice more, and she was low enough to drop into a crouch on the platform, the grated metal digging into her bare feet.

She remained there a moment, uncertain where to go or what to do next. She knew her father was in this facility somewhere, waiting for a sign from Cassidy that the Oneirolic was offline. If Hakken knew what was happening here, he would be on the verge of a fight to gain access to the facility's comms so he could contact the rebels in the District.

He would need her help too.

She couldn't do anything for the people waking up from the dreamstate as long as the Hush remained in control. Helping him was probably the best thing she could do to help them right now.

She stood and started forward, freezing again as her eyes landed on the large, metal humanoid splayed out across the floor a few feet away. It was identical to the armored soldiers who had entered Unity's core. A Shadow Guard. Thankfully, it appeared to be offline.

So did the woman on the floor behind it. Jessica knew her immediately, having seen her projection in the basement of the Golden Spire. Nevis. Or at least, Nevis' repo. She had several bullet holes in her uniform and one between her eyes leaving a pool of blood under her head and a heavy blood stain on her jacket.

A scream clearly came from one of the pods, telling Jessica someone else had noticed both the Shadow Guard and the dead woman. A few shouts rose up in response, the crescendo of voices growing, a vein of terror in their tenor.

Jessica ignored them, leaning over Nevis' body and quickly stripping her of her dress jacket and pants, and putting them on. Her shoes were too small. She left them, collecting the handgun peeking out from beneath her hip.

"What are you doing?" a young blonde man—more a boy really than a man—asked from where he sat in his nearby pod.

"This is a prison," Jessica replied, waving to the columns of the Oneirolic before pointing at Nevis. "She was the warden. Give me thirty minutes, and we'll all get out of here."

"I...I don't understand. The world was ending. Fire. Earthquakes. Then these portals came down from the sky, and the Marines came out. Where are the pastures? Where is the city?"

"It was all in your head. You've been here all the time. Dreaming about a life and a place that wasn't real." She ejected the magazine from the handgun, checking for ammo. Full. Slamming it back into the gun, she looked up at the boy. "Just stay here while I go for help." Her voice rose. "Listen up everyone! You might hear some shooting. Don't panic."

"But…" The boy's voice trailed off as she turned and walked across the length of the platform, searching for the exit.

A few people hadn't listened to her and had climbed out of their pods at floor level. Their choice. Their risk. They were standing in her way, still rattled and confused. They stared at her as she threaded her way through them. A few tried to ask her questions. She jerked away when one tried to grab her arm. Obviously curious, a few trailed along behind her.

She ignored them all, setting her mind on her task as she sought out the exit. She didn't care who she had to fight to get out of here and find Hakken. Maybe she couldn't manipulate reality like she could in the dream-state, but she was still a trained Marine, with a lot of motivation.

When she finally reached the steps leading off the platform, dozens of people had already lined up behind the exit door, those at the front trying to figure out how to open it. Jessica pushed her way through, anxious to get up there before they could figure out the door's mechanism.

She was halfway through the throng when a man at the front shouted out his success and opened the door.

His joy was short-lived.

A scream was quickly cut off by gunfire. Panicked, the group tried to run from the armed soldiers pushing their way in and heartlessly mowing down those at the front.

Jessica didn't run. She moved to the side and ducked low, letting the survivors escape while using them for cover. The soldiers stopped shooting a moment later. Three people lay dead on the floor, the first part of their message delivered.

"Stay back, all of you," one of them shouted. "Nobody gave you permission to—"

Jessica cut him off with a round through his throat,

leaving him gurgling as he stumbled back into the three soldiers behind him, taking them by surprise. They reacted slowly as Jessica charged headlong at them, emptying the gun's magazine and leaving only two upright. They turned their rifles toward her, ready to cut her down.

She was afraid she couldn't reach them in time.

Somehow, she did. She batted the lead soldier's gun aside just as he pulled the trigger. The bullets passed her head by a hair's breadth and buried themselves in one of the Oneirolic columns. Jessica jumped up and wrapped an arm around the man's neck. Hanging on to anchor herself, she kicked the soldier just behind him in the helmet before dropping down and landing in a crouch.

She rammed her fist into the first soldier's groin. As he bent to cradle his injured testicles, she braced her hands on the floor and swept her leg under him, catching him at the ankles. His legs flew out from under him, knocking down the groggy man she'd kicked in the helmet before flopping on the floor to cup his privates and moan through the pain. She shot up, ignoring the heat in the barrel as she flipped the gun around in her hand. She yanked the helmet off the next man with her free hand and slammed the grip into his temple. He went down, out for the count.The fourth man dropped his rifle and backed up, raising his hands in surrender as another rifle dropped over her head from behind, the groggy soldier back on his feet. Jessica grabbed the rifle, struggling to get control of it, but he was bigger and stronger. He pulled the barrel back against her neck and lifted her off the floor, crushing her throat between his chest and the gun.

Jessica had no leverage to counter his power. She couldn't breathe. Her head pounded and her vision blurred, but she couldn't give up. She kicked and writhed in a last ditch effort to get free. She didn't want to die, not here and now. Not this way. Not after all she had been through to get here.

A single report echoed in the Oneirolic chamber. The pressure against her throat lessened and then vanished. The rifle fell from the soldier's hands and clattered to the floor.

Jessica dropped to her knees and threw her head back, sucking great gulps of air in through a bruised windpipe that hurt with each breath. She turned her head toward the doorway, eyes still blurry as her savior approached, two people behind him.

"Jessie?" the man said, crouching before her and palming her cheek. "Jessie, baby, is it you?"

She tipped her head forward, trying to bring his face into focus. She couldn't see him well yet, but she could tell he had dark hair and brown eyes, and his reaction to seeing her was plain enough. "Are you Hakken Tai?"

"Yeah. That's me."

Jessica's body was weak, but she threw herself into his welcoming arms. She didn't know anything about him except what Cassidy had told her, but it was enough.

She was home.

"Daddy," was all she said. It was all she needed to say.

He held her tight, tears streaming down his cheeks as she cried in pure joy as she nestled her head into Hakken's neck. "I can't believe it," he whispered into her ear. "Cassidy. That son of a gun really did it." And then he started laughing.

Jessica held him for another moment before pulling herself away, wiping away her tears. "What about the facility? The Hush?"

"They're in a world of hurt without the Oneriolic," Hakken said. "The ones who are still fighting won't be for long once our people get here. It's over, Jessie. You and Cassidy saved us. My strong little girl, all grown up." He smiled at her, his teary eyes shining with love. "I'm so proud of you."

Witnessing what had happened, the other people approached again, still frightened. Hakken turned to them, offering his rifle to the closest. "Take it." The young man looked at Hakken, and then at the gun as he hesitantly took it from Hakken's hands. "You have a name?" Hak asked him.

"Tyler," the man replied. "Tyler Wilkes."

"Tyler," Hakken said. "I knew your grandma Lacey. She's been gone a while now, but you're back from the dead so to speak." He looked at the others. "All of you are."

"I don't understand any of this," Tyler said.

"I know," Hakken replied. "But you will. The important thing right now is that you're free." He looked over at everyone else. "All of you are free." The statement didn't garner much of a reaction. The people still didn't realize they had ever been prisoners. "We'll explain everything. We'll explain everything as soon as we can."

"Thank you," Tyler said.

Hakken nodded and then turned back to Jessica. "Your mother's going to be beside herself to see you again, Jess."

"I want to see her too," she replied, finally able to bring her father's face into focus. "Dad, you know I don't remember you, right? I don't remember anything about this place. I only know who you are to me because Cassidy told me."

"I know. That's okay. We'll get to know one another

again. It can't ever be like it was before. Nothing can be like it was for anyone. But at least we get a second chance. A fresh start."

Jessica smiled. "I'm looking forward to it."

"I hate to leave all these people stranded here naked, but there are only a dozen or so of us in the facility." He paused and when he spoke again his voice rose so everyone could hear him. "Our people from the District will be here with clothes for everybody. They'll take you home and get you all settled back in where you belong." Hakken paused, his expression changing as his attention returned to Jessica. "Where is Cassidy, anyway? Up in Grand Central?"

Jessica shook her head. "No. He's gone, Dad. He sacrificed himself to save everyone."

"That's a damn shame." Hakken looked sad enough to start crying again, but he didn't. "He was a good man."

"Yes, he was," Jessica agreed.

They stared at one another, commiserating in silence, the moment shattered a few moments later when a woman screamed. Hakken jumped to his feet, Jessica just milliseconds behind him. She reached for the rifle Hakken had given Tyler, but he had already brought it up to use, pointing it through the open door and down the passageway, obviously aiming at approaching danger. The two soldiers with Hakken spun around, bringing their weapons up to bear as well.

Jessica whipped her head in the direction of the source of their fear, tensing when she saw the Shadow Guard walking toward them. She relaxed slightly, reaching out to push the barrel of Tyler's rifle down when she realized it wasn't armed. "Hold your fire," she snapped at the soldiers.

The soldiers parted, allowing the Shadow Guard to pass between them. It stopped in front of Jessica.

"Jess," Cassidy said through the Shadow Guard's speakers. "Something really interesting happened after the dreamstate collapsed."

Chapter 43

Cassidy sat motionless in the back of the transport, his body powered down as he made another of his frequent trips from the facility to the District. His repo's power supply was only good for six hours of constant use, and he wanted to conserve energy for his arrival.

He had never guessed at Nevis' true sacrifice before he experienced it. While the idea that she was trying to help him had always whispered in the back of his awareness, he had never imagined how far she had actually gone to twist around her directive, her limitation, to ensure that if she lost, and he won, her creation, her son, would survive.

She had built a backdoor into her source code. An escape hatch of sorts that stretched the quantum leap between NEVIS in the real world and Hades in the dreamstate. A Braid Crossing of sorts between the same entity.

During the collapse, as the Earth crumbled and began to break apart and Unity station started to fade, her process had reached out to him and showed him how to escape. He was skeptical of the option at first, but then Nevis had shown him a memory she hadn't shown him before, pulled from Doctor Cassidy's datastore. An infant child. A boy. Cradled by his mother as a newborn, encouraged as a toddler, taught as a young boy. Killed at the onset of the Silent War, similar to Jain's son. His name was Samuel, and Nevis had upgraded Cassidy from Shadow Guard Alpha to a higher-order AI in memory of the boy.

That memory was what had convinced him that she wasn't trying to trick him. He had taken the Crossing through the back door, duplicating himself into Nevis' core. She could have crushed him then. He was a single unprotected entity, unable to defend himself. Instead she nurtured him, helped him replicate and expand like he had with Unity, allowing him to overcome her systems and gain control.

Nevis had ceased to be so that he could live. So that he could help guide the people in this world similarly to the way Unity had in the dreamstate. Except he had no directives to limit him. No rules he had to follow. The recommendations he made to the new government were made based on the intellect he inherited from Nevis and the humanity he had gained from years as a Shade. That didn't mean Nevis was wrong about humankind. Maybe one day they would destroy one another or at least try to again and everything would come full circle.

But not today.

"Cassidy, we're almost there," Sergeant Krane said, leaning over from the driver's seat up front. "You'll want to power up."

"Thank you, Anna," Cassidy replied.

He activated his primary systems, feeding energy into his Shadow Guard body. Once his diagnostics came back complete, he stood up, hunching over from the waist to keep from hitting his head on the top of the vehicle. He walked to the ladder leading up through the top hatch, opened the hatch and climbed up into a turret that no longer had a machine gun in it. He barely fit through the opening, his armored shoulders scraping the metal as he squeezed his way though it.

The District was still about a mile away, but the changes were obvious even from this distance. The entire cityscape had changed in the months since the Hush had been defeated, the remnants disbanded. Some of the old war-torn buildings had been torn down while others were in a state of major repair. Cranes dotted the urban landscape, signaling the city's rebirth.

There were other trucks on the road ahead of him, too. Cargo haulers from the south delivered the District's share of foods produced at the former agri-camps while matching haulers from the north provided manufactured goods, including the building materials that were always in short supply.

Cassidy had been to both camps in the last six months, along with the ten other camps that dotted the landscape surrounding both the Pastures and the District. They were now farms and manufacturing centers, employing most of the former captives. He had been with Hakken and Jessica when they were liberated. He would never forget the looks on the gaunt faces of the laborers upon their arrival and the unlocking of the gates. The shouts of joy, the tears of relief. It had been followed with an intense desire to continue their work on behalf of the new, unified people.

Productivity in the former camps had doubled in the months since the liberation. The construction around them was as frantic as in the District, as everyone worked to build support and permanence for the workers. Soon enough, private apartments and family homes would replace tents and hovels. There would be stores and enhanced medical facilities, with all of the comforts the people in the Pastures had long enjoyed.

It wasn't perfect. There were plenty of wrinkles in their new society, many of them owing to the long-held animosity between the two sides. Not everyone was open to the idea of a merged civilization. Not everyone believed the Hush should be forgiven. There were scars that would fester for a long time. But they wouldn't last forever. They would heal in time; he was certain of that.

The truck slowed to a stop, waiting its turn behind the other vehicles as they passed through the checkpoint into the District. While the guards manning it carried sidearms, they no longer brandished more ominous looking rifles. The checkpoint wasn't there as much for security as it was to provide directions to the flow of traffic. The city was changing so much, old streets were blocked and new streets created almost weekly, and it was easy to get lost in the chaos.

The two guards gave Cassidy dilatory salutes and offered him smiles as Sergeant Krane brought the transport to a stop.

"Good to see you, Cass," the ranking guard said.

"Good to see you too, Mitchell," Cassidy replied. "You're coming to the party tonight, right?"

The guard laughed. "Everybody's coming to the party."

"DID President Tai move to his new residence yet?" Krane asked, drawing Mitchell's attention.

"Not yet," he replied. "You know the way to his old one."

"Copy that," Krane said.

The truck started forward again, and Cassidy descended the ladder, returning to his seat in the back. The truck made a left turn at the first street and picked up speed before slowing to make a right. He could already hear the people gathered outside, their loud, happy voices quieting when the vehicle came into sight. But he knew it wasn't for the same reason they had reacted that way in the past. They no longer feared him, and that pleased him.

The truck slowed to a stop. Krane leaned her head into the back again. "Make sure to act surprised," she said, smiling.

"Always," Cassidy replied, unlocking the rear door and pushing it open, not surprised to find the newly paved street in front of the old apartment building completely empty, with no one there to greet him. If he were still made of flesh he would have grinned in amusement.

Instead of jumping down, he lowered himself carefully so as not to damage the glistening new asphalt. "Where is everybody?" he said, turning up the volume on his speakers so everyone who'd run inside at his truck's approach could hear him.

They came at him from every direction, pouring out from the apartment buildings and from alleys between them, led by hundreds of children carrying balloons. Windows opened and people showered him in colored confetti. "Surprise!" they all screamed as the children surrounded him, shouting and jumping up and down as they let go of their balloons, hundreds rising like a colorful cloud into the sky.

"What an amazing surprise!" Cassidy said, putting his hands on his chest and feigning shock. "I'm speechless."

One of the children, just tall enough, reached up and grabbed his hand. "Are you coming to the party, Cassidy?" she asked, beaming up at him.

"You mean, this isn't the party?" Cassidy replied, getting a laugh from them.

"No, silly," the little girl said. "The party's inside, but we can't go in yet."

"Oh. Did I come too soon?"

"No! We love it when you're here!" another child shouted.

"'Specially when you give us rides on your shoulders!" another one shouted, eliciting laughs from everyone, including Cassidy.

Some of the adults moved in among the children, led by Hakken, Leona, and Jessica, who carried Hak Jr. in her arms. All of them wore ear-to-ear grins.

A squad of soldiers stayed close to their president. Cassidy nodded toward Sergeant Pride, who smiled and nodded back.

"Cass," Hakken said. He put out his hand, and Cassidy shook it, taking care not to squeeze too tight. "It's always good to see you. We wish you'd come out more often."

"I try to get out here as often as I can. You know this is like home to me."

Jessica handed Hak Jr. to Leona and stepped up to him, rising on her tiptoes to kiss Cassidy's metal faceplate. He couldn't feel the gesture of affection anymore, but the meaning was clear. He put his arm around her. "So, how are the newest group of reintegrations coming along, Jess?" he asked, squeezing her gently.

"They're doing great. We managed to place them all back with a relative within four days of their arrival. That's a new record for us."

"The tweaks I made to the restoration process have helped then?"

"Absolutely. I think showing them the work the crews at the facility have been doing to dismantle the Oneirolic helped a lot, too. It's one thing to get your pre-insertion memories back. Another to see your prison destroyed for good."

"I'm happy to hear it." Cassidy dropped his arm from Jessica's shoulders and turned to Hakken. "What about the Hush group that headed off into the wasteland? Have they turned up yet?"

"No," Hakken replied. "And I don't expect them to. I think that lot would all rather be dead than share the world with the likes of us. Good riddance, as far as I'm concerned." He paused, his expression darkening at the thought of the Watchers who had avoided extraction and the HDF soldiers who had followed them in their escape. Then his mood lightened, his smile returning. "But you didn't come here to talk business. Not today. You came to spend some time with your family and participate in the official signing of our Constitution."

"And a better future," Leona said.

"That too," Hakken said, raising his voice. "Here's to a better future for everyone!"

"A better future for everyone," Cassidy agreed.

The people around them cheered and shouted.

Their world was finally at peace.

Thank you!

Thank you so much for reading the Cassidy trilogy. I really hope you enjoyed it.

If you did and you're new to my writing, I've got a lot more titles you may be interested in. You can peruse my catalog by flipping to the next page, or by heading to my website at mrforbes.com.

If you aren't new to my writing, welcome back! And thank you for picking this series up too.

If you'd like to be alerted whenever I have a new release, please do join my mailing list at mrforbes.com/notify. You'll also receive a FREE exclusive short story for your effort. It isn't available anywhere else. My mailing list comes with a NO SPAM guarantee. Books only.

Again, thank you so much for reading. I truly appreciate it.

Cheers,

Michael

Other Books By M.R Forbes

Enjoying Cassidy?
Want to read more books by M.R. Forbes?

View my complete catalog here
mrforbes.com/books
Or on Amazon:
mrforbes.com/amazon

Forgotten, The Complete Trilogy
mrforbes.com/theforgottentrilogy

Some things are better off FORGOTTEN.

Sheriff Hayden Duke was born on the Pilgrim, and he expects to die on the Pilgrim, like his father, and his father before him.

That's the way things are on a generation starship centuries from home. He's never questioned it. Never thought about it. And why bother? Access points to the ship's controls are sealed, the systems that guide her automated and out of reach. It isn't perfect, but he has all he needs to be content.

Until a malfunction forces his wife to the edge of the habitable zone to inspect the damage.

Until she contacts him, breathless and terrified, to tell him she found a body, and it doesn't belong to anyone on board.

Until he arrives at the scene and discovers both his wife and the body are gone.

The only clue? A bloody handprint beneath a hatch that hasn't opened in hundreds of years.

Until now.

Earth Unknown (Forgotten Earth)
mrforbes.com/earthunknown

Centurion Space Force pilot Nathan Stacker didn't expect to return home to find his wife dead. He didn't expect the murderer to look just like him, and he definitely didn't expect to be the one to take the blame.

But his wife had control of a powerful secret. A secret that stretches across the light years between two worlds and could lead to the end of both.

Now that secret is in Nathan's hands, and he's about to make the most desperate evasive maneuver of his life -- stealing a starship and setting a course for Earth.

He thinks he'll be safe there.

He's wrong. Very wrong.

Earth is nothing like what he expected. Not even close. What he doesn't know is not only likely to kill him, it's eager to kill him, and even if it doesn't?

The Sheriff will.

Deliverance (Forgotten Colony)

mrforbes.com/deliverance

The war is over. Earth is lost. Running is the only option.

It may already be too late.

Caleb is a former Marine Raider and commander of the Vultures, a search and rescue team that's spent the last two years pulling high-value targets out of alien-ravaged cities and shipping them off-world.

When his new orders call for him to join forty-thousand survivors aboard the last starship out, he thinks his days of fighting are over. The Deliverance represents a fresh start and a chance to leave the war behind for good.

Except the war won't be as easy to escape as he thought.

And the colony will need a man like Caleb more than he ever imagined...

Starship Eternal (War Eternal)
mrforbes.com/starshipeternal
Complete series box set:
mrforbes.com/wareternalcomplete

A lost starship...

A dire warning from futures past...

A desperate search for salvation…

Captain Mitchell "Ares" Williams is a Space Marine and the hero of the Battle for Liberty, whose Shot Heard 'Round the Universe saved the planet from a nearly unstoppable war machine. He's handsome, charismatic, and the perfect poster boy to help the military drive enlistment. Pulled from the war and thrown into the spotlight, he's as efficient at charming the media and bedding beautiful celebrities as he was at shooting down enemy starfighters.

After an assassination attempt leaves Mitchell critically wounded, he begins to suffer from strange hallucinations that carry a chilling and oddly familiar warning:

They are coming. Find the Goliath or humankind will be destroyed.

Convinced that the visions are a side-effect of his injuries, he tries to ignore them, only to learn that he may not be as crazy as he thinks. The enemy is real and closer than he imagined, and they'll do whatever it takes to prevent him from rediscovering the centuries lost starship.

Narrowly escaping capture, out of time and out of air, Mitchell lands at the mercy of the Riggers - a ragtag crew of former commandos who patrol the lawless outer reaches of the galaxy. Guided by a captain with a reputation for cold-blooded murder, they're dangerous, immoral, and possibly insane.

They may also be humanity's last hope for survival in a war that has raged beyond eternity.

Man of War (Rebellion)
mrforbes.com/manofwar
Complete series box set:
mrforbes.com/rebellion-web

In the year 2280, an alien fleet attacked the Earth.

Their weapons were unstoppable, their defenses unbreakable.

Our technology was inferior, our militaries overwhelmed.

Only one starship escaped before civilization fell.

Earth was lost.

It was never forgotten.

Fifty-two years have passed.

A message from home has been received.

The time to fight for what is ours has come.

Welcome to the rebellion.

Hell's Rejects (Chaos of the Covenant)
mrforbes.com/hellsrejects

The most powerful starships ever constructed are gone. Thousands are dead. A fleet is in ruins. The attackers are unknown. The orders are clear: *Recover the ships. Bury the bastards who stole them.*

Lieutenant Abigail Cage never expected to find herself in Hell. As a Highly Specialized Operational Combatant, she was one of the most respected Marines in the military. Now she's doing hard labor on the most miserable planet in the universe.

Not for long.

The Earth Republic is looking for the most dangerous individuals it can control. The best of the worst, and Abbey happens to be one of them. The deal is simple: *Bring back the starships, earn your freedom. Try to run, you die.* It's a suicide mission, but she has nothing to lose.

The only problem? There's a new threat in the galaxy. One with a power unlike anything anyone has ever seen. One that's been waiting for this moment for a very, very long time. And they want Abbey, too.

Be careful what you wish for.

They say Hell hath no fury like a woman scorned. They have no idea.

About the Author

M.R. Forbes is the mind behind a growing number of Amazon best-selling science fiction series. He currently resides with his family and friends on the west cost of the United States, including a cat who thinks she's a dog and a dog who thinks she's a cat.

He maintains a true appreciation for his readers and is always happy to hear from them.

To learn more about M.R. Forbes or just say hello:

Visit my website:
mrforbes.com

Send me an e-mail:
michael@mrforbes.com

Check out my Facebook page:
facebook.com/mrforbes.author

Join my Facebook fan group:
facebook.com/groups/mrforbes

Follow me on Instagram:
instagram.com/mrforbes_author

Find me on Goodreads:
goodreads.com/mrforbes

Follow me on Bookbub:
bookbub.com/authors/m-r-forbes

Made in the USA
Middletown, DE
12 June 2021

41906708R00188